Scourge
OF THE
Seas
of Time (and Space)

Enjoy Darling under the Jolly Roger!

Catherine Lundoff

CATHERINE LUNDOFF
editor

QUEEN
of
SWORDS
PRESS

Contents

CONTENTS, continued

Dedicated to all our favorite pirates.

Introduction

W HY PIRATES? WHY NOT PIRATES, I say! I am a lifelong fan of fictional and (some) historical pirates. Pirates have always represented freedom and adventure and swordplay and many of the things that I find irresistible. I was 9 when I first read Robert Louis Stevenson's *Treasure Island*, 11 when I read Raphael Sabatini's *Captain Blood* and 13 when I saw Tyrone Power and Maureen O'Hara in *The Black Swan*. By then, I was hooked. I watched or read almost anything featuring pirates that came my way. I enjoyed Geena Davis and Frank Langella in *Cutthroat Island*, tolerated *Hook*, chortled my way through *The Ice Pirates*. I have even written the occasional pirate story myself, including two featuring Jacquotte Delahaye (sometimes known as "Back from the Dead Red") and one about Anne Bonny and Mary Read. Fictional pirates are, let's face it, fun.

Of course, pirates were (and are) also bloodthirsty, cruel and terrible and those aspects of their stories cannot be ignored. Contemporary pirates, real or fictional, are much more complicated figures than the pirates of my youth: the romantic,

1

wronged noblemen driven to sea by injustice, kidnapped youths of stout heart and true and all the other imaginary heroes that sailed under the Jolly Roger.

I wanted to know more about those complicated pirates. Where were the queer women, the gay and bi men who I knew had to be there, the pirates who weren't white dudes who looked like Errol Flynn? I dove into nonfiction. I researched the Barbary Pirates and Grace O'Malley, and rejoiced in my initial discovery of Anne Bonny and Mary Read. I read about Ching Shih and her fleet of 300 junks. I read tomes about pirate cultures and history.

But I never completely abandoned the pirates of fiction. Modern pirates, at least the fictional ones, are no longer all male or all white or all heterosexual. Television shows like *Crossbones* and *Black Sails* and movies like the seeming endless *Pirates of the Caribbean* franchise depict people drawn to piracy from a wide range of cultures and backgrounds, and even sexual orientations. There are comics like *Raven: The Pirate Princess, I Was Kidnapped by Lesbian Space Pirates from Outer Space* and *Polly and the Pirates* that are filled with the adventures of a diverse range of female pirates. Authors from Tim Powers to Tanith Lee, Jane Yolen and Alex Acks have portrayed even more kinds of pirates, from the historical to the fantastical and beyond. At last, fictional piracy is beginning to reflect the rainbow skull and crossbones that a number of historians have suggested that it was.

I wanted an anthology with some of that diversity and range, so when I put out a call for pirate stories, I encouraged international contributors and made it an "open to all orientations and sexualities" call. I was very pleased to get nearly 100 submissions, from a total of fourteen countries. I read about lesbian pirates, gay pirates, bi pirates, transgender pirates and heterosexual pirates, as well as a number of tales in which sexual orientation wasn't specified. I got stories set in the Caribbean, the Mediterranean, the South China Sea, the Indian Ocean and outer space, amongst other locations. Stories were set in ancient Greece, in Viking-era Scandinavia and in the Golden Age of Piracy, along with many other time periods. It made for some terrific reading.

This volume represents some of my favorites amongst those stories, which I hope will also become some of yours. Author Elliott Dunstan writes about the aftermath of Trojan War and how one of Homer's neglected characters turns pirate in "Andromache's War." A.J. Fitzwater gives us a new installment of their dapper lesbian capybara pirate saga in "The Search for the Heart of the Ocean." Ginn Hale maroons her gay pirate hero on a fantastical island to find himself again in "Treasured Island" while Matisse Mozer sends his heroine across dimensions into new dangers in "Rosa, the Dimension Pirate." Ed Grabianowski takes us to a world of fantastical horror and introduces us to Jagga, a pirate captain turned demon hunter, in "The Doomed Amulet of Erum Vahl" while Ashley Deng sails us into the Barbary Coast from an another world in "The Seafarer."

And that's not all. Author Joyce Chng weaves a tale of new-found love and revenge in the South China Sea in "Saints and Bodhisattvas" while Michael Merriam takes us to the stars and a reluctant pirate crew forced to fight a terrible foe in "Tenari." Mharie West's family of bisexual poly Viking pirates must combat intolerance and persecution in "Serpent's Tail." Geonn Cannon's pirate captain carves out a new life for herself and her crew during the Golden Age of Piracy in "Rib of Man." A wounded pirate risks capture and destruction by her greatest enemy to save her shipmates in Megan Arkenberg's "Between the Devil and the Deep Blue Sea." Soumya Sundar Mukherjee's teenage heroine must battle pirates, mechabeasts and even a robot to save her father and herself in "The Dead Pirate's Cave," while Peter Golubock's pirate captain sails the former streets of post-climate apocalypse New York City in "After the Deluge." Su Haddrell gives us a woman pirate who needs allies and finds an unlikely one in the swamps of Louisiana in "A Smuggler's Pact" while Caroline Sciriha's pirate hero seeks redemption in "A Crooked Road Home."

Welcome aboard the *Scourge of the Seas of Time (and Space)*! Keep your blade sharp and step lively. We sail with the tide.

Treasured Island

By Ginn Hale

H OW I CAME TO BE marooned on the back of a wandering
island is a matter of some debate. Bosun Lisboa would
no doubt maintain that I received a rightful punishment for
attempting to incite a mutiny against our brawny, blond Captain
Alvim. But I would argue that I simply surveyed the ragged,
bare-foot crew as to how many members might enjoy a respite
from murdering sailors and plundering great stores of half-
rotten bananas. I'd wondered if anyone else desired to return
to familiar home-shores. Perhaps take up fishing as a source of
income.

After the months we'd spent chasing fruitless rumors of
Captain Barradas' hidden treasure and slaughtering entire
crews of little merchant ships for their pitiful stores, fishing
didn't sound so bad to many.

Before you laugh, allow me to point out that a good number
of us came from fishing families before we were pressed
by naval recruiters or captured by privateers. All I know of

navigation and sailing, I learned while hunting the vast silver shoals of sun skates and dragon eels that swam in the shadows of Reinazona's wandering islands. It wasn't the easiest of work nor the safest of trades but then, neither is piracy.

And truth be told, I'd felt far cleaner back when I'd reeked of fish guts and eel shit.

So, after another evening swabbing blood off the deck and listening to the screams coming from the sad little captive in our captain's cabin, I felt a change of occupation might be worth pondering. In hindsight, I acknowledge that I shouldn't have pondered so very loudly. But I'd been under the influence of rum and remorse. And a little more rum, after that. I may have referred to Lisboa as toadspunk; I may have called the captain a turd in a velvet coat — that's beside the point.

The trouble was that Captain Alvim had only just done-in our previous captain — Easal, was his name, I think — who'd only been leading us a week since he himself had done away with the captain before him. There had been a few before that as well. Sometimes, even I forgot that it had been Captain Barradas — him of the maps and riddles and the lost treasure — who'd had me dragged from my little fishing boat to serve as their Almagua navigator. "In the service of our Queen," he'd assured me.

But the wandering islands he expected me to find a way through were strangers to me, nothing like those I'd grown up among. And of course it hadn't taken long before Barradas' patriotic privateering gave way to preying upon any ships he encountered amidst the ever-changing shores of the Laquerla Ocean.

All in all, it made for an uneasy history. And there was me, in the middle of it, sick and drunk. I still argue that I didn't deserve to stand beneath the mizzen-mast, accused of inciting mutiny. Though I readily admit to having upped my stew on the captain's shoes.

Of course, the crew couldn't just murder me and toss my body in the ocean. Deadly bad luck killing an Almagua at sea, even one as defiled with bloodshed as me. Too much of a chance that my fishy spirit would take to the waves howling murder and raise up those black whales on my granny's side of the family. I swore to them that I'd do it too.

"They will rise up and crack this ship in half!" I punched my right hand in the air, displaying the blue tattoo of my clan. "And they will drag each and every man of you down to a deep, cold hell, where my ghost will play mermaid melodies on your bones!"

Bosun Lisboa looked alarmed, though he tried to hide his fear by bowing his face down into his thick black beard. Captain Alvim still held his pistol to my head but I felt his hand tremble.

"It's a doomed captain who curses himself and his whole crew," I pitched my voice not to reach him, but the fearful men surrounding us. If I didn't spark a mutiny in my life I certainly meant to with my death. It was the very least I could do for the man threatening to blow my brains out.

Alvim lowered his pistol.

An hour later the captain and bosun decided to let me set course for the nearest wandering island. Then they'd throw me overboard so that I might swim to the shore. If I got tangled in the island's stinging tentacles, well that would be between me and the island, none of their doing. That was Bosun Lisboa's reasoning and many agreed with him.

The evening I was to be tossed over, the red-haired eunuchs, Akwa and Rui, brought me a canteen of fresh water and a strip of dried squid. They'd been the only survivors of an Imperial

Indaji pleasure ship that we sank three years ago and neither wanted to make an enemy of a ghost. They requested that I tell my grandmother of their kindness, and I agreed.

After that, Dalir, who was long limbed, dark haired and only a few years older than me, crouched beside me. A decade past, he'd fled gambling debts in the opal kingdom of Muqadas only to lose his liberty at a card table in some pirate nest on the Laquerla coast. Now he traded me his prized knife in exchange for a kiss and my lucky dice. I realized that there were tears in his eyes and I supposed those nights sharing hammocks and hand jobs must have meant more to him than he ever said. I gave him my last three gold coins telling him that they would only weigh me down in the waves.

Then I went into the dark water and swam beneath a full yellow moon.

Back home, I'd thought our flotillas of islands, drifting across straights and forming ephemeral archipelagos, were immense. But the wandering islands of the Laquerla Ocean made them seem small as man-o-war jellyfish. Tendrils, thick as tree trunks, and scarlet fan-like gills hung around me and stretched all the way into the lightless depths. What creatures they hunted down there, I couldn't say. I simply thanked the Great Brine that none of the silver stinging tendrils cared for so small a catch as me.

Though one eel did snap at the buckle of my shoe before retreating back to its lair.

Even in the dark I could see brilliant corals ringing the wandering island like a reef. I nicked my hands and shins, making my way to the sandy beach. I would have laid down there and slept, I was so tired, but the big spider crabs clambering ashore all around me inspired me with enough worry to keep me from flopping there like easy carrion beneath their fist-sized claws. I staggered to a stand of fig trees and managed to climb up to a branch, which I lashed myself to with my belt, and dozed.

I woke as the sun rose, and for the first time I took in whole forests of tree ferns, figs and palms spreading for miles before me. Above them, morning mist condensed and cascaded down jewel blue sail-fins like waterfalls tumbling down sapphire cliffs. Generation after generation of seabird and bat colonies had added guano to the fertile soil that blanketed the wandering island's thick shell. When I descended from the tree I realized that the island's back had long ago become as earthy as land. The pulse of its heart was only a soft hum beneath my feet.

Still, I took a few hours that first day to dig deep and climb down to where I could lay my bruised hands on the turquoise blue scales of the island's warm shell and give it my thanks and seven drops of my blood. "I mean you no harm, Traveler. For all I eat or drink, I'll give back my share of piss and droppings. For your shelter, I will praise you to the sun and the moon and I will stand for you against the flames. And if I die here, my bones and body are yours too, but my soul, that's mine alone." I started to rise but then knelt again and added. "If my granny is down where you can reach her, tell her I say hello and that I haven't forgotten home, no matter how far I've roamed."

With that done, I set about exploring to find shelter, fresh water and what I could eat. Along the way I also began discovering what all wanted to eat me.

The biggest of the spider crabs hunted inland a good distance, but only at night, and as vicious as those claws of theirs looked, they were nothing compared with the massive beaks of the giant gold-plumed birds that stalked the forest in pairs. They stood far too tall and heavy for flight but weren't anything like the paunchy green auks that I'd known back home. I nearly shit myself when two of the sleek, gold giants tore through the tree ferns, charging me. I dived to the left, drawing my knife, but the birds couldn't have cared less. They bounded past, stretched up to their full height and ripped a python from a tree branch. Between then they tore the writhing creature in half then they gulped it down as easy as a pair of robins dispatching worms. They took crabs and turtles as well. That evening, I saw the pair feed the crabs to nestlings the size of ponies.

After that, I listened closely for the flutter of feathers and the excited clicks the giant gold birds issued as they hunted. When I stole eggs, they came from the nests of much smaller terns and gulls. I slept uneasily and took pains to avoid the hills of palm fronds that formed the gold birds' nests. They seemed to feed happily enough without my scrawny meat.

Biting flies, on the other hand, delighted in my pitiful taste. Over the course of passing months, I think they must have drained enough blood to fill another of me entirely. I made a joke to myself that a great swarm of them might steal my moldering jacket and fly across the ocean to impersonate me on the step of my poor mother's door.

"Pascoal!" I imagined her calling out to the swarm of flies as she hefted her swatter. "I hardly recognized you!"

I laughed to myself and then felt a wave of sorrow as I recalled my mother's fragrant hearth and my nimble sisters stitching nets and teasing me for throwing flowers at the shipwright's handsome son. I remembered the crunch of our shell path beneath my feet as I used to pelt from the house to greet my uncle on his way home from the market. The memories were like a treasury of beautiful glass that cut too deeply.

After that, I tried not to think of my family again.

I found respite from the insects and the gold birds by climbing high up to the oldest expanse of the island where cold winds drove against the immense blue sail-fins. Hills of moss mounded up over the remains of ancient fallen trees. Bats sang for the love of date palms all night long. I sang back to them and to the moon as it winked in and out of the clouds. I allowed a love-struck beetle to steal the remaining buckle of my shoe and I named the tiny orange frogs I discovered living in the freshwater hollows where I drank. Vaz became my favorite because he fearlessly clambered up to my shoulder and trilled hilarious songs of courtship, while I gathered eggs and dates.

I felt myself becoming lonely and strange.

All the while the island roiled up great waves as its siphons pulsed and its sail-fins caught fresh winds. New constellations climbed up into the night sky and the sun never seemed to sink in the same direction. Rains fell but the island skirted the towering black masses of typhoons as they skated over the ocean. Twice lances of searing lightning struck the island. Both times I raced through the forest to the fires. I fought through smoke to reach the orange flames and I suffocated them with heaps of mud before they could burn down to the island's shell.

Wandering islands will douse their own fires if they feel them. But little of the life clinging to the island would survive the decent down into the cold ocean depths. My granny had told stories of entire cities lost to a single errant spark. She'd always reminded me that before all else, we Almagua protect the wandering islands that provide us with our sustenance. And though this Laquerla island was an ancient stranger to me, it did my spirit good to fight those fires. The blisters reminded me that I could do something more than plunder and drink. I began to remember how it felt to have courage and to care for something more than my own skin.

As the smoke drifted from the dying remnants of the second fire, I noticed a pair of gold birds stalking between the steaming tree ferns. They kicked the ground, and at first I thought they were hunting charred snakes. But then I saw one deliberately smother a heap of stray embers beneath its tough feet. Then the bird caught sight of me and cocked its head, as if studying my smoke-streaked figure. I crushed out an ember under my filthy shoe, and I waited for the pair to charge me. Instead, one sang out a long low trill and its mate answered. Then the pair slowly strolled past, so close that I could smell their sweet plumes and see the faint pattern of blue speckles that decorated their tail feathers.

I took a charred snake for myself and hiked back up to my post in the heights, wondering if the gold birds too were guardians of this place—a strange clan of Almagua.

Vaz, my favorite frog, sang me to sleep.

Several nights after, I woke to see luminescent plumes trailing the island and lighting up miles of the black sea. I dreamed that an even more immense island floated in the heavens, filling the sky with vast sprays of glittering stars as it spilled its semen across the firmament. When I woke, I wondered if I might be going a little mad and I only just caught myself before I asked the question of the orange frog chirping on my shoulder.

From time to time, I thought I sighted ships on the horizon, but they never came close. Though more and more often, I glimpsed the green vistas of other wandering islands, drifting like mirages of true land.

One afternoon I woke late, feeling feverish, to discover that a huge flock of jewel red hummingbirds had invaded the island. They swarmed over the trees and surrounded the pools of fresh water. I stumbled after one, dazzled by its iridescent plumage and the astounding beat of its wings.

Then all at once the mossy ground gave way beneath me. I fell into a dark crevasse and struck planks of rotted wood so hard that I broke through into a second level. The hummingbird darted above me for a moment, then flashed away. I struggled to catch my breath, and simply lay there almost afraid to notice how badly I'd been hurt or how far I'd fallen. I needed to get up and get out before more ground tumbled down on top of me, but I couldn't move.

A numb darkness engulfed me.

I don't know how much time passed before I came to, but the sun seemed to have drifted far across the sky.

Shafts of late afternoon sunlight filtered down and glinted across heaps of Indaji gold and Maqadas silver. One of the rotted barrels that I'd smashed through bled out a pool of pearls all around my prone body. Small chests of jeweled baubles stood all around me. A Reinazona sword lay atop one, wrapped in a decayed leather sheath bearing the emblem of an eagle. As my eyes adjusted to the gloom I made out the skeletal remains of the five captives whom Captain Barradas had forced to carry his treasure when he'd hidden it away, fearing it would fall into the hands of naval officials dispatched to bring him home to face his queen's justice.

But he never lived to see the fleet of warships with their decks of guns and endless yards of sails. Instead, he'd died at the end of his first mate's sabre for depriving his crew of their share of plunder. And four years on, the remnants of Barradas' crew and a host of others still hunted the ever-changing seas searching for that narrow stretch of land where riches of every nation waited for the taking. Over those years, the stories of the wild captain's riddles had grown, along with rumors of maps and tales of ghosts tearing at sails and spinning compasses like whirlpools. The scale of Barradas' plunder grew from a haul that had weighed down our single sloop, to vast caverns, piled with more gold than ten galleons could hold. Pirate captains, naval commanders, merchant princes and even wealthy naturalists sought the treasure. And their fascination doomed countless numbers of us, pressed into their service. So many lives had been sacrificed for this shining, dank place and the riches it held.

And now it was all mine and all utterly worthless to me. I laughed so hard that I cried.

Then I wept for a time longer.

After I wiped my face and managed to pull my aching body upright, I staggered to the corner where the five corpses huddled atop each other. The chains that once secured their ankles had fallen from their bones and the bullets that had killed them lay hidden beneath colonies of white mushrooms. I barely remembered the captive's faces or names, but I still placed my hand on each of their skulls and wished their spirits to find release from this hole. I left a gold coin for each of them among their finger bones.

"Blue skies and shining stars await you," I said for I could offer them nothing else. Not holy blessings or the return of their bones to their homelands. "I wish you peace at our parting."

I took the sword and then I pushed the casks and chests together to form several precarious steps. My left shoulder nagged at the effort and my back ached, but the sound of thunder filled me with fear. I didn't want to be trapped in this hole when the rain came and turned the ground above me to a suffocating mud. I needed to be out if lightning struck the island and ignited a fire.

I strained for a handhold, digging at dirt and decayed moss. Again, the thunder, loud as cannon fire cracked through the air. At last, I caught a tangle of roots that held my weight. In a frantic scramble, I clambered out of the gold-filled grave.

Overhead, dark storm clouds hung like black banners across a golden sunset. Out on the indigo-blue ocean, a fast-moving sloop-of-war, flying a blood-red flag fired upon a narrow brigantine—a Reinazona merchant vessel, I guessed from her display of flags. The sloop I recognized at once even through the coming darkness and the distance of forest and sea. Barradas' *Morsa*, the ship I'd been hurled from months ago.

If Captain Alvim still commanded her, then no quarter would be given to the sailors or passengers aboard the brigantine. Their only hope would be to repel the *Morsa* or to outrun her. Slack sails and still air made me fear that the brigantine couldn't depend upon speed. The little ship shuddered in the water as cannon shot tore into her. Still, her crew managed to turn on the *Morsa* and return a volley of fire. Smoke billowed up from the guns of both ships. Twice more the heavy guns thundered as timbers splintered.

Then the *Morsa*'s foremast cracked and she veered to the side. At once the brigantine turned, not in pursuit but catching a gust of wind and making for the cover of my island. The *Morsa* fired after her. Cannon ball after cannon ball ripped through the ship. Her mizzen-mast crumpled, and a gaping hole opened in her hull. Then another.

The ocean gleamed with the brilliant colors of the setting sun as the brigantine sank before my eyes.

None aboard the *Morsa* sent out rescue boats, not even to seize survivors for ransom. I wondered if their supplies had run so low that they couldn't afford to feed even a single man more, or if Captain Alvim's cruelty had led more kind-hearted men like Akwa and Dalir to think drowning would be a better death than what awaited any captive in the captain's cabin.

Dread filled my bruised chest. I watched the *Morsa* slowly turn towards my island.

They would come ashore for fresh water, to hunt food, and to cut timbers to make repairs. They would come and shoot the gold birds and build fires. If I attempted to stop them, they would likely shoot me dead as well. If I didn't stop them, then all this wilderness and beauty around me would be lost beneath the waves. And I'd likely drown too.

While I stood, pondering what I could do, I noticed a form bobbing through the breakers. Then climbing across the coral. A survivor from the brigantine. A second followed after. They both hauled themselves onto the narrow stretch of beach and for an instant I couldn't imagine what had befallen them to make then hunch in such strange positions. Then I realized they were giant turtles that the crew must have taken for their meat. Only a day before their futures would have seemed doomed, and yet now only they of an entire brigantine survived.

Something in the improbability of their persistence offered me a spark of hope.

I studied Captain Barradas' sword, while out across the sea, two ship's boats cast off from the *Morsa*. The jolly boat carried five men, the longboat brought nine. That meant fourteen of the *Morsa*'s crew of twenty were bound my way. At the prow of the longboat I sighted Captain Alvim's white plumed hat fluttering like a beckoning hand.

I picked my way quickly through the forest and descended to the beach. The setting sun turned the pale sand red and the foam of the breakers a bloody pink. The hulking turtles hunched together like amorous boulders and paid me no mind at all.

My old crewmates didn't notice my presence either. They were too caught up in struggling to pull their boats across the coral while avoiding the claws of curious spider crabs. Their faces seemed more deeply lined than I remembered, and shots of white hair streaked both Bosun Lisboa's red beard and the temples of Dalir's black hair. Only Captain Alvim, with his broad shoulders, jaunty hat and bright velvet coat struck me as unchanged by the long months at sea. It seemed almost as if the exhaustion and weakness of his crew fed him — or perhaps it simply allowed him to sleep easy at night, knowing them to be too worn down to resist him.

"Stop where you are, my old mates! This island isn't yours to lay claim to." I didn't wait for them to get clear of the lapping breakers before I called out from the shadows of the trees. "I'll offer you fresh water and wood, but no more beyond that."

Alvim lifted his pistol, but in the twilight he couldn't pick me out from the shadows of the trees I stood beside. In any case, I'd seen him come ashore. Seawater still dribbled from the barrel of his gun. His powder was soaked through.

"Pascoal?" Dalir's face lit with fondness, but several of the others appeared fearful. No doubt a few thought me a ghost. Akwa pressed his palms together and bowed his head in the gesture I'd seen him perform over sailors' corpses many times before. Bosun Lisboa scowled warily into the forest behind me. Gold birds stalked between the trees pacing to the beach for their evening crab hunts. Several of the men stumbled back into the surf as they too glimpsed the silhouettes of the giant birds.

For an instant I thought that my bluster combined with the unnerving shadows would be enough to send them back to their ship. But I should have known better. Alvim was many things, but never a coward. He took three steps inland and planted himself like a hero posing for a portrait.

"Come out from the shadows if you dare, Pascoal," he shouted. "Or would you have me run you down like a cowering dog?"

Oh, I'd have loved to see him try to catch me through the forest gloom, but that wouldn't stop the rest of the crew from building their fires.

"Now my mother would say that every dog has his day." I moved a little to the left and then stepped out from the trees a few feet from where the captain and the crew expected me. "So here I am, meeting you on land where you are no more of a captain than am I."

Alvim pulled the trigger of his pistol and got nothing for the effort but an impotent click. Behind him the rest of the crew exchanged curious glances. Dalir looked relieved. None of the crew reached for their own weapons and I realized that they weren't, any of them, about to join Alvim against me, not here on my island.

I grinned at Alvim, and anger colored his face. Like a jackass, he hurled his pistol to the sand.

But then he drew his cutlass. The sight of the gleaming naked blade sent a shiver of fear through my gut. He excelled at murdering men with that sword. Rarely did he make the end painless or quick. He took delight in slicing off fingers, ears and the tips of noses and chins. As he closed in on me, I nearly did turn and run.

But the sand beneath my feet seemed to hold me firm.

Gold had never struck me as so precious that it merited fighting over—not when the sea boasted fish enough to keep a family happy and fed. Killing for the sake of plunder had only made me sick with myself. So sickened that I'd rather have died under the mizzenmast than have gone on under Alvim's command. But this island with its gold birds, flocks of bats and little orange frogs, had nursed my ruined spirit, and reminded me that there were things in the world worth defending.

Even worth dying for.

I lifted Barradas' sword and parried Alvim's first thrust. He struck again, fast and with force enough to send me staggering a step back. I blocked another hard, ringing blow and felt Alvim's rage shudder up the length of my sword to shake through my hand. He roared obscenities as he slashed for my face, then swung his cutlass low to sweep through my left knee.

I leapt back. The tip of his sword scraped across my shin. The heat of blood also poured down my left shoulder, though I'd hardly noticed when Alvim landed the glancing blow. My heart beat like the wings of a hummingbird and my arms already ached. This was his way, wearing down my strength while he bled me steadily by a thousand cuts.

But not this time. "You're just a swarm of biting flies in need of a swatter," I said, and for an instant it seemed to take him entirely off guard. I lunged and sliced through the chest of his coat before he pivoted and parried my blade. As we circled each other on the sand, I glimpsed Dalir and remembered the knife he'd given me. Not so long as a cutlass, but it had kept its razor edge for months, like a promise.

A gold bird let out a low booming cry and Alvim and all the ship's crew glanced to the forest.

I lunged. Alvim blocked the thrust of my sword arm. But he missed the sliver of silver that I drove into his chest with my left hand. I bounded back but not before Alvim slammed his cutlass across the side of my skull. Blood and a dizzying flurry of stars filled my vision. I stumbled and fell to my knees.

Alvim grinned. I wondered that he could still be standing, unless he'd had no heart for Dalir's knife to pierce. The hilt jutted from his chest. He swayed over me but still raised his cutlass.

Then the whole island seemed to give a little shudder, like the slightest sigh. I rocked with the island's motion. Sand slid beneath Alvim's boots. He stumbled, then tumbled backwards and rolled to the water's edge like a velvet rag. There he lay perfectly still, sand crusting his wide, dead eyes. I stared at him with a dazed sort of wonder. A spider crab edged towards him. Then two more.

I expected to feel claws snap at my bleeding flesh any moment, as well. Instead, Dalir's hand supported my back as he knelt beside me.

"Well done, Pascoal," Dalir wiped the blood from my eyes with the sleeve of his shirt. "Even Bosun Lisboa is on your side this time. We're all past ready to sail home. Barradas' treasure can sink to the bottom of the sea as far as we are concerned."

I laughed. Much later, Dalir laughed at the irony of his words as well.

Of course, there is no end to the tall tales about how I and the surviving crew of the *Morsa* made our fortunes and sailed the ship back to our home shores. Dalir claims that an army of mermaids showered our deck with pearls in a hopeless attempt to win me from his arms. Awka has spun many a fine story of how we dived for sunken cities of gold—my sisters adore his books. Bosun Lisboa likes to boast that he discovered a treasure map tattooed on the back of a blind man's eyelids. No doubt, my sisters will enjoy his book too.

But I will tell you truly. I brought home a fortune only because I befriended a wandering island that had no use for burdensome treasure. It was already alive with far greater riches.

The Seafarer

By Ashley Deng

O N THIS, HIS FIRST TRIP back to his homeland, Drasio has almost forgotten his old name. He shed it years ago—and with it, his old life—in favour of a new identity in a new land. But as the sounds of his old language and the smells of his old country fill the air he breathes, he feels it resurface in his memory like jetsam. Whispers of Berber and Arabic drift over the surface of the water, as his ship, the *Rose Star*, emerges out of the Karranean Sea and into the Mediterranean. They had crossed the Barrier by night and overhead the stars had changed, carrying with them a wave of bittersweet nostalgia. He watches the Three Dancers fade into Orion, watches the Gelgys turn into Argo Navis, the *tide* giving way to the *ship*.

He feels a hand on his shoulder while his head is still craned to the sky, watching the night come into clarity. He turns to the blonde-haired woman beside him as she grins reassuringly. *Larza*, he thinks, *as lithe as a dancer and as deadly as the tides.*

"Your first trip back across the Barrier," she says, squeezing his shoulder. "Congratulations."

"Thank you," Drasio replies. "But please, don't discredit yourself. Where would a captain be without his quartermaster?"

"*Temporary* quartermaster," she chides, shaking her head so that blonde curls accented with sea glass and shells fall over her shoulders. She is only his ship's quartermaster for this one trip, to aid him in navigating the Barrier between Ardán and the Maghreb, but he considers her far more than a temporary fixture to his crew. "But you —" she pushes him forward with both of her hands. " — should be addressing your ship."

Drasio stumbles forward with a grin; Larza is stronger than she looks and has never been afraid to show it. He turns to his men, gathered on the upper decks. There are orbs of light floating where lanterns should be, illuminating the *Rose Star* in the midst of darkness. He reaches out a hand and summons another light, larger and brighter than the others. It floats upward, coming to a rest above his head. He raises his arms with a warm smile as his men turn their attention to him, the captain addressing his crew.

He thanks them, wholeheartedly, arms wide as if he could embrace them from where he stood. "A captain could not ask for a better crew," he continues, lowering his hands to rest on the wooden railing before him. "For so few can safely navigate the seas of the Barrier. I pray we remain successful in future voyages even without our expert and beautiful quartermaster."

Larza, behind him, laughs. "You flatter me, Drasio," she says with a grin.

A voice from below calls from the crowd. "He flatters everyone!" the sailor exclaims, hands cupped around his mouth.

"Are you jealous, Almet?" asks Larza.

"Hardly! Even in Ardán, I wouldn't dare sleep with my superiors."

Drasio shrugs off the implication and smiles away the conversation. He turns it back to matters at hand, reaching out to rein in the lights that float overhead. They dim as they drift toward him in a sea of fading stars. "I would also like to issue a reminder to everyone on this ship that our voyage is not one of trade. Our profits on this trip will be far greater with the acquisition of the Ottoman war ship, with its gold and its guns, so that we may return another day for trade or conquest." He raises his hand above his head, drawing the light of the orb back into him. "At dawn, we raise the black." A chorus of cheers erupts from his crew, eager for a good hunt and a hearty fight. Drasio raises his voice for the first time this evening amid the roar below, projecting each word with increasing volume. "There will be no prisoners."

THE AIR ITSELF SMELLS DIFFERENT over the Mediterranean. Where Drasio finds the Karreanan smells sweetly of fruit and musk, the Mediterranean smells murkier and saline. He resists the urge to reach past the hull of his ship, to touch the water and taste it once more. The ship sways with the waves, though his men have dropped anchor. They await the dawn in not-so-hushed tones as they settle for the night. He, too, retires to his captain's chambers. There, he finds his quartermaster with a book in her hands and an amused look on her face. By now, he's used to her unannounced visits, and while they are so often unexpected, rarely are they unwelcome. She flips through the pages before waving it in front of him.

"A collection of Arabic poetry," she says.

"I have many," he replies simply.

"I thought you didn't miss Algiers." She closes the book, placing it neatly on his desk. "These are hard to find in Ardán."

"I don't, but the beauty of the poetry was hard to leave behind." He sits at his desk and runs a finger across the spine. "This one was given to me by Ariyl; the rest I found on my own."

Larza pulls up a chair and sits adjacent to him. She has toned down her dress for the expedition to neutral-coloured trousers and a thin, white blouse. But she still wears orange pigments in dots around her eyes, a jewelled ring pierced through a delicate nose, and her pierced nipples poke through the fabric of her shirt. "Does Ariyl know your given name?" she asks, curiosity glinting in her eyes.

"No," says Drasio as he reaches for the bottle at the corner of his desk. He swallows that memory with a swig of the seaweed liquor, coating his throat with sugar and salt. The alcohol settles in a burn in his stomach. "As far as anyone is aware, I am no less Ardani than you are. Or perhaps even more than you, given your mother's heritage."

Larza nods. A northerner by blood, she was born and raised in the south. But her blonde hair and grey eyes accent her pale olive skin, and on any given day, she walks as a ghost amongst the darker-skinned and darker-haired natives of Ardán. "Perhaps one day you'll tell me?"

Drasio downs more liquor and chases it with mango juice, grimacing at the thought of a name he no longer felt was his own. He looks over at his best friend, shrugs off the notion. "That name doesn't belong to me, although I wish I could say it no longer holds a bearing to my being." He opens the book before him, runs his fingers along the words printed on the page. "Surely you understand that. Ardán is no stranger a land than Béallic to the north; is it not a country where people choose to set aside past identities? In Ardán, we are all Ardani." He thinks of the Ardani he has met, the countless men and women whose ancestors were born in lands familiar to him but strange to them: Turkey, Greece, Morocco, Tripoli, Tunis, Algiers. Echoes of a world he had left behind.

"Those who manage to cross the Barrier and find themselves on land, yes." Larza reaches for the liquor and pours some into a glass, swirling it with her fingers as she adds some mango juice. "But still, there are some who grow melancholic for their homelands or cannot adjust to their new lives. You, on the other hand, hardly miss Algiers." A ghost of a smile grows on her face. "You've never told me why."

"The government that controls Algiers has sought to keep my people down for centuries. They would rather see us enslaved or killed than free." Drasio grins bitterly. He remembers receiving news of executions of his loved ones while he was at sea. He remembers the stories of Berbers pulled from their homes and forced into slavery. He skims the poetry on the page, the language here soft and kind and almost foreign to the hatred spat at his people. "They took my parents when I was young. They almost killed me and my crew when we refused to back down. And while I nearly died when crossing the Barrier, I would surely have died had I stayed in Algiers."

He pauses and closes the book, hiding away its words between the covers.

Larza looks at him sympathetically in the dim light. "Are you not proud of your people? Do you feel shame for your given name?"

Drasio shakes his head. "I was not given a Berber name," he replies. "In Ardán, all are welcome in the new land. But in the Maghreb — in Algiers — despite my people having been there before, we are enslaved and suppressed." He glances outside through the windows, over the horizon where he knows there will be land; to a country he once called his own. And he speaks, with a level voice and determination. "I want to see it burn."

WHEN DAWN BREAKS OVER THE *Rose Star,* Larza is already barking orders at the crew. Drasio hears her from his quarters and suspects she slept poorly. Rarely does she jump straight into the thrall of what would otherwise be a quiet morning. He pulls a map from the shelf and carries it with him onto the upper decks, where his crew is raising the anchor and letting fly the sheets. He meets Larza at the rear of the ship, climbing onto the railing above the stern. She smiles and waves and wishes him good morning. Slowly, she raises her right arm and the ship lurches forward; the calm waters below kicking up waves as she pushes and pulls until they're moving at sailing speeds.

Drasio watches the sails, strained from the wind. He smiles. *Larza, who breathes life into the tides,* he had once called her. He remembers her laugh when he was first granted his powers by the mages of Béallic, when light came to him in clusters of stars around his body. *Drasio,* she had said, *who brings light into the darkness.*

Larza jumps down from the rail, tugs the map from under his arm, and unfurls it before them. On it are the routes they had secured weeks ago, of war ships and galleons moving across the Mediterranean, marked in red. In green, dotted sparely across the waters, are the entry and exit points into the Barrier. "We should be crossing paths with the *Two Lions* if our schedule is to be believed," she says, tapping a tailored nail to their current location. "But given that we're on a trade route, we may be more likely to run into a galleon. I hope you're all right with a potential cargo ship. There will be guns, though not quite as many."

"I want the *Two Lions,*" mutters Drasio. "Ardán will be in need of an updated fleet if we are to continue patrolling the waters of the Barrier. Our fleet is falling gravely behind the technology of this realm and if we are to continue trading in the Maghreb, we should at least *look* like the ships we are pretending to be. Besides, if I can weaken the Ottomans by even one ship, I would consider this voyage a success."

Larza rolls the map tightly, pressing her lips together in a smirk. "But you'll be back for more."

"Of course." He offers a hand to take the map, but she shakes her head and slides it under her arm.

"I'll take this back in," she says. "I refuse to let you hole yourself back into your cabin until the first signs of contact." There is amusement in her voice, and her tone is light-hearted, but he knows she is serious. He opens his mouth to object but thinks himself better. She's right, of course, and he would likely just let his anger fester away if he did.

"Are you like this on your own ship too?" he asks with a smile.

"As in, do I act like a captain? Of course I do." She grins. "Although I do have a *very* competent quartermaster."

"I should hope your wife is as competent as you are. Things must run smoothly between the two of you."

Larza's face lights up, an idea on her tongue. "There's your answer!" she exclaims. "What about Nyralt? I've heard he's an excellent sailor."

Drasio smiles at the mention of his lover but knows, in his heart, it wouldn't be a good decision. "He's more of a fisherman," he replies. "Life as a pirate would not suit him well."

She nods, considering his words. "You'll will find someone."

THEY SAIL FOR HOURS, CIRCLING the waters, before the sails of another ship peek over the horizon. He hears Almet call from above, "Dutch galleon! Two hours north!"

The mood on the *Rose Star* shifts. Drasio swears the wind's picked up, leaving his crew now bristling with anticipation. Their calls to each other grow louder and more eager as they scramble to turn their ship north. Drasio stands by the wheel, contemplating whether he should raise the black now, to signal their presence as a pirate's ship. He thinks to the flags they have brought on this trip—of the colours of Tripoli, of Morocco, of Tunis, of Spain—and he decides that they should be Tunis. He calls for the flag to be drawn, and the blue, green, and red stripes fly high on the ensign post behind him.

Larza, at his side, hands him a spyglass and mutters an "I told you" before sauntering off to join the rest of their crew. Drasio raises the lens to his eye and spots the masts over the horizon, the red stripe of the Dutch flag just bright enough to stand out against the sky and sea. He mutters to himself, remembering that they used to be orange. He preferred the orange. It stood out from the colours of the British and French fleets.

Drasio lowers the spyglass and collapses it. They are still at least an hour away from any combat, but he is as anxious as his crew and itching for a fight. It only dawns on him then—as he watches the horizon where the Dutch ship sails—that, for the first time in too many years, he has returned as a pirate to the Mediterranean. He glances over his crew and realizes, too, that he is the only man here returning and that for his crew, these are foreign waters. And while it had been decades since he had left Algiers, he has hardly aged beyond his thirty years—kept young by the magic granted to him by the mages. He watches Larza as she climbs the mainmast with an ease his men lack; there's a grace to her movements and a hidden strength in her stride that she gained with her training with the mages. And while he had done the same training, he never quite thought he had the same grace.

It takes an hour before they begin their hunt. The tension he feels only grows heavier when he sees the Dutch galleon turn toward them rather than away, picking up in speed. He extends the spyglass, raises it to his eye, and frowns. Not Dutch, perhaps. Not anymore.

"Be prepared for a fight!" he calls, running to find Larza. "Those below—ready the guns! All above—ready your eye-pieces!" He hands Larza the telescope.

"You're not scared, are you?" she asks as she raises the spyglass to her eye.

"Not scared," Drasio replies. "I'm surprised."

She hums. "I suspect they're doing exactly what we're doing. This should be interesting." She shoves the spyglass back in Drasio's hands. "But for a career pirate like you, this shouldn't be a problem."

Drasio lets loose a chuckle. "By Ardani standards, I'm more of a privateer," he says. "The crown pays us—it's hardly illegal."

"*Former* career pirate then," she replies, jabbing a finger at his chest and grinning. "Happy?"

"Captain!" Ilario this time, on lookout. Drasio cranes his neck to face him. "There's been a change in their flag."

Through the telescope, Drasio sees the red half-moon of the Ottomans replace the stripes of the Dutch. They are close enough now that he can see the men on board, and he wonders whether it would be wise to remove their flags altogether or to signal that they are a pirate ship. He watches the Ottoman ship sail closer with growing displeasure. He worries about what exactly may be on board that ship. Larza, next to him, glances at him hesitantly. "Strike our colours," he says. "And raise the black. Let them know we aren't some merchant ship to be taken."

Larza smiles and calls out the orders to the rest of their crew. His men scramble to switch out their flags, the anticipation of action buzzing through the air. Larza stands at the bow, readying herself to climb onto the rail at a moment's notice.

Drasio watches the galleon anxiously. They are close enough for cannon fire, but no guns are trained in their direction. The galleon begins its slow turn towards them, coming in as close as it can, and though they are still several hundred meters away, he can see their captain. He waits at the quarterdeck, hands behind his back. Drasio grimaces. He suspects they both have the same intentions: to board the other ship.

Drasio surveys the *Rose Star* and its crew, ensuring they're all wearing their eyepieces – wooden coverings with thin slits that were designed for his crew and his crew alone. They were made specially to withstand his style of combat.

The galleon approaches. Four hundred meters now. Three hundred. He grips his sword with his left hand, raises his right above his head. He watches the men of the galleon prepare their ropes and weapons, watches Larza out of the corner of his eye as she drops to the water below and shakes the sea beneath them. He smiles as the Ottomans back away out of surprise, and he stands his ground while some shoot their guns as they retreat. Both ships lurch back and forth and Larza slides across the water with a grin on her face, a dancer among the waves.

The crew of the *Rose Star* readies themselves and fires their guns at the Ottomans across from them. They throw their ropes, preparing to board, calling to each other in a mix of Ardani and Arabic. Drasio sees their captain walk to the side of the ship, shielding his eyes with his hand as the light above him grows in intensity.

His men have taken ships like this countless times before in the Karranean. They know when to board: right before the light blinds their victims and right before Larza pulls a wave between the ships, taking as many of the enemy crew as possible.

Drasio watches their captain raise his gun, still shielding his eyes, and he calls out — in Arabic, not Ardani — to his crew, "Their captain's mine!" He wants him to know. Drasio's lip curls in a snarl. He wants their captain afraid.

He lowers his arm as the light slowly reaches its peak intensity; his men run and climb aboard the other ship, their swords unsheathed, their guns cocked. And then, light engulfs both ships, drowns them in white. The sound of swords clashing, and the cries of combat and slaughter fill the air.

Drasio unsheathes his sword, climbs aboard, and holds tightly to the rails as the water below him explodes. The waves rock both ships, a wall of water between them. His men hold steady while the others fall off the sides. The ship rocks back again, crashing down to its upright position and Drasio slides to regain his footing. By now, the light has receded.

The Ottoman captain, brandishing his sword, runs toward him and brings his blade down, but Drasio is faster. He leaps out of the way, parrying his blade, and manages a closer look at the man before him. Not an Ottoman by birth, no. He is blonde and blue-eyed, though he wears the clothes of the Ottomans and carries an Ottoman sabre. Drasio grimaces as he slashes at the captain, managing to tear into his jacket, but no more. He parries another attack, taking the blade and pulling it out of the captain's hand.

His opponent simply stares at him, teeth barred. "Devil," he sneers in accented Arabic. "Demon."

"You must be Dutch." Drasio moves closer to the Ottoman captain. He lowers his sword but keeps it ready. "Following the likes of Suleiman Reis, Murat Reis, Zymen Danseker, hm?"

The other captain raises his gun, cocking it and aiming with shaky hands. "You blinded us," he stammers. "You moved these waters—what black magic do you possess?" He shoots, but the bullet breezes past Drasio's shoulder. The man's hands still shake. Drasio glances around briefly and finds that the fighting around them seems to have calmed, with only a few of the Ottoman men remaining on their feet.

Drasio pushes aside the gun with the tip of his sword, looks at the captain with contempt. "What is it about you Dutch and the Ottomans? You're one of countless other corsairs who've left behind your countrymen because it's more profitable with the Turkish," he says as he takes the gun from the captain's grip. He throws the gun aside, picks up a discarded sword from the ground, and offers it to him. "Either way," he continues, "I don't give a shit who you work for, this encounter's outcome would have hardly changed. But seeing that you've joined the Ottomans makes this all the more sweet." The other captain keeps silent, eyeing the sword being extended to him, hilt-first. By now, a crowd has gathered around them. "Should you defeat me in combat, I will leave you your ship and its goods. My men and I will retreat without further conflict."

The Ottoman captain snarls. "You've killed my crew." He takes the sword with a heavy hand.

"So you won't fight me?" Drasio is almost disappointed, but the Ottoman captain rushes toward him, sword extended to impale. Drasio grins, side-steps out of the way and parries the blade. "You will fight then." He slashes at the captain's arm, but then he falls to the ground as his legs are swept from under him. He rolls out of the way of an incoming slash, dragging his sword upward as he pulls himself to his feet, nicking the other captain on the shins. Drasio ducks the swing of the other's sword, grabbing his wrist with his left hand and cutting the Ottoman captain in the shoulder. He pulls out the blade and strikes again, forcing the Ottoman to drop his sword with cries of pain. Drasio grits his teeth together in a grimace.

"Demon," says the Ottoman, seething.

"No such thing," Drasio replies. He tightens his grip on the other captain's wrist, feeling the bones crack from the force.

The Ottoman's sword falls to the deck. Drasio digs his sword in deeper, and the Ottoman captain cries out. He swings his arm at Drasio's elbow, attempting to knock his grip loose. Drasio frowns, feeling a bruise forming right above his elbow. The Ottoman strikes again, but this time with something sharp, nestling itself into Drasio's arm. Drasio swears, half in Arabic, half in Ardani, pulling out his sword and watching the bloodied blade drip onto the wood below. The Ottoman cracks a smile. Drasio's own right arm is bleeding now, throbbing in pain, but he knows he can fight through it.

In the Ottoman captain's hand is a dagger, small and thin. It must have been holstered to his belt. Drasio is surprised he missed it. The Ottoman lunges at him again. This time, he is using his left arm. And while his opponent is now clumsier and less precise, his attacks are far more chaotic. Drasio finds himself on the defensive, keeping his sword's point trained at him to maintain a distance. He waits for an opening and strikes his left wrist, knocking the dagger out of his opponent's hand and slicing part of it off in the process. Drasio steps in, kicks the Ottoman down to his knees, and uses both hands to drive his sword into the man's chest through his collarbone. The other captain slumps forward and dies with a gasp.

Around him, his men are quiet. Ardani pirates do not celebrate deaths in a duel. Instead, there are nods of encouragement, of acknowledgement that the ship is theirs.

Drasio pulls out his sword, reaches down to the dead captain's jacket, and wipes his blade clean. He grits his teeth as he inspects his wound, extending his arm only to be met with a stabbing pain. The wound isn't large but it's strategically placed, and he pulls off the sash of the dead captain and ties it around his elbow. It'll heal, but he'll need to be careful.

Larza sits watching from the quarterdeck. He isn't sure when she climbed on board, or how long she had been watching, but he nods to her. She jumps off, puts a hand on his shoulder, and walks him to the ladder leading to the lower decks. "What do you wager we have below?" she asks.

Drasio presses his lips together in a frown. "You know the answer."

"I do." She begins her descent before him, jumping off halfway down the ladder. "It's no Ottoman war ship. That would probably have been easier."

Below, Ilario greets them before the closed door to the cargo hold. There is blood below, and a few of his men are clearing out the dead bodies, piling them to the side. "We've counted thirty guns on board," he says in his native Ardani.

Drasio nods. The *Two Lions* likely would've had at least fifty, given the size of the ship. But he presses on. "And inside there?"

Ilario steps out of the way, opening the door. "Uh, see for yourself."

Drasio isn't sure what he's expecting. Spices? Weapons? Alcohol? No, he knows what he's expecting, deep in his gut. Inside, he sees around two hundred Europeans, chained at the wrists and ankles. The hold smells of urine and gods-know what else; they've been beaten and bruised and emaciated. The few that look in his direction are scarred with defeat while the others hang their heads low. He groans inwardly, his heart turning at the sight. This is a slave ship. He should've known the moment he saw the Ottoman flag.

"Should we kill them?" asks Ilario. "Your orders were no prisoners but we thought you'd want to see this for yourself. They're all in poor shape and Larza may have injured a few earlier. The conditions are such shit I'm honestly not sure what was inflicted on them before or—"

Drasio cuts him off. "Well, we can't just let them loose in Europe!" he sneers. He pushes Ilario out of the cargo hold, his eyes wide as he holds his arms up defensively. Larza follows closely behind. "They've already seen us—they may be prisoners, but even animals know the seas do not move in the ways Larza has granted us. What would you have us do?" Those last words come out in a growl.

"Bribe them perhaps?" continues Ilario, meek. "We have little need for the gold that's in the captain's cabin."

"We can always use the gold," Drasio mutters. He turns to Larza for suggestions. There is an underlying bureaucracy at play here, and one only he and Larza are familiar with. They have been trained by the mages to maintain order across the Barrier, to ensure that the two realms stay separate and safe. This is, as far as he is concerned, a complete breach of their orders.

"We aren't supposed to traffic people across the Barrier," she replies, crossing her arms. "Too many lost find their way already and most of them simply don't adjust." She sighs. "If we do return them to Europe, what are the odds their stories will be believed? Is there any possible way to spare these poor mortals?"

Ilario seems disappointed and slightly put off from the use of the word *mortals*. He frowns. "So killing them isn't an option?"

"I refuse to kill slaves," replies Drasio. He glances at the cargo hold. "If we take them to Béallic, they would be guaranteed free of any risk of becoming a slave. This will always be a risk when trading in the Mediterranean. The pirates here traffic people more than any other goods."

"You know, Lord Blaire won't be happy with this," says Larza.

"Lucian can go fuck himself," Drasio mutters. He thinks of the face of Lord Lucian Blaire of the High Council of Mages. He thinks of his wealth and his status and wishes for a moment he knew what it was like to fear for his life. That Lucian would perhaps for one moment have to face a decision such as this. After all, what does Lucian know of slavery? Drasio grimaces at the thought and weighs the potential capture of the *Two Lions* against the slaves he now finds himself responsible for. He considers the conquest of an actual Ottoman ship, knowing that he may have missed the opportunity altogether.

And he resigns himself to the thought, makes peace with the situation he's in. Returning these slaves to Europe could mean danger, but bringing them to Béallic would mean freedom. He turns to Ilario. "Unchain them," he says. "We'll bring them across the Barrier and send them north after that."

Ilario nods. "They're going to be useless on this trip, you know," he says.

"You'll find a way."

Larza begins her climb back to the upper decks, with Drasio behind her. She offers a hand at the top of the ladder, which Drasio gladly takes with his uninjured arm. She pulls him to his feet. "Have you given up on the *Two Lions*?" she asks, a coy smile on her face.

"I may have," he replies. "It's no Ottoman war ship, but they have a dead slave trader and a stolen galleon."

"And one less shipment of slaves," she adds. She takes the wheel, resting her tiny frame against it. "Béallic is terribly underpopulated anyway. We'd be doing Lucian a favour."

"So you'll defend me?"

"Of course I will."

Drasio smiles. "The *best* quartermaster. What will I do without you?"

"You'll find a new one," she says with a grin.

DRASIO, DESPITE HIS INJURED ARM, still helps his crew wrap and discard the bodies of the dead into the waters. He notices the light drain from the sky into bloodied reds and dusty purples and watches the clouds paint themselves over relatively calm skies. He wraps the Ottoman captain with his dagger and sword rather than taking them for himself. It is a tradition he learned from the Ardani pirates, to honour the dead by returning to them their weapons, especially in a duel. Almet helps him lift the body over the side and into the water below. The captain's body plunges into the depths briefly before resurfacing and floating away.

The wind picks up. It carries with it a chill that he feels through his jacket and a buffeting humidity laced with salt and flora. He squeezes his injured elbow, feels the heat of it even over his shirt. He pulls his jacket close around him, taking in a deep breath of the air. There's a feeling in his gut of an on-coming storm, instinct developed from decades of life at sea. He looks to the sky as the night settles in and watches the stars twinkle into existence. This is his first trip back to the Mediterranean, and he hadn't even stopped in the Maghreb proper. He smiles to himself as he finds the North Star. He'll be back, and he prays to the Three Dancers of another sky that he will be more ready then.

He climbs back aboard the *Rose Star*, watching Larza shuffle around the slaves on their ship, Ilario attempting to show them the ropes—quite literally. He takes his place at the helm of his ship, calling for his men to raise the anchor. Almet walks up to him with a long silken ribbon covered in chains, enough to have been from his entire crew. He thanks him, unhooking a necklace from around his own neck and looping it through one of the holes of the ribbon. An Ardani charm, for good luck. He kisses it, prays to the Gelgys for a safe trip home, and tosses it over and into the waters.

Larza, on the galleon, waves to him. She stands at the stern and pushes the waves in their favour. On both ships, the sails fly, catching wind and pulling them forward.

Drasio wishes his crew a safe voyage, in the Ardani tongue that's grown natural to him. In the hours they spend sailing back towards the Barrier, the night falls heavy on the sky, and he watches it change, watches the Argo Navis fade into fogged night. His crew sing songs of Ardán, telling stories of the sea-faring people who long ago settled in the land they now call home – that he too now calls home. He remembers his talk with Larza and thinks that perhaps, he should collect more books of Ardani poetry. And that perhaps, on his next trip, he will have distanced himself from Algiers, from his old name. He smiles. That would be nice.

Saints and Bodhisattvas

By Joyce Chng

WHERE THE STRAITS INTERLACED EACH other with the confluences of currents and trade routes was the famed Golden Chersonese, a beacon of light, the center of all wealth and riches. Saints and bodhisattvas met there, allies in the interexchange of spirituality and learning. You would find your path there, they said. You would never hunger nor would you thirst. Bewitching creatures lurked in the Golden Chersonese, fantastic animals that populated your mind's bestiary. Birds of paradise with tails that flamed like the sun, dragons with large flickering tongues and poisonous saliva, and large cats that roared and founded a city. It lured many explorers, sailors of the sea and wind. It lured me.

I was born in the middle, a straddler between two worlds, one of the sea and one of solid land. The midwife laughed and said I was destined to ride the waves, breathing both ocean air and the sap of sea almond and angsana trees easily. Ibu was perturbed by the midwife's words, but she only held me, so she said, trying to protect me from the elements. I was in the middle, where the currents of life swirled like whirlpools forming at the wake of ships. At two, I was already swimming. At four, I stood at the prow of a skiff, the sea breeze on my face, the sea singing in my veins. At ten, I joined my father in his travels. I remembered soaring sunbaked stupas, the Sanskrit and Pali of saffron-robed monks, and the solemn tolling of gereja bells on Formosa's hill. I remembered the fragrance of spices and sandalwood wafting through the narrow streets of Melaka, the cries of the vendors hawking their wares.

When I turned eighteen, I was given my own perahu. Rare for a girl, but I was never a girl, never a boy either. I wore a lacy kebaya at home, a simple chinon and baggy trousers at sea. My hair was bound tight. I swung on ropes, unencumbered by loose strands of hair. My right hand held a dao, a gift from a friend whom I saved. His ship burned, his cargo gone, but he lived. He was grateful to be alive. I was a saint for saving him.

I fought with his dao, now my dao. With it, I explored the Golden Chersonese.

Then, she came into my life like a bodhisattva.

MY MEN WERE LOUDLY DISCUSSING the merits of cooking while they repaired my ship. Away from home, they longed for their homes so they distracted themselves with repair work. Sleek, sharp of prow, my ship cut through the sea like a kris. Yet it was not invincible against the forces of nature. Wood wore down easily, got chipped and sometimes dented. The underside of the ship had to be scraped thoroughly. Months at sea meant abundant growth of sea life. The sharp edges of the shells on the ship's sides hurt our exposed skin.

They joked about making seafood kari with the mussels as they removed them. On lean days we often picked them off the sides of the ship and ate them boiled in coconut water. I never liked them. I craved my mother's ulam. I missed the cleansing taste of the finely chopped herbs and the bitterness of the fried shallots. But to play along, I laughed with them, like the way my father had taught me. In their eyes, I was the towkay's son.

The last raid saw our rival, another band of lanun, trying to escape. In their panic, they rammed the prow of their perahu into the side of my ship. The sound of it made me sick to the stomach. It reminded me of breaking bones. We were lucky water didn't seep in. We limped into our port, our lives and cargo intact. I was livid. We would have to spend the whole month repairing the ship and miss a season of plying the sea before the torrential rains returned. I hated returning to port and having to wait the rains out. For the repairs, I traded in a new chest of precious Chinese silk in exchange for tools and timber. I had intended the chest to be sold to a buyer. It felt like a bad start.

Around this time, the dry season was nearing its end, ready to go but unwilling to leave. The land was parched, the grass a brittle brown, and the wind hot against my cheeks. It blew in gusts, stirring up puffs of dust from the ground. A large desiccated spider tumbled across my sandaled feet. The withdrawing tide exposed the seabed rippling with life. Tiny fish darted in the pools of clear water. Crabs waved their pincer claws. I leaned back into the warm sand, my arm across my eyes, glad for some respite. I only wanted the repairs done as soon as possible. The heat lulled me into a light nap.

I heard someone walking towards me, footsteps crunching on the sand. I glimpsed beaded slippers glittering vivid red and green. Beaded slippers? I raised my face then to the glare of the afternoon sun. She stood before me, imperious, the sunlight outlining a slim figure clothed in a vivid sea-green kebaya and red sarong. Young nonyas were usually accompanied by a stern matronly chaperone when they left their house, if they ever left it at all. They led sheltered lives. What a rare occurrence indeed.

"You must be the captain of the *Sri Matahari*," the voice was young and confident, clear with precise pronunciation of the patois spoken in our parts of the Golden Chersonese. I got up quickly, dusting my chinon and trousers as I surveyed the girl in front of me.

Her hair was a light brown. Under the sun, the strands shimmered gold. Her skin was the color of my own: the color of a Peranakan child - olive with subtle shades of perang. Her dark eyes were large and bright with a lively intelligence. Portuguese Kristang, then. There was a large population of them in this part of Melaka. They were mostly fishermen. The wealthier ones ran shipping consortiums.

"I am," I said briskly.

"I have a request...a job for you," the young woman continued without any introduction. "I will pay you."

I smiled wryly. "I won't agree to any request without knowing the name of my potential hirer."

Her full lips twitched. She must have pouted a lot as a child. She schooled her irritation with a smile too. "I am Maria."

"What can I do for you, Maria?" I stifled my own chuckle. She must have thought I was a man.

She leaned forward suddenly, her manner at once shy and conspiring. Something flashed bright at her neck. A silver necklace. "I want you to kill a man."

"Kill a man?"

I raised an eyebrow. I had encountered such requests before and twice I refused them very politely. I wasn't an assassin.

"Captain Neo," Maria said severely.

"So you do know my name. Back to my question: Kill a man?"

"Not so loud!" the young woman snorted. My first mate, Halim, looked up sharply. He was always alert and quick to respond. That was why he was my father's first mate and now mine. Only he knew who I actually was.

"I am not a killer," I shook my head.

"You are lanun. Lanun kill people," Maria pushed on. I frowned. I was beginning to dislike her attitude. I wanted her to go away. "You are not averse to killing."

"You must have mistaken me for something I am not. I am just a simple trader," I said very mildly. My men knew that particular tone very well. Suddenly, all repair work stopped and the men stood up, very slowly, with hands on their parangs and kris knives, glaring darkly at her. "You have such a low opinion of us. We are not the ruffians you think we are."

"Ai meu Deus!" Maria said angrily. She had noticed their reaction. She was no fool.

"I know that expression, senhora. You don't have to swear."

"I would like you to hunt down the man who killed my father," Maria whispered, her voice harsh, almost guttural. Her eyes were wet with unshed tears and she clearly hated showing that weakness in front of me and my men. "I know who and what you really are. *Please help me.*"

Her voice tugged at something in me. Loss. Pain. Despair. I thought of my father, already several years dead. He died when I was twenty, a victim of the prolonged coughing sickness.

"*Please.* Que os santos te abençoem." *May the saints bless you.*

I knew the phrase. All the captains who plied the Golden Chersonese learned the two or three languages spoken at the major and minor ports, besides the "port tongue," which was a mixture of all thelanguages together. I glanced at the silver necklace on her neck. It was a small crucifix. Serani. Most of the Portuguese Kristang were called Serani by the rest.

Against my better judgment, I nodded.

Her full name was Maria Fernandes.

Once she was perceived as non-threatening, my men went back to repairing the ship, their voices loud enough to be heard from the deck where I invited Maria for freshly brewed Ceylon tea. I did so, because it was the right way to show hospitality to guests, and because this was the way my father had taught me. It was also a good way to gauge my guest face to face, over tea and preserved sweetmeats from my own personal store.

Maria took off her slippers to walk up the wooden plank, even mincing daintily across without losing her balance. She politely declined my helping hand to step into the ship. Her sarong restricted her movements, yet she moved quickly and with grace. Soon, she sat, legs tucked under her, while I poured the tea into delicate porcelain cups. They were the craze at the moment, all the way from China. She nibbled on the sweetmeats, complimenting the taste of the sugared dry hawthorn. I sipped my tea, wondering who she really was, where her family lived.

"I am an orphan," she said without being prompted. "If you are curious as I think you are. I was adopted by a Peranakan family. But I left on amiable terms. This kebaya and sarong... they belong to a friend who took me in out of pity." She lapsed into silence, staring into the sea. Heat shimmered over the horizon. The sky was a clear blue.

"Ah, I see," I said. "How will you pay me? This is a business transaction."

She looked up, her eyes wide, her nostrils flaring. I realized she was afraid. "I will...pay you once the deed is done. At the meantime, please grant me permission to work onboard your ship."

"This is still very vague, Maria. I can't work on the basis of empty terms. My men need payment. Let me remind you that we are all rough people," I shook my head. "We are all used to rough and hard work."

Maria stared hard at me. "I have heard rumors about you, that you are actually a woman in disguise. I can work just as hard as a man."

"What if I am?" I challenged back, suddenly angry at the intrusion of my privacy. Rumors were often spread by jealous gossip and idle chatter. "Can you handle a weapon? Will you faint at the sight of blood?"

"NO!" her shout startled me with its sheer vehemence. "I am not some fragile flower! If it's handling weapons you want, I can do it. Teach me!" She spat the words out as if they bothered her.

"Well, then," I said finally. "My ship's still being repaired. We can't leave immediately."

"I can wait," Maria pouted. "Even if it means a month."

Halim chose this time to pop up, peering straight into the ship at us. He was a wiry man, built for the sea. Age had grizzled his temples, but his eyes were still sharp, his tongue even sharper. I saw him as a father of sorts, a replacement for my own. He wore his customary dark sarong and left his torso bare. His family kris hung by his side. "Adakah semua dalam keadaan yang baik?" he asked, glancing at Maria sternly. Maria glared back, unafraid.

"We are well," I smiled, waving him away. "Don't worry."

My first mate nodded curtly and ducked back out into the afternoon sun, shouting orders to the crew to stop lazing around. Maria left her tea untouched. "I have no family left," she said.

"We will talk more tomorrow," I said, suddenly tired. Maria's presence had stirred emotions I'd thought were gone. I missed my family.

I WOKE UP FROM A dream where my mother was making sambal with the batugiling. Her strong hands rolled the stone cylindrical pestle across the large mortar board. I could hear the stone grinding against the chilli and herbs. Somewhere, someone was singing. The smell of the chopped galangal and chilli being mixed intoxicated me. My heart ached with longing. I opened my mouth to say something to my ibu...only to peer up, sore and ill-rested, at the ceiling of my cabin.

I found Maria waiting for me at the bottom of the ship. It was barely morning yet. The tide had rolled in and the hint of rain was in the air. The men slept in, wrapped in their sarongs. Only Halim seemed awake. He was idly fishing, but I knew he was also alert and listening for any sign of trouble.

She had not slept. She was still wearing her kebaya and was wrapped in a tattered shawl. I glanced down at her feet. Bare. The beaded slippers were gone.

"Are you comfortable?" I asked. Maria smiled wanly at me. "We walk barefoot on the ship. Are you sure you don't need protection for your feet?" My own were callused from years on board ships.

She only nodded. The sky was beginning to lighten. A sliver of golden orange peered over the east. Was Maria the kind to bolt? Time to seal the agreement. I spat into my right hand and extended it to Maria. Without hesitation, she spat into her right palm and then pressed it against mine. She didn't even flinch.

"Your life is now mine and my life is now yours," I intoned the formal phrase used amongst people of our particular trade. "You share your food with us and we share our food with you. We eat the same food. We breathe the same air. The sea protects you and me."

"Amém," Maria said, crossing herself. My lips quirked. I decided I was going to like her.

"Let's break fast," I walked towards Halim who had started a fire to grill the ikan kuning he'd caught. "And let us get you something to wear. That finery has to go."

"Please let me keep the kebaya," Maria hurried to join me. "I want to remember something from my former life."

"Of course," I answered coolly. The cooking fish smelled delicious.

We found headgear, a plain grey chinon and dark green trousers for Maria. The cloth cap came from Halim's own pile of clothing, the chinon and trousers from my chest since we shared a similar body type. Divested of her kebaya and sarong, Maria looked like a boy in her new clothes, her hair tied up into a tight bun and hidden under the cap. She wore no weapon yet. Her necklace still hung on her neck.

She ate with what seemed like a healthy appetite, picking the flesh off the fish bone with her fingers and chewing the whole fish head before chasing it down with more Ceylon tea.

"The ship's not ready yet," Halim reported. "We need one day more."

"Our men are hardworking," I said. My first mate grinned, a flash of white teeth.

"They are motivated by the sea," he said, before leaning closer, darting a quick look at Maria who remained ignored by the rest of the men who swarmed over the ship. "You trust *her*?"

"Hers is a blood feud. She seeks revenge."

"Keep an eye on her, kapitan. I would rather have her off the ship."

"She has no family."

Halim snorted. "That's the reason given by half of our men. And...she's...you know...a woman..." He let the sentence trail into silence.

"You said that about me a long time ago."

"You are our towkay's child."

"Son. Our towkay's *son*."

Halim's face reddened. "Kapitan, you proved yourself on the sea. Her? I am not sure, though I have heard that there are women on the other ships too, just as fierce and bloodthirsty as men."

"Let her go clean the ship's deck first," I said finally, wrapping my headgear around my head. "That's her first test."

By mid-day, Maria hung around like a bedraggled ghost. The ship floor was scrubbed but she was thorough.

"Not bad," Halim said, sounding unconvinced.

"Let her mend the sails," I said.

By evening, she sat, looking pale. The sails were mended, the tears neatly sewn. She managed to get the tools from the men who treated her as some sort of novelty. Halim made seafood kari, the spices courtesy from our own supplies, the fish and shrimp netted from the day's catch. Maria received her coconut husk-bowl of kari and retreated to the prow of the ship where she ate alone.

"Now let us see if she decides to stay," I nibbled at my own food.

I WAS WOKEN UP BY the sound of splashing water and the smell of cooking fire. I peered out from my cabin. Maria was boiling water in the tin kettle. Fish was already cooking on wooden skewers she picked from the fallen twigs beneath the portia trees. She had caught enough for all of us.

I smiled.

SRI MATAHARI CUT THROUGH THE water, as if relieved to be released from confinement. Her sails caught the wind full. I heard them humming their familiar song. Around me, the men went about their usual duties, checking the ropes, the hooks and sharpening their weapons. Halim stood at the lookout, his eyes watching everything. Our pilot, Abdullah, steered the rudder. He had an intuitive touch when it came to guiding the ship.

"Maria!" I barked.

She ran up quickly. Her eyes sparkled. I could feel her excitement. So far she had shown no seasickness. She didn't seem to mind the sea. Perhaps, somewhere in her blood, there was seawater.

"Where does the murderer of your father live?" I asked.

"Temasek," she replied quickly, her voice cold. "He lives on Temasek."

WHILE *SRI MATAHARI* SAILED, I taught Maria basic weapon drills. I couldn't possibly teach her all the things I knew. Instead, I chose one weapon and stuck to it. Maria handled the dagger easily. Block, attack, strike. Block, attack, strike. I knew the men watched the practice from the corner of their eyes, still painfully polite and reluctant to engage her with their activities.

"You need to be more aggressive," I pushed her. " Attack me. The people you meet later will not be nice nor will they be gentle."

Maria gritted her teeth. She had stopped pouting. In fact, I had not seen her pout since she came aboard. She came at me, her guard open. I stepped aside and twisted her arm. She struggled.

"Again," I said. I released her. She didn't rub her arm. Instead, she inhaled deeply, closing her eyes, before opening them again. She rushed, I evaded, only to have her side-step me. Her foot caught me off-balance. I tripped and stumbled. The men chuckled.

She reached down to help me up. Her grip was strong. I got to my feet. I could smell Maria. She smelled of spices and sweat. Her hair oil was not unpleasant, her body soft and warm. I felt my body respond, a flush of moist heat between my legs. The response surprised me. I had never felt like this before.

Before I could speak, she had placed her dagger onto my bare neck. I felt the cold edge press gently against the skin. "Surprise," she whispered in my ear. "*You have thick soles. I think you need shoes.*" She smirked.

"Beginner's luck." I pulled away, scowling at her. "Well done and thank you, no. I don't."

HALIM SIGHTED THE SHIP FROM a distance.

We were nearing Temasek, having navigated the complex network of small islands and sandy shoals surrounding the island. Maria had spent the week on the ship learning how to steer the rudder, wrestle and hone her fighting skills, and scrub the deck with coconut-husk bristles. The week had passed uneventfully. The season had only begun. Most ships would only emerge from their hideouts and ports once the merchant ships arrived. The ones plying the straits now were either fishermen or...people like us.

I had grown used to watching Maria prepare hot water and food every morning. I...grappled with the surge of emotions and physical sensations whenever I saw her. I dreaded and craved standing next to her. She was the saint I couldn't bear to touch, a bodhisattva so holy I felt guilty for even walking close to her. An exquisite and rare beautiful bird-of-paradise. Yet, she saw me as her captain and the person whom she had hired to kill her father's murderer. The voice of reason in me warned me to stay far away from her and maintain an air of business. I had never had a woman on board my ship. Halim was right. It stirred up *things* in me.

The men were not immune either. One by one, they started to drift close to her, so that they could catch a glimpse of her before scuttling away with their dignity intact. A couple of them tried to share food with her. When she washed herself with the clean water we stored in barrels, everyone pretended not to see. We draped a sheet across her part of the ship to cordon off the area. Yet, she didn't seem interested in any of the men. She treated them like older brothers. Strange and distant older brothers.

Kill the murderer, get my payment, and we would be rid of her. These thoughts filled my head.

Where would she go once the deed was done?

"Perahu!" Halim shouted.

IT SLID IN CONFIDENTLY, LIKE a hunting shark lured by blood and the prospect of a meal. The perahu was of the same make as *Sri Matahari*. Its sails were angled sharply. The captain was banking on speed. There were lanun who prided themselves on their attack skills. Many were hit-and-run experts: attack their opponent or a merchant, take what they needed, kill everyone aboard. I had seen ships adrift at sea, the crew dead and the cargo stolen. Most of the time, we just sailed past and offered a prayer.

What else could we do?

There were ten figures standing at the side of the ship, their weapons drawn. They were ready to board. Their pilot was steering the perahu so that it was heading at us directly. They were ready to board and kill. Abdullah yanked at the rudder and *Sri Matahari* moved, pulling away. It was our own tactic, to draw the enemy into a circling dance. "Let them give chase," I said, my heart pounding. I relished the taste of the hunt. My blood was singing in my veins. Beside me, Maria swallowed convulsively. Her eyes widened.

The lanun drew close, enough to see their features. Their faces showed a range of colors: perang and putih. There were three Dutch men among them. Some of the Dutch decided to stay after incursions into the area. Most had moved to Batavia where I heard they wreaked havoc and were terrible masters. They had fought with the Portuguese for territory and local rulers used them as pawns to their own bid to power. These

Dutch men looked battle-hardened, their skin thick and leathery, their eyes fierce. They wore the same clothing with the rest. They had thrown in their lot with these lanun.

"Short sabers," Halim muttered darkly. "Probably stolen." He hated the Dutch.

Maria gripped her dagger with a wild look on her face. She seemed to have seen something...someone on the ship.

"What's wrong, Maria?" I said.

"It's *him*. I recognize him. He's there on the ship!" Her voice trembled, halfway between fear and exhilaration.

"Who's he?" I growled.

"My father's killer. One of the white men! There, look, he's wearing headgear!"

I saw him. He was a middle-aged man with white hair and grizzled face. Tall and lanky, he leaned heavily to his left. Old injury?

"Are you sure?" Halim snapped.

"Yes!" Maria shivered. "Yes!"

"You ready?" I asked her. "Are you sure?" I repeated Halim's question.

"Yes, I am."

"Abdullah, we are going in," I shouted.

Abdullah needed no further instruction. *Sri Matahari* began her attack run.

"HE KILLED YOUR FATHER?" I whispered.

"Yes, he did. They fought over something a long time ago. They were...friends. He killed papa. He killed him and Mama pined to her death. I saw her die. I was only ten. *Ten*. I want to kill him for what he did to Papa and Mama. He destroyed my family!" Maria's knuckles were white, her breathing shallow. Her eyes, though, blazed with hatred.

"Today you get to kill him and avenge them," I said.

We drew close enough to board. The lanun yelled curses at us. My men hurled the boarding hooks.

With a laugh, I leaped across, my dao aimed at the captain of the ship.

HE WAS AN OLD MAN, even older than Halim but he fought harder than a cornered harimau. Still, I managed to subdue him, kicking him hard in the ribs. He fell hard backwards, his head hitting the boards. Dark blood seeped beneath the head. His men roared, having witnessed the death of their captain. They were going to fight even more viciously now.

In the tumult of combat, I didn't see Maria. Everybody was busy killing or trying not to get themselves killed.

The chaos parted, to reveal Maria confronting the Dutchman who killed her father. Her eyes screamed death. She yelled a stream of Portuguese words so obscure I didn't understand most of them. Only "death" and "go to hell" made sense.

The man seemed to freeze, as if he recognized her, before he launched into a series of slashing cuts to drive her off. He wanted to kill her.

Maria ducked, dodging the saber. The silver necklace swung, catching the light of the sun. Then my line of vision was hindered by a tumbling mess of wrestling men. When they rolled away, I looked desperately for Maria. What I saw sent shocks up my back.

The Dutchman had her pinned to the floor, his saber tip pointed towards her throat. She was resisting him as fiercely and strongly as she could, spitting into his face. He swore and cursed at her. Suddenly, he grunted and his entire body stiffened. Maria had somehow managed to shove her dagger deep in his chest.

"Go to hell," I heard her say in Portuguese. The man didn't respond. He was already dead. She looked disgusted as she pushed the corpse off her body and pulled the dagger out of its chest. There was a deep hole, welling quickly with thick red heart's blood.

By this time, the battle was done. The remaining crew members begged for mercy, only to have Halim slit their throats with his kris. The rest of my men went about the dead bodies, making sure the crew remained dead. The ship was carrying stolen cargo: three boles of expensive Chinese silk and two large cedarwood chests. Upon opening the chests, we found eighty gold and silver ingots in each. They must have recently attacked a merchant ship to have such riches. We were in luck. I thanked all the deities, even the saints and bodhisattvas. I was already planning to give some of the gold to Ibu in my next visit to my family home.

Dagger in hand, Maria stood in the sea of corpses, staring numbly at the dead men, including the body of her father's killer.

"It's done," she said in a soft voice. "Rest in peace, Papa and Mama."

She didn't cry. After wiping her dagger clean of blood, she helped the men carry the cargo across the plank, back to our ship.

We left the perahu adrift, the fate of every lanun who died at sea. *Sri Matahari* sailed away, richer and heavier.

"I AM VOIDING OUR AGREEMENT," I told Maria when the ship found shelter at a quiet mangrove swamp. Halim was wading in the soft mud, ready to hunt for the large meaty crabs. We would celebrate later with a meal of boiled mud crab.

"Why? I promised to pay you," Maria sputtered. She seemed to have weathered her first kill well.

"We have two chests of ingots. I am going to give you eight of the gold ones. I hope you can start a new life with them."

"Eight gold ones," Maria let her words trail off.

"We will drop you back in port tomorrow," I said. "Go back to your friend. Pay her one gold ingot as compensation."

"No, I want to stay," Maria said firmly. "I want to stay on the ship. With you."

"I am not your protector."

"You are not," Maria said. "But we swore an oath, remember? *Your life is now mine and my life is now yours.*"

"Ah."

"I want to uphold our oath," she said, watching Halim catch his first mud crab. He was chuckling away like a little boy with his first catch, his face and legs smeared with mud. The men laughed too. It had been a bountiful day.

"I want to travel the Golden Chersonese with the ship... with you," she continued, her gaze returning to rest on me. She was very close now. I could smell her. She washed herself thoroughly with our water after the encounter with the lanun. She bore the fragrance of sea salt. Her dagger rested tucked in her belt. "I want to know you better," she said shyly.

My heart rose at those words. I tried to maintain a stern demeanor. "You might get more than what you bargained for."

"The Peranakan matriarch bitch made me do all the menial chores," Maria snorted. "I can endure *anything*."

"Anything? Including me? I can be rather unbearable, just ask Halim," I replied. "Are you sure?"

"You are interesting, Captain Neo," Maria giggled.

"I am only *interesting*?"

Maria laughed her first real laugh. Such a wonderful sound. The men glanced quickly at her, startled by her sudden gaiety.

"Of course," her eyes sparkled merrily. "That is why I want to know you better."

"Indeed," I said. "Indeed."

SO, YOU CAME INTO MY life like a bodhisattva. We sailed the Golden Chersonese together, you and me, straddlers between the worlds. With two of the gold ingots, I bought you a pair of new boots, no more beaded slippers, but in the latest fashions outside the Golden Chersonese. They were apparently the rage in the courts of the kings and queens. They were made of the finest leather, with the tracery of yellow flower embroidery curling along the edges and the softest of velvet lining their insides. You laughed and said you could run faster with bare feet. "Don't be silly," you said as the sun rose above us in reds and oranges.

I laughed back. You kept the shoes in your private wooden box with the kebaya and sarong. You still wore your silver necklace.

And all was right in the world again.

The Doomed Amulet of Erum Vahl

By Ed Grabianowski

CAPTAIN JAGGA CROUCHED BY THE quarterdeck rail. Beside her, the steady rattle of lead shot striking the side of the ship rang in her ears. "Hard to port. Put on speed, Tripton!"

The sailing master, his demeanor that of an aggravated professor, was scrambling on all fours above a hatch on the gun deck. "Hard to port," he yelled down into the opening, then turned back to Jagga. "We can't do both at the same time, you know."

Below, the helmsman heard Tripton's call and pushed hard on the whipstaff, cranking the rudder far beneath him and shunting the ship to port. *The Hammer of Triel* groaned and came about.

The chatter of gunfire and other projectiles against the hull let up for a moment, and Jagga dared a look over the rail. To starboard was the lush jungle shore of Brathi; just aft were the low-slung, golden gunboats of the Redhands, mercenaries hired to protect the coastal trade routes. The same trade Jagga intended to take a piece of for herself. She flashed a manic smile at Tripton. "Do what you can, sir."

Tripton looked up toward the fore of the ship, one last futile spray of lead peppering the rail to his right. The carefully sculpted goatee and wire spectacles riding low on his nose gave him a delicate look, but his skin was weathered and brown, and his gentle, precise voice changed to a sailor's rough bark when he relayed orders for the captain. "Oi lads, straighten out and away from the shore, full sail. Got to get off these breakers." The crew, no longer ducking rifle fire, moved about the rigging and set *The Hammer of Triel* on her new course.

Jagga watched the gunboats give up the chase and fade into the distance. She'd lost this engagement by coming in too far from shore, her four-mast barque easy to spot against the horizon. The Redhands had been ready for her, and Jagga wasn't overly fond of a fair fight. "Tripton," she called mildly. "A word please."

He joined her on the quarterdeck and they watched the coast recede behind and to starboard, the sleek ship gaining speed as it got farther from shore, slicing along the ocean swells rather than crashing through breaking waves. They were headed south, the wind at their back, the sky clear and blue, though the air was thick with humidity. Jagga eyed Tripton's heavy leather coat. "How you can bear the heat in that thing? I don't think I've ever seen you take it off."

He turned slightly and brushed away some lead shot that was embedded in the folds and creases of the coat, not quite resisting the urge to grin. Jagga laughed.

"My aim is to go another day south and try our luck again," she said. "I consider this a trial run. Now we know the merchants hire mercenaries, and they have guns. Not very good guns, but those Redhand gunboats are too small and fast for us to hit with our cannons."

Tripton shrugged. "I don't see as we have much choice. We can't very well return north. Not without an impressively large amount of gold to bribe our way past your many *admirers*."

Jagga knew her reputation. They called her Jagga the Ripper, or Jagga the Bitter, or Jagga the Thorn of Gael. In the darker corners of Ulsh and Covengate they had much fouler names for her, filthy epithets that made her smile when she heard them. She'd spent the last year flying the jade flag of the Azeth Rebellion on *The Hammer of Triel's* mast, patrolling the coast of Ulsh for any shipping between Ulshan loyalists and the exiled royal family. The Azethans paid her well, but when the King of Ulsh came roaring into Jaidh Bay with a full war fleet, she slipped away and headed south. She'd backed a rebellion, the rebellion had been crushed, and now it was Jagga who was in exile. The Ulshans knew *The Hammer of Triel* well, its low hull painted gloss black, Jagga at the helm, unmistakable, pale and tall, black hair chopped at ear length like an afterthought, tattoos winding along her arms and up her neck. Going back meant braving either the Ulshan navy or the knife-sharp ice floes of the far Upper Sea.

"The wind blows south. We go south," she said. "And hope it's a wind of good fortune."

Tripton snorted.

THEY SAILED THE REST OF that day, keeping the coast just in sight. Once the sun set, they anchored, unwilling to sail blindly into unknown waters. The northern kingdoms, consumed by centuries of savage war, had little contact with Brathi. Only in recent years had traders and explorers crossing the Ulash Mountains returned laden with silver and jade, and tales of a rich confederation of city-states united by a tightly controlled merchant's alliance. Jagga, so inspired, had decided to try her luck, guessing shipments along the coast would be ripe for plundering.

Come morning, massive pillars of dark cloud thrust high into the western sky, far inland. Jagga stood at the forecastle with Myelle, her quartermaster, beside her. Myelle was startlingly thin, with a braided beard hanging to his waist. He eyed the distant storms. "If those clouds aren't wrung out by the time they reach the coast they could be a problem."

Jagga nodded. "Think how fast we'll move under sail in a hurricane." She gave Myelle a jovial elbow, but he was unamused.

The crew of thirty-five was generally in agreement with Jagga's plan to look for Brathi merchants a little less prepared than the ones they'd faced the day before. Decisions on the *Hammer* were made on a semi-democratic basis, mainly because the majority opinion could hold sway by force, though it was expected that Jagga would encourage consensus at knifepoint from time to time. But just before midday, the coast changed, and so did the plan. The jungle gave way suddenly to a rough brown desert just a few miles wide, so sparse they could see where the foliage continued again farther along the coast. It was as if something had taken a massive bite out of the jungle, leaving a three-mile semi-circle of bare sand.

In the center of this desolate spot, just a few hundred yards from shore, stood a black temple, a pyramid with four tall monoliths, one at each corner. It gleamed in the sun as if it was carved from solid obsidian. Tripton and Jagga stood at the quarterdeck rail squinting at the strange edifice. Tripton withdrew a small spyglass from his coat and took a closer look. "Well, shit," he said.

Jagga took the spyglass, and after a moment scanning the weathered yellow shoreline she saw what Tripton had seen. There was a woman fleeing the black temple. She'd seen their sails and was waving her arms frantically at them. Jagga lowered the spyglass and looked at Tripton. "Well, shit."

Jagga gathered the crew to convince them it would be worthwhile to have a look at the temple, that it was bound to house valuable relics or hidden chambers of gold. But they'd been with Jagga too long, and knew better. A crewman named Plagg spoke up first. "Yer jus' soft-hearted, Jagga, and always will be."

"Jagga the Kind," someone called out in a high-pitched, singsong voice.

"It's a woman in distress, then?" shouted someone else. "Jagga just wants someone soft for her bed!"

The crew roared, Jagga along with them. "Jagga the Seducer," she cried. "Oh, I see I've no secrets from you lot. But mates, you can't see much at this distance. She might have a face like a walrus and naught but three teeth."

As the crew laughed, Jagga heard Tripton murmur, "Jagga the Not Terribly Picky When It's Been Rather a Long Time."

Jagga's only reaction was to show the crew that half-crazed grin. "Bring her in close and we'll take the ship's boat to shore. Maybe bring back a prize or two."

THE WOMAN WADED OUT TO greet them. She was young, maybe twenty, with a tangle of dark hair and a semi-feral gleam in her eyes. She wore only a simple cotton shift, which covered her from neck to feet but was rendered nearly transparent by the spray of the ocean waves. Jagga caught herself staring.

"Neri," the young woman said, pointing to the center of her chest.

Myelle stepped forward. "Greetings, Neri. I am Myelle and this is Captain Jagga. Are you in danger?" He spoke in Brathi — not perfectly, but he alone among the crew had traveled far enough south to learn a little of that sweetly flowing language.

Neri's face lit up and she replied in rapid Brathi, pointing frantically back toward the temple.

"Slow down, Neri. Slow," Myelle said.

She took a deep breath. "Eiyeria o considorae delomelai. An hah haani ery. Soenisohn sepidesonn eiyerio," Myelle translated. "It is a haunted place. Something hunts me. I am alone and must escape this place."

Jagga nodded. "We'll have a look." She waved the crew forward with her, striding across the sand toward the temple.

"No!" Neri cried. She reached for Jagga and clutched at her arm, pulling her back toward the sea. "No, please." She said these words in Covantish, the North's most common tongue.

Jagga gave Myelle a wink, then reached up to place a hand on Neri's cheek. "It's okay, girl. We're warriors. Whatever hunts you, we'll destroy."

Neri sobbed, "No," and pressed her face to Jagga's shoulder.

The crew turned in unison to stare up at the massive temple. It seemed to cast a shadow on them, though the sun was nearly straight overhead. The oily iridescence of the walls towering over them felt deeply unnatural. The side of the temple facing them appeared to have no door, although the seams of massive bricks could be seen at this distance. Its strange, baleful presence felt like cold hands tugging at their spines.

"Eh, I'm no ancientologist, captain," Plagg said. "I'm good at aiming cannons and climbing rigging and naught else. Something's wrong with that place, there is, and I don't think I'd like to go inside it."

The rest of the crew muttered agreement.

Jagga held her gaze on the temple, one arm carelessly looped around the small of Neri's back. The salt air of the sea and the warmth of the girl in her arms swayed her. "Hurry back to the ship, then. If we're going to make a habit of running away, we might as well be quick about it."

As the ship's boat made its way through the waves back to *The Hammer of Triel*, no one looked back. No one wanted to feel the presence of the obsidian crypt again. No one saw the sand at the shore stir and shimmer. And if they had, they still might not have seen the cold yellow eyes glaring out of the impossible shadows at them.

THE HATCH LEADING DOWN TO the hold was already open when they climbed back aboard the ship. One of the crew pointed at Neri and offered a crooked, malevolent grin. "Down you go with the rest of the cargo."

Jagga came over the rail. "No." She didn't yell; in fact, she spoke rather gently, but there was no mistaking the command in her voice. It was rare for the crew to hear that tone—Jagga knew she couldn't lead a crew of misfits and outlaws with too tight a fist, but her sharp wits and tightly muscled arms had earned her enough respect to demand authority when needed. The barbed blades she wore on each hip functioned as her badges of office. "Myelle, bring fresh water up, and some food. I fear she hasn't eaten in days."

"Very well."

While Myelle went into the hold, Jagga led Neri to the quarterdeck and through the small door into her captain's quarters. Digging through a half-empty chest, Jagga emerged with some clothes that were, if not clean, at least dry and better suited for life on a ship. "Here, these are for you. I'll wait outside while you..."

Before Jagga could finish, Neri had dropped her cotton shift around her ankles, and Jagga discovered that Neri was wearing one other thing: an amulet, wrought of flat black iron in the shape of an elaborate and unfamiliar symbol, hung from a twisted length of rope around her neck. It fell just between Neri's bare breasts, a harsh contrast with the lush umber of her skin. The amulet wasn't the first thing Jagga looked at, but when she did, she felt a cold, uneasy tension in her gut, a strange echo of the feeling she had standing near the black temple. She lifted her gaze to Neri's eyes and saw gratitude there, and an invitation. Jagga swallowed, her throat suddenly dry. "Your...your food will be waiting on deck." And she left Neri alone.

The Hammer of Triel was quickly underway again. Jagga, Neri, and Myelle spent much of the afternoon on the forecastle, learning each other's languages. Neri knew more Covantish than expected, so they were soon deep in conversation without Myelle's translations. He left to grimace and glare at the rest of the crew, one of his favorite ways to pass the time at sea.

"My town was attacked, my family killed," Neri said. "I fled into the jungle and stumbled upon the temple. I was desperate for shelter, but I fear my presence there awakened something."

"Who attacked your town?"

Neri paused, narrowing her eyes against the low afternoon sun. "The town lies near the coast. Raiders from the interior come to disrupt the silver trade."

Jagga felt an unfamiliar pang of guilt. "Ah. And something came after you at the temple?"

"A phantom. It came out of the shadows."

"Well. You're a long way from there now. You may be stuck with us for a while, though. We're not often welcome at coastal towns."

Neri smiled. "I understand. I don't know where to go. For now, I just want to keep moving."

They stayed in each other's company quietly for a time, listening to the thud of waves slapping the hull, the sails snapping in the wind. Sea birds turned and dove into the sparkling water. Neri finally broke the silence. "Thank you."

"It's a bad habit of mine, rescuing people," Jagga said.

"No, a *good* habit. You are kind." Neri leaned her head to Jagga's shoulder, and the only thing that tarnished Jagga's joy at this was the fact that most of the crew was likely watching. She'd never hear the end of it. She took a short step away.

"There is a reasonably comfortable sack of grain in a storeroom beside the galley. You can sleep there if you like, or on deck if the weather holds."

Neri nodded, giving Jagga an odd half smile. The lowering sun set her eyes aglow, and Jagga caught herself staring again. When the sun dropped below the horizon, Neri simply turned and headed toward Jagga's quarters. Jagga followed and found her waiting there. She locked the door and pushed Neri onto the bed, kissing her with a hunger and need that was both welcomed and returned.

Entwined, they slept little, Neri's body flowing like a river goddess, Jagga's muscles tensing and releasing. But Neri would not remove the amulet, and even at the height of passion, Jagga found it disquieting.

Later, unable to sleep, Jagga dressed and slipped out of bed to walk the deck. A lantern, turned low, hung aft, though the silver moon did more to banish the darkness. She stood still, looking over the ship, letting her eyes adjust. A sound came from the bow, clear and cold in the silence of the night watch. It was both familiar and wrong, like a long blade drawn across a leather strap, oily and slithering in a way that made Jagga grind her teeth unconsciously. Then there was a wet tearing noise and the low sound of a man moaning.

Jagga fell into a fighting stance, but she'd left her blades in her quarters. Empty-handed, she ran across the deck and found Plagg lying in a pool of his own blood, his throat torn open. Before she could cry out an alarm, a man-shaped figure emerged from the shadows by the bow rail, thin and wiry, cast in jet and shrouded in churning shreds of smoke, backlit by the moon. From its face shone malevolent yellow eyes, and when its mouth fell gaping open, there was nothing inside but a vast and starless void.

"Murder!" Jagga shouted. "We're boarded!"

The night watch, up in the rigging, had not even been aware that anything was aboard. Jagga's call was echoed across the ship, but before anyone could reach her, the creature lunged. Black claws like needles slashed, Jagga leaning back just enough to avoid getting her throat sliced open. She was filled with a malignant feeling, but far stronger now, stronger even than what she'd felt on the beach.

Behind her, Jagga heard a voice cry, "No!" The creature looked past her, then darted across the deck. Jagga turned to see it striding straight at Neri, who'd emerged from the stern-castle clutching a sheet around her body. The crew was rushing onto the deck, armed and confused. The cloud of shadow and smoke that shrouded the thing made it hard for anyone to take aim. Jagga alone gave chase.

Neri stumbled backward, the sheet falling away. The creature pounced, and as Jagga ran, she could see the ochre glow of its eyes bathing Neri's terrified face.

But it didn't attack. As Jagga sprinted, she saw that it held the amulet in its vicious claws, gazing at it with eyes wide, slitted pupils flaring with lust. Neri arched her body away, the rope on the amulet taut around her neck.

"It must not have it," Neri said, gasping.

Jagga tucked her shoulder down and slammed into the creature at a full run, knocking it off of Neri as she tumbled after it. Its body was disconcertingly soft and when she touched it, Jagga was wracked with nausea, her throat clenching against the sudden urge to vomit.

She staggered to her feet. It hissed at her, flexing its claws. There was the crack of a pistol, and the creature gave a short shriek as it dissolved into a small mote of shadow that vanished into the night air.

"Cold iron shot," Tripton said. Smoke rose from the barrel of his gun.

Jagga watched Neri retrieve her sheet. She reached down to touch the amulet, but Neri turned away. "Explain this to me."

Neri's eyes dropped. She huddled under the sheet. "I found it in the temple."

"But you know something about it. You knew that that thing shouldn't get its claws on it. Why?"

"The amulet is the Black Key. That was a...a god, I think. Its name is Erum Vahl. If it holds the Key, the world unravels. It's hard for me to say. I saw a vision when I first held the Key. That is how I know."

"And it's been chasing you ever since?"

Neri's eyes were dark pools, tears cascading from them to splash her cheeks. "Yes. It came to my town. It kills and kills. I fled to save the others there, to save anyone else I know from this fate. But each time I escape, each time anyone injures it, it returns."

As Jagga stood thinking, from the forecastle came a despairing cry. "Oi, it's done for poor Plagg, what a bloody crime this is." As the crew gathered up Plagg's remains, Jagga felt their fear turning to anger.

"I'm bound to protect you, Neri. I have that much honor, at least. Give me the amulet."

Neri wiped her face, her expression growing stern. "Never. It is my burden. I would flee my entire life to save anyone else from this endless tragedy."

"Ah," Jagga said softly. She sank to one knee, her face close to Neri's. "But I don't think you're the wandering kind, sweet one." She kissed Neri's face, salty from the sea and tears. They returned to the captain's quarters. Myelle gave quiet orders to the crew, who obeyed him in sullen silence.

THE CREATURE CAME AGAIN THE next night, but they were ready, lanterns on every mast to dispel its foul shadows, each crew member armed with cold iron shot. When it returned two nights later, Jagga took a wound in her shoulder, her skin shredded by its vile claws. She spent the following day clammy and heaving, wracked by a ceaseless ache that left her arm nearly useless.

On the fourth night the shadow god manifested in the bilge and crept through the bowels of the ship, murdering seven of the crew before Myelle drove it off with an iron sword. The crew seethed with anger and Jagga knew it. Still she spent hours with Neri, talking and caressing. She didn't have the words in any language to describe her feelings. But she knew something had to change.

"Why not throw it into the deeps and be done with the damned amulet?" asked Old Jonn, the ship's cook. His tone suggested he wouldn't bother removing the amulet from Neri before casting it overboard.

"It would find it," Neri said. "It will find it anywhere. And then all this," she waved her hand as if to encompass the entire world, "Will become ash."

"Tripton, bring her about and tack into the wind. Head back north," Jagga said.

He tilted his head in confusion.

"We're taking Neri home."

The crew muttered, but Neri only sighed. Later, Jagga found her weeping in their quarters.

"Please don't," she whispered. "Please do not send everyone I know and love in this world to their deaths."

"I'm not." Jagga coiled her body around Neri, running her rough hands over Neri's skin. As Neri relaxed into Jagga's arms, Jagga deftly gripped the amulet and snapped the rope that held it. "Just me."

IT TOOK A WEEK RUNNING against the wind to get back to the black temple, battling the creature each night. Wearing the amulet now, Jagga caught a glimpse of the visions Neri spoke of: a sky blackened by ash, the ocean boiling, and the name etched in her mind—Erum Vahl. They traveled another day past the temple to get closer to Neri's town, though as they passed the glittering black pyramid, she felt it pulling at her like the tongue of a great beast drawing her into its mouth. That final night, with the ship at anchor and the shadow god temporarily banished after a hard battle, Jagga sent the crew below. She and Neri slept at the bow, lying naked in each other's arms under the slowly turning stars and the soft touch of the sea breeze. Jagga found herself kissing tears from Neri's face again, mingled with her own this time.

In the morning, Jagga rowed Neri to shore alone, and they embraced on the beach.

"Be safe, sweet one. Return to your home and live and love for all your days."

Neri kissed Jagga hard, then turned and ran into the trees.

When Jagga returned to *The Hammer of Triel*, her face was grim. "I am Jagga the Accursed, now. Jagga the Hunted. Jagga, of Neri's Heart." Her voice grew coarse with emotion. "We head back north, then west past Ulsh. From there, I don't know. I'll keep moving as I always have, and battle Erum Vahl every night. You can stay with me or not, but you've all tasted the shadow god's breath. You know what it means to carry this."

She held the Black Key up, the iron oily and hot in her fingers.

"You can try to take my ship from me if you choose." The blades at her hips glimmered darkly in the low morning sun. "But I've fought worse."

Jagga's gaze fell on the empty beach, and she felt an ache she couldn't name.

"When night falls, I'll be waiting."

Serpent's Tail

By Mharie West

Thorgest Ketilson woke badly since he had entered his forty-fourth year. Each day, he felt like there was wool between his ears. This time was no different.

"Up, Ref." Makarios' voice had that particular snap which meant weapons were out, and so Thorgest was scrabbling for his sword, even as he got out of his blanket and to his feet as best he could. His long plaited hair swung behind him as he steadied himself. Blinking the sleep from his eyes, he saw with dismay that the rowing had stopped and every man was on his feet. Ulf had his sword out and something hot and out of control shone in his eyes.

"You jump when your harlot asks, hey, Ref?"

Thorgest's mind raced. He *thought* that the inn door had creaked too loudly the night before they left port. He kept his sword low, but poised and ready nonetheless.

"I jump for no one."

Ulf sneered. "Then does he jump for you, your foreign boy?" He pointed his sword straight at Makarios, which was a threat and an insult combined. Thorgest ransacked his mouth and spat hard on the deck at Ulf's feet.

"We're in the middle of the fucking sea, Ulf. What do you think you can do here?" He brought his sword up and ready. Makarios moved to his flank, sword out too.

"Do you do it because you're too old to have kids anymore, she-fox?" Ulf taunted Thorgest with the feminine version of his nickname, Ref.

Thorgest gave an exaggerated sigh. "Really? How are such serious insults coming from a puppy-boy straight off his mother's tit?"

He saw the killing rage flare in Ulf's eyes then, which confirmed it hadn't been there before. Still, the young man hesitated.

Thorgest could understand why. No one else was making a move to help either of them, so all of a sudden Ulf was facing two seasoned, experienced fighters alone, on a trading ship in the middle of the ocean.

Ah, the boy was too young for trading. Barely older than Thorgest's oldest son. He needed a few more raids under his belt to get that fire out.

"I should kill you for what you've said," Thorgest said clearly. They all knew it was true. The right to kill after that sort of insult was enshrined in law. "I *could* kill you. But it would be dangerous for everyone else involved, so I'll see you when we've both got feet on dry land again."

"Coward!" Ulf snarled, looking a little like his lupine namesake. More quickly than Thorgest had expected, Ulf took the three short steps separating them and lunged.

It was a clumsy, showy blow, and for someone like Thorgest who'd been paid to kill in the great city Miklagard, it was child's play. He swept the point aside with the pommel of his sword then put all of his weight into shoving Ulf, chest to chest.

Ulf staggered backwards and fell. He kept the sword in his hand as he went down, and accidentally nicked his bench partner. The other man swore and punched Ulf in the side of the head.

Thorgest extended his sword and took half a step forwards, just to prove that he could finish it if he wanted, then stepped back. He looked at his crew…the crew he had thought was his. Several of them wouldn't meet his eye. It was a painful thing to see.

He wondered whether any of them were truly offended by the public unveiling that he and Makarios were lovers (a secret most of them had known at least something of previously), and which of them were simply excited by the idea of getting his ship if he was killed or outlawed. Or just at seeing him taken down a peg or two.

"I'll see you're all paid your share when we get in," he said at last, before sitting down on his bench and picking up his oar.

THE RESULT, ONCE THEY PULLED into home, was worse than Thorgest had feared. He had expected Ulf and maybe one other youngster to jump off the ship and try to stab him from the shallows. What he hadn't expected was an almost equal split of the crew of ten, eyeing each other warily as they stood in the foam.

"What are you *doing*?" he shouted. He pointed at Ulf, who was in the middle of his little group and looking much more confidant now. "He wants to kill me. I have every right to kill him. The rest of you shouldn't be involved, unless you really want to start blood-feuds for your children and *their* children." Without taking his eyes off Ulf's "crew," he pointed to the men who had gathered behind him and said, "You too. Don't you think I could handle this sapling with one hand tied behind my back? Go."

There was some mumbling. A familiar bulk settled at his side and Makarios whispered, "Never."

As everyone knew it would, that act of intimacy made the others charge.

It was four on two, but within the first frantic few strokes, two of them fell away. One had a slashed arm spouting blood, and Thorgest had simply clubbed the other one on the head and kicked him away. Now it was only Ulf and his benchmate. You bonded to your benchmate, it was a hard thing to turn away from, but Thorgest could see the doubt forming in the man's eyes.

Still, in they came again. He and Makarios were trying to not do real damage, and that was always a problem in a fight. Ulf feinted for Thorgest and let the deflection carry his blade straight into Makarios' face. His instant of satisfaction faded when Makarios stabbed him in his sword arm. Thorgest took the opportunity and made the split-second decision. The law was on his side. His sword pierced into Ulf's stomach, and he angled it as high as he could to try and find the heart and cause a quick death.

"*Nithing!*" came a shout from where the rest of Ulf's supporters had run to the crowds on shore. Thorgest stared at them in disbelief and pointed at Ulf, who was gurgling and turning the wet sand brown.

"He's dead because he called me that."

"You can't kill us all!" Under the hostile eyes of his former friends and neighbours, who crowded close to let him know he wasn't allowed any of the cargo, Thorgest did the only thing he could. He and Makarios emptied their ship chests into their sacks and prepared to leave. "Look at me, Maka," Thorgest muttered as they lifted their spare clothes and a few days of uneaten rations.

"I'll live, Ref." Makarios' olive skin was slick and red from cheek to collar.

"I can see your cheekbone." It glinted like moonlight in the gaping red flesh.

"And you've seen it before."

They trudged away from the ship. The hostility from the crowd was now palpable. They might have killed their accuser but they hadn't denied anything, which was basically the same as admitting everything, and it was probably only a matter of moments before someone started spinning the tale that Ulf hadn't deserved to die.

But after an hour or two, they felt fairly certain no one was following them. Thorgest turned to Makarios and scraped some dried blood from his lip away with his fingernail. "I'll get to Kupsi if I can and we'll round up some of the old crew and meet you at the cove where I've kept the Serpent." He hadn't rowed in the Serpent for years. It was a light, fast ship, which had been perfect, back in the day, for raiding round coastlines.

"But—"

Good, he was glad that Makarios was uncomfortable about going back to activities best suited to hot-headed youths like Ulf. "Get home, Maka." It was a journey of several hours and doubtless some hotheads would now have a head start. "Sewenna knows what to do if anything happens," he said, more to convince himself than anything else.

"More than both of us put together," Makarios agreed, then leaned in and gave Thorgest the bloodiest kiss they'd shared since Thorgest has lost most of his nose in a battle fifteen years ago. "Meet you at the Serpent."

Sewenna the Blind, they called her in the village, along with a number of unflattering things: nag, leech, English. That last one was true, though she hadn't set foot on her homeland since Ref had snatched her away twenty years ago. The other two might be true, too. People could think what they liked. But 'blind' wasn't true. At least, not how everybody thought.

True, she couldn't see facial expressions and couldn't see when the ground rose or fell, and certainly couldn't see her neighbour's fine stitch-work. But none of that was really necessary. She could see shapes, colours and movement, she could hear well, and her children joked that she had magic fingers due to their sensitivity.

That night, she was grateful they thought her black-bound and helpless.

She woke with a start. There was nothing unusual in this; it was the price she paid for paying more attention to sounds than most. Still, there was something about the silence this time that scared her. She concentrated into the quiet, letting it fill her while she waited for it to be disturbed again.

A clink.

A weapon.

There was absolutely no good reason for someone to be trying to silently move a weapon right outside their house.

As quietly as she possibly could, she rose from the bench she slept on and walked slowly and carefully around the fire to where her sons slept on benches on the other side.

"Ssh," she whispered into their ears even as she shook them back and forth to rouse them. When they were younger, she had taught them to write runes by tracing them on sand, mud, and their skin. She did this now, urgently, aware that every second she was spending was a waste: úr for iron, madr for man.

Her younger son, Godgest went straight for his belt knife and was half upright by the time she pinched him, hard. For once in her life, she was glad for the elder boy, Thorkell, who thought and moved more slowly. Silence was ringing in her ears like a bell. She whispered to each boy, her words soft and gastlike on the air. They had an escape route, though it had been created when the children were too young to remember, and if they took that path rather than make a stupid heroic stand in the house, then they might all survive.

Boys informed, she went back round to Thora. Her daughter was already sitting up, jaw set and clutching her own belt knife. The noises were getting louder and Thora had always had better hearing than her brothers anyway.

"There's more than one, Mama."

Sewenna nodded slowly. Understandable. One man might consider himself able to kill two women in their sleep, but her sons posed a more significant problem.

This was definitely a murder attempt. A humiliation or a threat would have been delivered in daylight, or with great noise. But this was a cowardly, dishonourable murder attempt: killing a family in their sleep in the dead of night with no chance for them to fight back. It should ruin all who took part in it. So why was it happening? What had prompted it?

She thought that she knew. When your household was built like theirs, you knew it was just a matter of time before your society couldn't tolerate you any longer.

MINUTES LATER, THEY SMELLED SMOKE. In the darkness, the flickers of fire at the door were so stark in contrast that even Sewenna could make them out. There was more noise coming from outside now: low, angry male voices. Sewenna cast a nervous look at the other end of the house, where she knew a stout wooden bar blocked the door and wondered if someone out there was gaining a conscience before it was too late.

Luckily they had nearly finished moving all of the massive pile of old furs that lay in one area of the floor. They would have been at least thirty seconds faster, but Godgest and Thorkell had kept scuttling up and down and returning with sacks that clinked. If she had to guess, Thorkell had grabbed a half-finished axe-head he'd discarded two days ago and Godgest had grabbed a fire-poker. She tried not to snap at them about it. Neither of them were little boys anymore and she was lucky they had listened to her at all and not stormed straight out of the house, waving their puny bits of iron.

Also, if she was fair, she'd admit that she'd stopped and tied a full purse to her belt while she was pulling on her outer dress. Job done, she lifted the final fur away for the first time in fifteen years and the children all made noises of surprise as the wooden trapdoor was revealed. She tugged at the handle. It stuck. One, two, three hands joined hers and heaved, and the trapdoor opened. Even to her eyes, its square black maw looked uninviting.

"*Where* did you say this goes again, Mama?" Godgest whispered.

"Helvegr," Thora said with typically bitter humour. The Road to Hel.

Sewenna rolled her eyes at their melodrama. They hadn't even thought of the really terrifying bit: that the tunnel could cave in when they were inside it, and that they could end up suffocating underground as their home burned.

Ha. Lovely.

The front door was starting to catch light properly now. The shadows it cast made her children look much older than they were.

"Thorkell, you first." She shuffled aside to let him peer into it. Now she elaborated on what she'd told them earlier, "It was measured for your father so you should have enough space to move forwards with your knees and elbows. Eventually, you'll hit another wooden trapdoor. You'll end up in the old outhouse — yes, the one we used to tell you was rotting and full of ants. There should be a big wooden peg in the back wall; if you pull it out, the whole wall will fall away. Try to do that quietly. It backs straight onto the copse. Hide in there and wait for me."

"No, I'll go last, Mama." Godgest. Always Godgest. He stood in front of her with that silly patchy beard he was so proud of, stubbornly folding his arms. She could see the stupid poker dangling from his belt.

"No." She was calm but firm. He scowled so hard that she could see it distort the blur of his face.

"Yes!"

"I should really go last. I can stand heat better than the rest of you," Thorkell, an apprentice blacksmith, pointed out.

"I'd rather crisp and know you were all in there, getting away," Sewenna said bluntly.

Thora sighed loudly at them all and plunged into the hole like a diver. Sewenna's stomach dropped to her feet as she imagined the potential for slow suffocation.

"Wait a bit before following," she advised Thorkell. "You don't want her to accidentally kick you in the face." Just three years ago, she'd had a swollen, bruised face for days when they'd crawled into it to test it and Makarios had panicked in front of her.

Smoke was starting to fill the room beyond what they could usually tolerate. She hoped that the stout, hardened outer shell could withstand the fire for just a bit longer.

"Mama, I'm staying until you go!" Godgest hissed.

"Then we'll both die and that would be a pity." She stared at his face as the seconds ticked away in frantic heartbeats. People tended to react better when she stared at them like this, even though they were just blurs to her. "I'll be behind you. I promise."

She didn't *need* to see his eyes to know when he gave in.

True to her promise, she wriggled into the hole only thirty or so heartbeats behind him. She closed her eyes in the darkness and started to edge forwards on her knees and elbows, being careful with her feet. If they got tangled in her skirt, she might accidentally kick the wall. She knew how fragile the tunnel could be. And who knew how much air there was left? With three panting, wriggling bodies before her, and a fire behind them, perhaps it would run out soon. There had been no point in scaring the children, but that just meant that all the fear sat on her chest like a great toad.

The earth was freezing cold and damp around her, and small clods kept dropping onto her face. She imagined ghostly dwarven touches and shuddered. She thought that she could hear Godgest moving up ahead of her—and just for a terrible second, her mind told her that it wasn't her son and it wasn't moving away from her.

After what seemed like an eternity, when she was certain that she couldn't breathe another breath in this underground snake belly, she felt a sharp upwards tilt. Silently she thanked the Lord of her childhood and every god of her husband's, just in case any of them were listening. The next second, a white blur was waving in front of her face and she could hear Thorkell telling her to grab on.

She sat on the edge of the hole and spent a few precious moments trying to control her breathing so that they couldn't tell how badly she'd reacted down there. She noticed her filthy hands, felt the mud in her ears and up her calves. The others appeared equally as filthy, at least if the unusual darkness of their faces was anything to go by. At least one of them had badly chattering teeth. Probably Thora—she always did forget her cloak. Well, at least they might not be immediately recognisable.

"Have you got the wall open?" She coughed to try and cover up the alarming deep pitch of her voice.

"Of course!" Godgest's voice was strained. "I'm holding it ajar for us. We were just waiting for you."

She wriggled her toes to check how her leg muscles were doing. Minimal shaking. She'd be fine. "Let's go, then."

Thorkell took the other side of the loose wall and they lowered it slowly and carefully. One side snagged on a sapling, which was reassuring. If the trees had started to regrow around the gap they'd cut a few years ago, their escape should be less obvious. She put both hands out to navigate around the snagged door. Godgest made an abortive "helpful" gesture towards her and she hissed at him like a cat.

"Peer over the edge of the outhouse and tell me what you see," she demanded. It was her way of reminding him that he could be helpful in better ways. "Is anyone looking in this direction?"

"The-there's a lot of people, Mama." His voice trembled just a little. Thora crawled out of the opening on her hands and knees and took a look through the screening branches of a bush too. Even Thorkell had twisted round and was trying to see over his shoulder.

"No one's looking, Mama," Thora confirmed. "They're all crowded round the front, just...waiting." Now her voice wobbled.

Waiting for the screaming to start, Sewenna thought bitterly.

Never one to be outdone, Godgest interrupted when Thora drew breath, "There's probably half the village out there." He named a few of them.

The detached wall scraped against the rest of the outhouse. It sounded deafening. She'd just caught her movement in the edge of her vision — Thorkell had flinched, hard, and who could blame him when Godgest had just said Thorkell's future father in-law's name?

Enough. She shepherded them outside and then told them to try and prop the wall back up again. It was probably futile but the tiny attempt at covering their tracks made her feel better.

THEY PUSHED ONWARDS THROUGH THE trees — doubled over at first for cover under stunted thorn bushes and eventually standing taller as the trees around them matured and multiplied. From long habit, Thora went first. Not only was she the closest to Sewenna's height and so the best judge of obstacles, but her leading stopped the boys from arguing and fighting.

Sewenna's eyes were starting to hurt from pointless straining into the dark, so she closed them instead and trudged forwards. That meant she was the first to hear the sound of rapidly approaching footsteps. She opened her mouth and eyes.

And Thora screamed. Sewenna's heart tried to appear in her mouth and her feet simultaneously, and she charged forwards like a bear in the pit.

"Easy, my darling!" came a familiar voice. A familiar outline too, with a familiar way of standing.

Sewenna stopped dead. "Fuck you, Maka," she said instead of the hysterical giggle that wanted to come out.

"Mama!" Thorkell sounded so shocked that Sewenna had to remind herself of the language she'd caught him using when he'd got distracted at the forge yesterday. She put her hand on Thora's shoulder and separated Makarios and Thora from their hug. He obligingly hugged her instead, which hadn't been her intention, but she'd be lying to herself if she didn't admit that it was good to lean into his warm embrace for a second or two.

"What's going on?" The pommel of his sword was digging hard into her hip. It was unsheathed, which meant it was bloodied. She could smell blood too, standing this close to him.

He clasped her hand and squeezed it three times, an old sign for 'We'll discuss this later, not in front of the children.'

She frowned and went for a different question instead. "Where's Ref?" She ran her free hand over his face, and he flinched away as her fingers brushed something wet and ridged.

"He's heading for the Serpent."

"Ah." Sewenna let her eyes slide even more out of focus for a second as she tried to figure out which emotion was causing the sudden weight on her chest. She wasn't fond of that ship. She'd been *brought here* on that ship. But, more importantly right now, it was the fastest ship and the one that the fewest people knew about.

Makarios' hand on her elbow broke into her unpleasant thoughts.

"Let's go, yes?" He had already started walking before she said anything. Thora ceded head of their line to him and they shuffled on as fast as they could. The ship Makarios had mentioned was ten miles away, and they all knew that they needed to be out of sight when the sun came up.

Sewenna knew she was the big obstacle to that. They had to travel at her speed. Most of her slowness was due to the unfamiliar ground and a lifelong fear and avoidance of tripping and falling over obstacles she couldn't see: loose stones, a dip in the path, a rise in the path...anything, really. At this speed, it would take them maybe four hours. If she just straightened up and accepted that her family would catch her or pick her up if anything happened, they could maybe make it in three hours.

Come on. Speed up.

She walked on quickly, with her heart beating her throat. Every step felt like a disaster waiting to happen. Every sound could be an attacker bursting out of the trees. The moon was bright enough that people with normal eyesight would be content—that wasn't what you wanted when you were trying to escape.

"Who's joining us?" she asked after what felt like hours of tense trudging, when she couldn't quite bear keeping herself company anymore.

People had to be joining them, or they might as well have lain down in the house and drunk the smoke. Although they all knew how to row, the ship needed twenty people to row it most effectively, so six wouldn't be of any use at all.

"Not the usual crew." Makarios' voice was flat. "Ref's sent Kupsi as a messenger to round up some old favours."

Kupsi was a grizzled veteran of fifty who had known Ref since they went raiding together as young men. It made Sewenna feel a little better that he was still dependably around.

"Why not the usual crew?" That was Godgest. Sewenna guessed from the angry tone of his voice what he would be saying next, her most predictable child. "You can stop trying to keep secrets from us now. Someone's tried to kill us! In our beds! We deserve to know why!"

"He's got a good point," Thora said. "Father clearly did something. Did he kill someone?"

"Not unprovoked," Makarios muttered, half under his breath. He stopped so abruptly that Sewenna banged her nose on his shoulder, and turned to face them all. "You're right, you've got a point. Or rather, you've all got a choice and you've got to make it now."

Silence. In her mind Sewenna could see the shape of what Makarios was about to say, but, as if the situation was deliberately mirroring her eyesight, she couldn't make out the exact details.

"Ref and I are both outlaws now. For...well..." His head moved towards Sewenna, as if silently asking for help.

"For fucking."

Godgest. Why was it always Godgest? But no, Thora was nodding hard too. Makarios' face was still pointed towards Sewenna. She could see from the shadow pattern that his mouth was slightly open. Her mind, too, was blank. She'd always thought that she, Ref and Maka had kept their secret, but that instant, shared reaction surely meant that at the very least, the children had had suspicions.

"Ref can tell you more details if he wants when he gets to us," Makarios said eventually. "But the point is still the same. We're both outlaws — or I'm sure we will be once they get to the þing assembly. If you help us, you will be seen in a very bad light."

"What, like the light from the fire they used to burn us in our beds?" Thorkell hadn't spoken in at least an hour and his voice was gravelly. Sewenna raised her eyebrows at his dramatic pronouncement.

Godgest jeered, "What are you, a skald now?"

THEY WERE ALL STARTING TO stumble by the time that they reached the cove where the ship was stored. The distance wasn't necessarily the problem, but combined with sleep deprivation, worn-off adrenalin and the fact that in Thorkell's case, he had put on his old ruined shoes in his hurry to flee, it all added up to a grumpy, wobbly group. Makarios was the only one seemingly unaffected. At several points in the last mile or so, Sewenna had to outright lean on him, rather than just using his shoulder for guidance, and he had walked on despite his wound and her extra weight. Now he shepherded them under a cliff, up a pebbly slope and into a small cave. There was just enough room to fit everybody in.

He looked down at them with one hand on his sword and nodded unsmilingly. Sewenna thought, with a slightly hysterical laugh, that smiling was probably not an option for him right now.

The sun was rising now, casting pink and cream shadows over them all. Sewenna could have wept for relief at the resurgence of colour. She dealt so much better with the world when she could identify bits of it properly. She was tempted to look up at Makarios, get close enough to feel his breath on her face while she checked his gaping cut and she pretended not to want to kiss him for the children's sake. Instead of being that self-indulgent, she examined Thorkell's feet, made Thora sit down, and just...tried not to antagonise Godgest.

The image of her burning house kept creeping back into her mind. Money she hadn't been able to bring. Rugs and blankets, and the first horseshoe Thorkell had ever forged, which he'd given to her. Every single item of clothing other than what they stood in. All gone.

Shut up, Sewenna. She took a deep breath in and shut her eyes. Her eyelids let a single tear go free. *Just shut up. That won't help.*

THEY WERE TIGHTLY SNUGGLED UP against each other and feeling warm for the first time in hours. Thorkell was definitely asleep. It was always obvious when he was asleep. With his snoring deadening her hearing, Sewenna knew Thorgest had reached them, not because she'd heard or seen him, but because Makarios had, and the loosening of tension from his shoulders was obvious.

"He took his time," she whispered into the warm skin of his neck. Makarios laughed and staggered on sleepy legs out of the cave so that the rest of them could follow him.

Thorgest stood at the bottom of the slope looking, Sewenna thought, much like an engraving of Thor himself. He just needed a hammer instead of his sword. It was the ridiculously dramatic way that his waist-length curly red hair streamed out behind him. She couldn't wait for the wind direction to change and for that mane to thwack him firmly in the face.

Thora was the first to fling herself at her father and he picked her up and swung her around even though she was a young woman of fifteen. Fierce hugs followed for Thorkell and Godgest.

"I knew you'd get them out," he said to Sewenna, standing close enough to her that she could see most of his facial expression. Their foreheads rested together.

"You hoped," she replied even as her heart melted anew, because she'd been brutally honest by default for too many years to change now.

"I prayed." He touched his hammer amulet briefly. Then he pursed his lips and whistled a passable imitation of a cuckoo.

Suddenly, men materialised from the trees a few hundred feet away. Sewenna flinched backwards, then felt a lot better for it when she saw Makarios take his hand off his sword.

"Crew?" she asked Thorgest. He nodded. Over the thud of relief in her ears she asked the question that she knew from past experience was at the forefront of every rower's mind, "How on earth are we paying them, Ref?" She ran distracted fingers over his muddy and torn tunic sleeve. "Did you keep something from trading?" She could see he had a sack with him, but she very much doubted he'd been able to get away with much of value if people had been trying to kill them.

"Now, that's a question." Thorgest grinned. He put an arm round her waist and cupped her chin on his other hand. "When I found you, Sewenna —"

She opened her mouth to yelp "Found?!" but the sparkle in his eyes was too sweet.

"We weren't sure we would all make it back home, and we'd gotten a lot of stuff from those monks. So we hid it, and hoped that we could come back later for it."

"Ah." That was Makarios. He shuffled into the hug and they naturally let him in. He said sarcastically, "So, we're going in a raiding boat to find buried treasure. I can't wait."

Sewenna rolled her eyes but pecked him on his non-injured cheek anyway. She pulled away from the comfort of the hug, turned her face towards the grey blur of the sea, and took the first step towards the waiting Serpent.

Between the Devil and the Deep Blue Sea

By Megan Arkenberg

I WASN'T LIKING THE LOOK OF her—that smoky dark skin, those full hard lips, those big eyes as bright and hot as coals—but she was a lady, and the gents and me, we know how to treat ladies.

"Name's Sham," I said, and I even let her shake my hand, which I generally don't on account of some broken fingers that never healed right. I had Crow and Anny Pryce to thank for that, just like I did for a lot of things. "Short for Shamrock," I added, "in case you're wondering." I knew she was, of course, but it'd be rude to make a lady admit it.

She nodded, with a little smile that said I wasn't making her feel any better but thanks for trying. "You can call me Golden," she said. "Is your ship for hire, Miss Sham?"

First of all, I ain't "miss" *nobody*, and second, the *Ruby Prince* ain't mine strictly speaking. But I was taking the lady's name for a good omen and figured Captain Cat would do the same. "She sure is, Miss Golden. Where do you want to take her?"

She glanced at the dock over her shoulder. There wasn't nobody there I'd be worried about, just two old fishermen hauling in their catch and a pretty whore hauling hers, but Golden was twitching like a mouse in a cat's shadow. "Can I come on board?"

"What, you being followed?"

"Something like that."

I called over my shoulder to Cook's hand, a scrawny little kid we all called Cornflower on account of his eyes. "Hey, fling me a ladder for the lady on the dock!"

It took a little while—sometimes I think Cornflower's missing a knot or two in his rigging—but finally we got Golden up on deck and all the gents, including Captain Cat, gathered 'round for hearing.

"So what's the trouble, Miss Golden?" Cat asked. His birthing name is Thomas, but we called him Tomcat 'cause he's always on the prowl. He can be intimidating—over six feet tall, with wild red hair and eyes to match—but he was being real careful with Golden. Probably figured she was spooked enough already.

Golden looked down at her feet. Apparently she'd decided to get all the mud out in one spit, because her words came in a rush. "I was Duke Desmond of Glasshill's lover, up until two weeks ago."

"What happened two weeks ago?"

"He died."

I looked at Cat; his eyebrows were raised almost to the hem of his head-scarf. Golden blushed and spilled the rest even faster. "He was murdered. His nephew strangled him in his own bed and poisoned all five of his daughters."

"Sounds like his nephew wants to be Duke," Fairweather said. He may have a lucky name, but he's also got a maddening habit of stating the obvious. "What's this got to do with you?"

"I'm pregnant with Desmond's child."

Cat's response was exactly what you'd expect from a man who calls himself a Perfect Gentleman of Fortune; he pulled up a crate for her to sit on and sent Cornflower to grab a bottle of rum.

"Let me guess," I said as Golden tentatively licked the mouth of the bottle. Back in Coldcliff, where I'd grown up, Anny Pryce was Queen of the Sea and she'd taught us how politics worked themselves out. "Desmond's little ass of a nephew is trying to kill the baby."

Golden nodded. "I need to get away. There's a hiding place I know of, but it'll take a skilled crew to get there."

"And you can't hire a straight ship because...?"

She blushed again. "I'm dead broke."

Silence landed lead-heavy on the deck. Fairweather's thin lips twisted like he had something nippy to say, but old Mayborn shut him up with a glare.

It looked for a moment like nobody was going to talk. I drew myself up, big as I could muster, before somebody whipped out a knife. "We ain't taking on charity cases, Miss Golden."

"I didn't say I couldn't pay." She set the rum down hard on the deck by her knee. "That hiding place I'm headed to, it's the best you'll ever find. Unapproachable without a guide, and damn hard to reach even then. Straight ships wouldn't have any business with it, but for you gentlemen..." She looked up at Cat, her face set as stone. "I'm willing to share."

The silence came back, only now it was like a pot about to boil; smooth on the surface, bubbling underneath. The gents and me looked at each other, we all looked at Cat, and Cat looked like he'd just been served a brimming bowl of cream.

"Miss Golden," he said, bowing over her hand like she was Anny Pryce herself, "you have yourself a deal."

We hadn't been planning to leave Flintfield for another week or so, but Golden was sure as anything that she had the Duke's dogs on her tail and we needed to sail *now*. So I spent what was left of the day helping Mayborn mend the flying jib and tying down Cook's barrels with Cornflower and generally getting the *Prince* ready to jump. That ain't my usual job, of course—Cat signed me on as a cannon-master—but we needed all the hands we could get, wherever we could get 'em. Figured we wouldn't need the cannons on this jaunt, anyway.

Sometimes, I'm stupid as a ball of wet twine.

I was rubbing the knot-cramps out of my crooked knuckles, ready for a hot dinner and the gentle swing of my hammock, when Cat leapt down on the deck next to me and pointed at something on the docks.

"See that?"

I rolled my eyes. It was new-moon dark, and my sight ain't nearly as sharp as Cat's in the best of times. "What're you looking at?"

"That monster down at the edge of the docks. Look at her. She's like a mountain, and that's just what we can see above the water."

"Hush, you." I hit him across the shoulder. "She's a galleon, that's all. 'Sides, what're you worried about? You plan on taking her?"

"I'm afraid she might plan on taking *us*." Cat folded his arms on the rail and leaned out, the sea-wind blowing his hair across his face like ribbons of blood. I didn't like the way his eyes looked. "Sham, that's Crow's ship. And where Crow is, you know Anny Pryce is close behind."

"Damn." I knew it was just my imagination, but my hands seemed to ache worse just knowing Crow was nearby. "You think she's still out for me?"

"That's the same as asking if I think she's still breathing. Anny Pryce don't quit, not 'til she's got your skull as a hat-stand."

"Thanks for *that* lovely picture," I said. And all at once I felt like a length of rope someone's stretched too far to tie. My stomach was doing fancy little flips, and my knees were nothing but water. "Crow knows I'm on the *Prince*, Cat. He saw you pull me out of the water last time."

Cat pressed his hand against the small of my back, warm and steady. "They won't get you again, Shamrock. I won't let them."

I shook my head. There's no "let" when you're dealing with Anny Pryce.

"Anyway." Cat lifted his hand away and rolled his shoulders. "Just thought you should see. We'll be out by sun-up. They won't even know we were here."

"Yeah," I said. "I ain't worried."

But all that night I dreamed of Anny Pryce and her lead chains, and I woke up with my hands aching like blue-hot fire.

LIKE CAT PROMISED, WE WERE gone before sun-up, and Flintfield was just a brown smudge on the horizon when Golden finally crawled out of her cabin, walked up to the railing, and emptied her gut into the sea.

"Not liking the waves?" I asked. Making conversation with a sea-sick lady ain't exactly good manners, but it's not like I could ignore her when she was fluttering around in front of me.

Golden didn't seem to mind, anyway. She wiped her mouth with the back of her hand—and it looked strange, her face all apple-green and her palm pale as clover honey—and gave me a watery smile. "The baby's not liking the waves," she said. "Or mornings, for that matter."

I laughed a little. I knew how that worked. "Yeah. My sister had five sons. She carried easy, but...mornings."

Golden's big eyes narrowed. Then she shook herself like a dog. "Sorry," she said. "It's just hard for me to picture you with...I'm sorry."

"Ain't your fault." I clapped her on the shoulder, like she was one of the gents. "So how far along are you? You ain't showing yet."

And so we spent most of the morning talking about babies and growing bellies and letting out shirt hems, and then she ran some baby names by me that all sounded slimy and pretentious, though I didn't say so to her face. I knew Cat would laugh himself sick if I told him, but it was nice to have a lady on board, even one who looked so pretty it was sinister. I love the gents, but they ain't learned to make conversation—and especially not about babies.

Around noon, Cat sent me up to the 'nest with a spyglass and told me to look to the north. Now, Flintfield was straight west of us, and I figured if Crow was following, he'd be coming from that direction. There's nothing big north of Flintfield, nothing but Coldcliff, and if we had Crow *and* Anny Pryce on us at once, I was going to throw myself overboard now and save us all the trouble.

Then I saw the ship Cat was thinking about—little thing with a single mast—not Anny Pryce, not unless she'd gotten in some serious trouble since we last met, and I knew I wasn't that lucky. Which meant this ship wasn't chasing us.

Or if it *was* chasing us, it wasn't because of me.

"Fairweather!" I called. He scrambled and met me halfway down the 'nest ladder. "Where's Glasshill, anyway?"

He shrugged. "Can't say for certain. Why?"

"If it's anywhere north of here, I think Desmond's nephew is on our tail."

Fairweather squinted in the direction of the tiny ship. "That little thing? Ain't a match for the *Prince*. In fact..." He took the spyglass from me and held it up to my eye, nearly tipping us off the ladder in the process. "She's not even headed for us. Either he don't know how to set his sails, or he's going west on purpose."

"Oh," I said. "Good."

And if Fairweather believed me, he was even dumber than I give him credit for.

"Cat," I said that night, "I think the Duke's nephew is matching up with Crow."

We were alone by the wheel, each of us with a hand on it, though our course was straight through until dawn. Cat was looking up at the sky above us like a diamond-studded scarf, and I couldn't see his expression.

"Unfortunately," he said, "that makes a lot of sense. If that dinghy we saw today really belongs to the Duke, it'd be good for him to catch up with someone who knows the seas—someone who knows how to hunt."

"Someone like Crow." I rolled my shoulders, but it didn't make me any less tense. "I know I should be glad it's not me he's after, but somehow, I can't get up the gumption." I glanced at Cat out of the corner of my eye, but his face was still turned away from me. "What'd Golden tell you about her hiding place?"

"Nothin' more than how to get there. And that it takes a skilled crew."

"Crow's sure got one of those. Cat?" Finally, he looked at me. I swallowed hard. "You still so sure you ain't gonna let him catch me?"

"I'm sure." He nibbled his bottom lip, looked back up at the stars. "Besides, Sham, you killed Anny's best lieutenant once before. What makes you think you ain't able to do it again?"

SO THAT NIGHT, I DREAMED about Dragonfly.

People don't believe me when I say she made Crow look like a kitten, but it's true. In the beginning, Anny Pryce just kept Crow around for his pretty face; but Dragonfly started and ended as a weapon. She was tall and skinny and pale, not gray-white like Anny but a pale that was almost blue, and when she was a kid her daddy beat her and that's why her face never moved right. And she was scary. When you saw the bodies of the people Dragonfly killed, you weren't always sure they'd been people.

All that would have been fine, but around the time I turned seventeen—a year or two after I joined up with Cat—Dragonfly decided to go after my sister.

I still don't know why. Maybe Moirrey had done something to cross Anny Pryce, or maybe Dragonfly was just in a mood.

I just know what Dragonfly did to my sister, and if I told you, it'd take me all day and then some. I got sick when I first heard about it, and then I got mad. Real mad, the kind of mad you have to wake up from.

And I didn't wake up from it, not 'til I left a bag on Anny Pryce's doorstep with Dragonfly's head in it.

That's the reason Anny hates me, the reason she and Crow picked me up in a Crossgallow tavern and dragged me onto her ship so she could break all my fingers and burn her sign on my shoulder and throw me overboard to drown. You think that'd be enough to give a body nightmares, and you'd be right.

But my dream, it was worse than that, because Dragonfly was there chasing me along with Crow and Anny and the Duke's nephew, and Dragonfly was angrier than all the others because I'd killed her, and she wasn't afraid of nothing because she was already dead. I woke up before she caught me, and I was so damn grateful I cried until dawn.

DAYS PASSED—SLOWLY, THE WAY THEY do when you're out at sea with no clear idea of where you're going and a damn clear idea of what's coming behind you.

Golden wasn't giving the location of her hiding spot to no one but Cat, and his orders seemed designed to mess over any of the crew who was trying to guess where we were headed. That was fine by me; I just wanted to get Golden safe and have done with it. Every time I looked, there were sails on the horizon behind us, and I wouldn't've placed a bet on whether they were the Duke's or Crow's.

But I'll tell you something else that was shocking the smoke out of me; I was getting fond of Golden. Don't get me wrong, she was still too pretty by half. But there was brains beneath that beauty, and she knew something about making quick in a conversation.

Only problem with getting fond of people—that's when you start worrying about them. Soon, it wasn't just the thought of Crow that was keeping me up nights.

"What're you going to do if we get caught?" I asked Cat one morning. We had been working the wheel all night, and our faces matched the grayish-green of the eastern sky.

Cat gave me the most dashing smile he could manage. "We ain't going to get caught."

"Save the bragging for your whores."

He sighed, leaned forward and rested his chin on the rail. "How's our cannon compared to Crow's?"

It had been years since I was up close and personal with Crow's ship, but there's some things that stick in your memory like tar. "They'll make matchwood out of us before we reach the stations."

"Then we hand the lady over to the Duke-ling."

"Cat!"

He rolled his eyes up at me. "You got a better suggestion?"

"No." I swallowed hard. "Just don't get us caught, sweetheart."

TWO DAYS LATER, FAIRWEATHER JUMPED down from the 'nest with a look on his face like he'd seen his dead grandmother. "Captain!" he shouted. "Up ahead!"

So of course the whole crew dropped whatever they were doing and scrambled for the bow, even Golden, though she didn't scramble often on account of her seasickness. There were rocks up ahead, big and jagged and black, crinkled and shiny like burnt sugar. But it wasn't the rocks Fairweather was leaping crazy over; it was the whirlpool next to them.

We all stood still and silent for a moment. Then Golden let out a sigh like a gust of wind.

"Thank goodness!" she said. "Captain, it's a straight throw now."

"Straight between the Devil and the deep blue sea." Cat whistled through his teeth. "You don't lie when you call that the best hiding place we'll ever find."

"But you can do it?" It wasn't Golden who asked, but Cornflower, his bright eyes round as a pair of coins.

"Of course I can do it." Cat ruffled his hair absently. "Let's just hope our pursuit doesn't catch up to us before we get through."

And I tell you, that man should get a job with an acting troupe, 'cause his sense of timing is just peachy wonderful.

I SAID A WORD MY aunties would've washed my mouth out with lye for, and when that didn't take, I added some things about Crow's mother and a rabid cow. His ship was bloody huge, and it had come out of nowhere, right up on our tail. Golden took one look at it and fainted right into Cornflower's scrawny arms.

The short, crooked man on Crow's deck must have been the Duke's nephew. He had that look, like Power's second cousin, and a griminess about him like a kid reaching for someone else's toy. Crow was there, too, tall and dark and lovely, his black hair loose and whipping in the wind.

The woman—slight, white-haired, her long fingers curled on Crow's shoulder—was Anny Pryce.

"Cannons!" Cat shouted, but none of the crew moved. It was far too late for shooting things.

"Good morning, Captain!" Crow called, leaning over the railing like a lady waving farewell to her sailor. "Good thing we got to you before you disappeared into that lovely clump of rocks up ahead. Our dear friend the Duke would be so disappointed."

"You're an ass, Crow," I retorted. Cat flung out his arm to hold me back, but I ducked under and ran for the rail. The ships were close together, a lot closer than I think either Cat or Crow wanted to be, but Anny Pryce didn't believe in personal space. Suited me fine, too. "When'd you take to running the Duke of Glasshill's errands?"

"When we found out he was headed the same way we were." Crow's eyes twinkled like spilled oil. "For different reasons, of course."

Golden was coming to, moaning like a gale wind. The Duke, who until now had been looking slavishly from Crow to Anny Pryce, turned his beady little eyes over to the *Ruby Prince*. "There she is!" he shrieked. "Make them hand her over and let's get out of here."

"Calm yourself," Anny Pryce said.

If you ain't heard Anny Pryce's voice, I ain't sure I can describe it for you so you understand. Some voices are cold, but Anny's is just frigid. It turns steel brittle.

"As you can see, our dear friend the Duke judged it wise to abandon his ship for ours," she said. "We are not running his errands at all, girl. Consider him a hound on a scent — or a decoy."

I reckon the Duke and I were feeling about the same at that moment.

"We'd love for you to hand over Miss…Golden, is it?" Anny Pryce sneered, her mouth straight and flat as a blade. "But I'll settle for only you, Shamrock."

"No!" Cat shouted, and it was my turn to hold him back. I caught him, one hand on each of his shoulders, and stood between him and Anny.

"I told you, Cat, they'll make matchwood of us if we don't cooperate." He stilled some, but there was still murder in his eyes. "You're getting paid to get Golden to safety. Let them have me, and you can make it through the pass. Crow's ship is too big for them to follow."

Cat shrugged my hands off. "Listen to yourself, Sham! I said I won't hand you over to Anny Pryce, and I meant it."

"Maybe I ain't yours to hand over."

The color drained out of his face so fast, I thought I'd see it collecting in a stain around his collar. He took a tottering step back and passed a hand across his forehead. "I...damn, Shamrock, that's not what I meant."

"I know it ain't." I looked over my shoulder at Golden. She was slouched between Cornflower and Mayborn, looking sick and lost and determined all at the same time. Real lady, she was. I gave her what I hoped was a reassuring smile and turned back to Cat. "Take care of her, okay?"

"Shamrock!"

I grabbed a grappling line from the stack and flung it across to Anny Pryce.

Cat might've made a grab for me as I started to climb over — he can be an idiot sometimes, it sounds like something he'd do — but if so, the crew held him back. I dropped onto Crow's deck half an eternity later and held out my hands for Anny to tie together.

"Nice fingers," she said, flat as a paving stone.

I spat in her face, and Crow came up behind me, and there was a splitting pain in my head as everything went dark.

I WOKE UP IN THE brig, which was no surprise, but I hadn't expected the Duke to be keeping me company, trussed up in the corner like an autumn pig. Guess that's a lesson about working with Anny Pryce; she ain't for hire, even if you think she is.

My hands were tied behind my back, and someone — Crow, I'd bet, though it was probably Anny's idea — had woven the rope between my fingers, straining the joints so hard I thought they'd break again. Real carefully, I twisted to my feet like a cat and pressed my eye against a crack in the wooden wall. No good; Crow's brig was below the water line, and all I got was an eyeful of pitch. So I couldn't know for sure, but I hoped real hard that Cat had taken Golden through to her hiding place and forgotten about me, like he was supposed to.

The Duke squeaked something around the dirty rag in his mouth. I kicked at him half-heartedly and plopped down with my back to the wall. "Shut up," I said. "Greedy, murdering slime ain't my idea of a good roommate, neither."

He screwed up his forehead like he thought looking at me ugly would light me on fire.

Then the sound of footsteps came from behind the door, sharp and light and even. I sat up straight. Someone fumbled with the rusty lock, and the door swung in with a slow, screechy creak. Anny Pryce stood on the other side, smiling like Death at a duelists' society.

Up close, her face looked like a mask someone had stored in a dusty place for too long. Her mouth was dry and pale, and her eyes looked brittle. Back in Coldcliff people used to say that Anny Pryce was a handsome woman, but I can't figure out how they managed to tell. All I could see was the dryness.

"So you traded yourself for the girl," she said, sneering from me to the Duke and back again. "How...noble."

"Actually, you traded the girl for me. Went back on your word." I tilted my head, like I was considering. "Not very noble, but what should he've expected from your kind?"

Anny raised a single eyebrow. One of the only people I know of who can manage that expression without looking addled. "My kind?"

"Lying dogs who can't do their own dirty work."

Her slap came like a whip crack across my cheek. "Rest assured," she said, dragging me to my feet, "I won't be making that mistake again."

Crow came out of the shadows behind her like a ghost. He took me by the shoulders, and Anny led us out and up into the cool salty night.

The deck was lit up with little glass-paned lamps hung in the rigging. They threw their light over the water, all the way to the shiny clump of rocks that guarded Golden's hiding place—the shiny clump of rocks that was slipping farther away from us with each passing second. I prayed miserably that Cat wasn't going to try anything stupid.

"Evening, boys," she said. I gave her a funny look, 'cause that's the first time I heard a captain call her gents *boys*. It just ain't done. And it was damn clear she was mocking them, twisting her words around in her mouth like a harbormaster. "I don't suppose you all remember Shamrock?"

There were a few jeers, but not a whole lot. "I'm the one who killed Dragonfly," I said, to help them out a little. Everything in my gut felt like soured milk. I knew I was going to die; it couldn't hurt to make sure everyone knew why.

Crow gave me a shake and cut the rope from around my fingers. I rubbed my hands together and looked up at Anny

Pryce. I was expecting her to have a hanging rope out, or a gun at least, but she wasn't holding anything. Was she just going to throw me overboard again?

Then she held her hand out to one of the men, and he gave her a knife.

"You remember what Dragonfly did to Moirrey," she said. It wasn't a question, not even close, and it wasn't meant for anybody but me to hear. "You remember how they found her clothes in bloody shreds around the bedroom. You remember how the blood soaked into the plaster walls—that whole part of the house needed to be burned down. You remember that the biggest piece of her your mother found..." She held up her free hand and lowered the fingers, one by one, until only the smallest was left standing. "Don't you, Shamrock?"

"You're a bloody coward, Anny Pryce." I spat in her face again, and this time Crow didn't do anything to stop me. Anny just smiled and wiped her cheek with her sleeve. "You ain't got the guts to do any of that yourself, so you take credit for what your trained dogs do. I ain't afraid of you."

That last part was mostly a lie, of course. Mostly.

'Cause I had gotten away from Anny Pryce once before, and I had killed Dragonfly.

"You, now, Miss Queen-of-the-Sea," I said, "you're terrified of me. You're scared like a kid in the dark."

The crew laughed, as I expected they would—but not Anny. Her face went slack, like a sail with no wind.

"'Cause anything Dragonfly did, well, I can do better than that. *I killed Dragonfly.* Scary as she was, she's dead now, and it's all because of me. You can give orders real nice, and maybe if you try hard enough you can break a girl's fingers..." I wiggled my own hand, just like she'd raised hers. "But you're nowhere near me, Anny Pryce, and you know it."

She jumped at me, knife raised, about the same time Crow made a grab at me from behind. I dropped to the deck and rolled out from under them. Of course the crew wasn't just going to take that, and I was kicking for all I was worth, trying to keep their hands off of me. There was just one way for me to get out of here, I realized, and that was in the dark.

I grabbed a fistful of rigging and started climbing. The first lamp broke with just a jab of my elbow, and the second landed on the deck in a spray of glass and fire. Someone got his hand around my ankle before I had the third all the way loose, and suddenly I was on the deck myself, tilting my head crazily to avoid the burning oil.

Anny pressed her knee into my chest, driving the breath out of me. She pressed the knife deep against my cheek.

"Where did you think you were going, Shamrock?" Her voice was dry and breathless. "You're caught, girl. There's nothing here but the water and me."

"Between the Devil and the deep blue sea," I muttered.

And the third lamp snapped its rope.

I was hoping it would knock Anny Pryce insensible, and though I wasn't that lucky, she must've had a lump the size of a rook egg on her head the next morning. I didn't stick around to see. As soon as the pressure from her knee let up I rolled out from under her, dodged past Crow, and dove into the sea.

The water sprayed up icy and dark around my face. I moved my legs like I was walking up a steep hill and managed to keep my head above the surface. And it turned out to be a good thing I hadn't put all the lamps out, because a little sparkle of light still got out across the water and glistened on the rocks by Golden's hiding place.

I dove under the next few waves, until I got out to where the water was too dark for Crow's crew to see me clear. I ain't a great swimmer, but I'm better than most, and I had the threat of Anny Pryce to keep me moving. I closed my eyes, stretched my arms and kicked as hard as I could.

And didn't stop kicking 'til I heard the splash of oars by my head.

"Sham!" Warm hands reached down and closed around my shoulders. I pried my eyes open, sputtering and blinking through the salty water. Cat's face was pale as sailcloth as he lifted me up into the dinghy.

"Sham, you all right?"

He lay me on the floor of the boat, resting my head against his knees. I coughed until I could get words out. "We've got to keep meeting like this, Cat."

"I thought I lost you."

"Well, you thought wrong." I sat up, looked around the little boat. We were halfway between the sharp shiny rocks and the silent spinning of the whirlpool. If the dinghy were any bigger, I wouldn't've liked our chances. But Cat's hands were steady on the oars, and I knew I could trust him.

"What were you gonna do?" I asked, flat as I could. "Take on Crow in this mangy thing?"

He looked at me hard. And then his face broke with laughter, and I knew everything was going to be just fine.

Andromache's War

By Elliott Dunstan

ANDROMACHE—ONCE OF HYPOPLAKIA AND ONCE of Troy, and now of nowhere at all—watches the sky pass by behind her captor and master, the sea splash at the side of the penteconter, and dreams about home. Home is faces, long gone; home was burning, the last she saw it, a thousand voices crying out as they were slaughtered or captured; home is a memory.

"What's the matter, Andromache? Lost in thought again?" Neoptolemos is staring back at her, the pride of victory lighting up his face. It's been only a day since they put out from Troy, and her hands are still cold. The first morning without her son. The first morning alone.

-Hell hath no fury-

The anger starts slow, still smoldering as he turns back to stare out at the waves breaking at the prow. She gets to her feet, sandals soaking in the water at the bottom of the penteconter, and she strides down between the rowers. "More found than lost, my lord," she replies, and he starts, glancing down at her again as she climbs up to stand by him.

He laughs, and she stares at the pearly white of his teeth. He's young, too young to have so much blood on his hands. Her hands are so cold. So cold. "I thought you'd get a taste for the ocean." His hand strokes her waist, and the repulsion that runs through her like a shock is so violent, so brutal, that she almost jumps into the ocean herself, to be away from him. She'd be with Hector, and Astyanax, and the rest of her family and people.

-Hell hath no fury-

"Tell me, Neoptolemos, once more," she says it in a quiet, almost pleading tone, "why my son had to die."

His eyes blur with confusion for a second, eyes as blue as the ocean and the sky that meet behind him in the horizon, and then smoldering fury sets them alight like tinder to bark. Then—"Oh, yes. Hector's son. If I'd left him alive, he would want me dead. My father killed his; I'd be the target. Better to end the cycle now."

And in your favour. But Andromache just nods, the picture of innocence, of matronly subservience and understanding, and pretends not to be hearing the awful thud of a body falling off a wall, over and over again.

"So Hector kills Patroclus, Achilles kills Hector, you kill Hector's son so he won't kill you—the cycle ends there, then?"

Neoptolemos shrugs. "Unless there's some bastards I missed, the house of Priam is at an end."

It's never occurred to Andromache to count herself as part of any dynasty or house. She's a princess, of course. But to hear herself and Cassandra and Hecuba and so many other living, breathing souls denied and ignored, as if their souls passed on when their husbands did—

She touches the front of Neoptolemos's bronze armour, as if with admiration, and takes hold of a leather strap. Then in quiet, unassuming words, she says, "So is the house of Achilles."

And she shoves him with strength she didn't know she had, balancing the fates, and Neoptolemos topples over the prow of his ship, bronze armour glinting in the sunlight, boars-tusk helmet falling off his head and fair curls tossing this way and that in the salty wind.

He disappears under the wine-dark waves with a speed that surprises her, the armour he was so proud of weighing him down (and, she'll wager, all the lives that hang on it like heavy, sodden fruit).

Andromache has seen plenty of men fall in battle. They've fallen to their friends, to their enemies, and when the despair of the Achaean assault had built to the point of no escape, sometimes to the points of their own swords. But as she waits and watches the murderer of her son, her father-in-law, her people drown in the Aegean Sea, she scrubs her hands against each other with a sudden conscious knowledge that now, a man has fallen to her, and she cannot take it back.

Hell hath no fury like a woman with nothing left to lose.

~2~

HYPOPLAKIA – UNDER THE MOUNTAIN – is not quite big enough to be a city, not quite small enough to be a town, storied enough to matter, inconsequential enough that it could vanish without a trace. Herakles founded it generations before, named it Thebe, and all the following generations since called it something else to distinguish it from its cousin.

This is Andromache's homeland. Even more so, she is one daughter compared to seven sons, all competing to decide who will inherit their not-quite-city, to pay tribute to Troy, which will in turn pay tribute to the Hittites inland in their grand city—

It's no wonder that when Hector, son of Priam and prince of Troy, rides into Hypoplakia, there's not even the glimmer of suspicion in Andromache's mind that it has anything to do with *her*.

Except, of course, it does. Andromache is sitting in the olive grove when Hector comes to her. He asks her for her hand, like she is a princess with a dowry instead of an unwanted extra mouth to feed, and she accepts—it is her duty, after all, the first thing that Hypoplakia has asked of her, in her short life, and it's something she can do for her birthplace. Hector marries her in the olive grove, his hand warm in hers, and they ride away together. He whispers promises into her ear that they'll visit.

(When Hypoplakia burns to the ground under the greedy swords and chariots of the Achaeans, Hector holds her while she cries. He doesn't mock her. He swears that he will drive them off or die trying—and Andromache is struck by the sudden realization, *oh,* oh she does love him after all —and asks him please, please to stay with her.)

~3~

SHE TURNS FROM THE PROW, staring down at the rows and rows of oarsmen and trying to pretend that her heart isn't jumping into her throat with fear. In the middle, some of the other Trojan slaves are looking up at her with the selfsame fear, *Andromache what did you do* – but the Myrmidons are confused, angry, befuddled, trying to understand what has just happened.

Of course, she realizes, on the edge of desperate laughter. *The grandchild of the sea.* It won't be long before Neoptolemos resurfaces. How could she have been so foolish?

They're all waiting for the inevitable. Thetis will bring her grandchild back to the surface, and either she or Neoptolemos will execute Andromache for her insolence.

The ship rests in the dead wind, in haunting silence. Then, one by one, the Achaeans drop their oars and stand, staring up at the concubine, the murderer, still unsure whether she is blessed or cursed.

Even Andromache doesn't know. But when she turns and looks at the sea, the waters are dark and sad, but preternaturally calm. Judgment has been passed on Neoptolemos—and his fate has been decided, for better or worse.

Andromache opens and closes her hands, still cold from the sea-winds. Possessed by vengeance, or a tool of the gods' justice? She isn't sure anymore, if she ever was.

She looks back at the Myrmidons, and one of the men in the front meets her eyes, the same crossing-point reflected in his dark irises. "In Thessaly, a slave murdering her master earns the death penalty," he says calmly.

"It's a good thing we aren't in Thessaly," she shoots back, trying to remember to breathe.

"It is."

She exhales, shuddering. She's a princess, and if any of the men in front of her wanted her dead, they would have acted already. Besides, there are at least ten Trojan slaves to... forty Myrmidons. Never mind.

"It's a shame our king was standing so close to the prow. I was trying to save him."

The first Myrmidon's eyes bore into her like daggers, and she can feel more of them throughout the ship. But she walks down the ship again, keeping her back straight. "As his wife—" and isn't it wonderful how the truth becomes a tool, in the right hands? "I would like to make land and honour him. Of course,

I'm only a woman. I will need advisors to help me navigate home to Thessaly. Or wherever we choose to go." She chooses her words so carefully, they feel like scorpion's stings on her tongue. The temptation to scream in desperation *take me home* is so strong that it hurts. But if she knows nothing else, it's how to be a diplomat. It's how to promise exactly what she has and make it sound like more.

If she knows nothing else about men, she knows what they're greedy for.

"Neoptolemos's wife? Is that how you're playing this, woman?" comes the snort of derision. She turns and faces the man who spoke—tall, burly and dark-bearded.

She shoves down the fear she feels, knowing she's exposed in the flimsy dress she's wearing, knowing she looks nothing like a wife should. "He needed one."

"Concubines don't get a say. You can't slaughter a good man in cold blood and then steal his title." He spits at her, and it lands on her cheek.

Andromache wipes it away slowly, carefully, with ice in her eyes. "There are many things in this life I cannot do," she says, fixing her eyes on his and letting the sting come back into her voice. "I cannot bring any of my kinsmen back from Hades. I cannot rebuild the stones of Troy." Her cheeks light up with fury. "But I have seen my husband and son avenged. And I have spent ten years protecting my homeland. Whereas *you*," —her eyes sweep the Achaeans, battered and bruised and old and sore—"are your homes still waiting for you? Ten years gone? Ten years waging war on behalf of some king's pride?"

The man's eyes drop in shame, and his cheeks burn. Andromache takes a step closer to him, and pulls the short-sword from his belt, claiming it for her own, and lets the tip hover at his chest. "My name is Andromache. Not concubine. Not woman. Not Trojan. Andromache."

"Andromache," he spits.

"And I am the wife of Neoptolemos. He took me for his own, before any Argive wife, and he left no heir." She lowers the sword. "This ship belongs to me. If you have a problem with it, you may go down to the ocean floor and ask *him* for counsel."

His head bows in understanding. And then, so does the man next to him, and the next, and the next, until she's surrounded by bowed heads and fists on chests. "Andromache," they say as one, and suddenly she feels dizzy.

It wasn't supposed to work.

~4~

THAT NIGHT, SHE IS VISITED not by Hector (her dreams are not kind to her; the one face she wishes she could see again is lost to the underworld, possibly forever) but by Priam, his shamble accentuated in death, his beard long and twisted, his eyes closed in horror.

I tried, she says. *I tried.* But he shakes his head.

We hid. We all did. We put all our faith in one man —

Once again, Andromache tries to claim that she tried. But the sinking feeling in her chest tells her something different, that if she hadn't been a helpless woman, if she had been a warrior like Hector, she could have done more. Perhaps.

But it's hubris of the worst kind to believe she could have changed fate. She won't fall into that trap.

She looks down into the weight in her arms, expecting to see her son, but instead, there's only empty air. She can feel him, heavy and warm and sleeping, but there's nothing there. Only a distant wail, the sudden rush of air on her cheeks as she stands over the wall and reaches for him (too late), and the faraway, sudden, awful thud—

For a moment, she thinks she's woken up. It's not until she realizes she's surrounded by sisters that she realizes that she's still dreaming. Helen is the one she sees first.

I didn't mean to, Helen whispers. The face that launched a thousand ships is screwed up with tears, and Andromache may have killed a man, now, but Helen has killed thousands without lifting a finger, and the weight of them all sits on her back. *I didn't want this. I just wanted to be happy.*

Cassandra is hiding from Andromache, behind the priestess's veil. Andromache pushes past Helen (the sympathy is there, but it's not enough to blank out the unending fury) and tries to lift the veil, but all she can catch a glimpse of are the lips muttering words, over and over again. *What were you trying to tell me?* She wonders. *What were you trying to say?*

And then Hecuba. Her husband's mother, frail and strong all at once, gone mad at the sight of her children's bodies. The gods had spared her in some small way; she'd slipped out of Odysseus's chains in the form of a cat, but the small kindnesses made the rest of the cruelty hurt more. Here, in the fate-dream, she is young and tall but her eyes are white voids, staring deep into the past.

A warning, Andromache realizes. All three of them, a warning.

She wakes up with a start, the dawnlight filtering through the tent's thin fabric, and she gets to her feet. She goes down to the water, ignoring the men as they awake in bits and pieces. And she dips her head into the ocean, letting the past drift away as much as it can, washing away the stains from her eyes.

~5~

THE ACHAEAN WHO HAD SO quietly challenged and reassured her—the first one—is Phileas of Epirus, not even a Myrmidon at all. This puts her surprisingly at ease; that there's at least one person on board this ship that isn't tied to Achilles by blood, or a Trojan slave.

"You've got guts, for a woman," he says with a smile flickering around his mouth once she's lifted her head from the water.

"Is that a compliment?" she shoots back.

"You've also got a mouth."

She isn't sure how to respond to that. Slavery is meant to make her more obedient, but instead it's ruined her, taken away all the little rules she's spent her life following. She stares at the ground instead.

"You have no intention of going to Thessaly, do you?"

"Not if I can help it," she murmurs. "I don't foresee a warm welcome."

"Neither do I." He sits down next to her, tapping his sword against his knee. "What do you want, then?"

"Blood," the answer jumps into her throat before she can stifle it. It's a horrible answer. Vengeance solves nothing, but the blood-debt weighs on her shoulders, crying out to be paid.

Phileas hums thoughtfully at that. "You can only make somebody pay in blood once, that's the trouble. What do you do *after* you've slaughtered…well, I imagine your list is long. You've got more grievances than most."

"You've been paying attention."

"You're Hector's wife. Aren't you?"

"I imagine the rest of the crew is too stupid to put that together."

"More than you imagine. But no, most of us don't waste our time with the marriages and petty squabbles of the kings."

"Except when you fight their battles for ten years."

Phileas throws his head back and laughs. "Oh, you're *still* on about that. You don't know what Myrmidon currency is, do you?"

She wrings out the last drops of water from her thick, dark hair, watching him curiously. "No."

"Two things. Loyalty and gold."

"And yours?"

"More of the second than the first."

"You're not *really* from Epirus, are you?"

"Oh, I'm from Epirus. My *mother's* from Crete."

Andromache sighs, staring at Phileas with an unimpressed glare. "Of course she is. So unless I can pay them and earn their trust, I'll end up just as dead as Neoptolemos?"

"That's right."

"Why are you helping me?"

"Because, it might help you to know, nobody liked him." Phileas nods to her arm—or, more specifically, she realizes, at the bruises that have slid back into view, and she yanks her dress back over them. "Achilles was a hero—a bit of a loud-mouth, arrogant, but he had the *right* to be. He did great things. But nobody gets to ride on his father's fame with nothing to show for it except sacrilege and the murder of old men and children."

Andromache can feel the blood drain from her face, and she yanks her eyes away from Phileas. She doesn't want to think about it, but it's too late.

"My apologies, Your Highness."

"Don't," she mumbles. They sit there in silence for a moment, before she clears her throat. "So the rest – the Myrmidons – it's about whether they hate being led by a woman more or less than by a teenaged bully."

"Exactly."

"You're not filling me with confidence."

"You could always put me in charge."

"You're Cretan," she scoffed. "Not in a million years."

"That's just cruel."

She puts her hand back into the water, watching the waves crash over it — then looks up at the horizon, squinting at the blur on it. It's another ship, she realizes, and she's seen enough ships come into the Trojan harbour that she knows what it looks like when a ship is listing, trying to find ground.

And then, she knows what they're going to do.

"Myrmidons!" she calls out, and Phileas falls backwards in surprise, blinking up at her. "Arm yourselves, board the ship, and get ready for battle!"

"What are you doing?" Phileas hisses. But the power in her voice is doing something because, true to their nature as warriors, the Myrmidons are *obeying*, hearing the call of opportunity —

Andromache points out to the listing ship, and to the design she can just barely make out on the prow. "That's the ship of Diomedes," she says with a confidence she almost feels. "And I watched everything that went onto that ship." She can't help the giddy glee that fills her bones. "Time to pay my men."

Before she climbs onto the penteconter, she strokes her hand over the bronze ram on its front, and blesses it with every word she has. She doesn't know how to sail a ship — but she knows how to inspire confidence in the heart of men, and besides, that's what her generals are for.

The rest, she'll learn along the way.

~6~

THE NIGHT THEY BURY HECTOR, Andromache can hardly breathe. Looking at his defiled body is too hard – instead, she keeps her mourning to herself, and instead cradles Astyanax in her arms, whispering courage to him and hopes of vengeance. Even then, she knows, deep in her heart, that she will not get to see her son grow old; she takes the knowledge and buries it somewhere in her mind where she can forget, so she can still hope for victory against their ruthless besiegers.

Once the games have ended and the lights have gone out, she takes herself up to the wall and stares out at the massed troops by the shore. She's watched their number dwindle over the years and began to familiarize herself with their patterns. There is Nestor, the old king, with his pattern as he walks among the tents; Diomedes who tends to the herds when he can't sleep; and there, at the edge of the camp is Achilles. This is the first time in a long time Andromache has seen him alone, without Patroclus, and as much as she wants to hate him, as much as she wants to see him dead, she can't help but stare at the empty space by his side with sorrow.

How terrible it is, she thinks, that she can stare across the battlefield where her husband died and feel even a twinge of sympathy for his murderer? Then, she thinks, how terrible it is that instead of comfort in mourning, there is only more death to be found.

She holds Astyanax close, and whispers, "You will be a great king one day." She keeps going through the tears threatening to choke her. "A kind one. A good one. You'll make your father proud."

Astyanax looks up at her with his father's eyes and burbles into the empty darkness, and she buries her face into his mop of curls and cries.

~7~

"IF THIS IS A JOKE," Diomedes says with calm amusement, "it's an excellent one."

Andromache stands over him with her arms crossed. "This would be the part where you ask for mercy."

"From a woman with a sword?" he replies wryly. "I don't think so — *ow*," he complains peevishly as one of the Myrmidons pokes him with a spear-tip. "You've one breast too many to be an Amazon, you're disappointingly mortal, and I've got all my clothes on."

"I can change that."

"Suddenly I regret opening my mouth."

Andromache chuckles despite herself. She's starting to see what men got out of all their squabbling and warfare. She has no interest in taking slaves, though—just all the Trojan treasures that Diomedes 'liberated' for his own treasury. "Phileas, take some of the men and take everything you can carry."

"I'll have you know I won that all fair and square."

"And now I've won it back. If you didn't want to be pirated, you should have fixed your ship."

Diomedes huffs. "I've been at war for ten years. I deserve a break."

"I was at war for ten years and *lost*. Save it."

He sighs. "Will you at least untie me before you leave?"

"Hmm... No."

"Gorgon."

"Achaean."

"That's not an insult."

"Not to you, perhaps," she shoots back with a curve of her lip, and the paling of his face is all the gratification she needs. She lets her men rummage through the treasure, and she strides back onto her ship, feeling her back straighten and her messy braids tumble down her back.

Once they've set sail again, Diomedes's ship scuppered and floundering behind them, the Myrmidons behind her let out a cheer.

"Where to next, my lady?" comes the cry from the oars, and she turns at the prow, eyes glittering.

"Wherever we want. But first, let's make land. Time to celebrate."

~8~

IT'S A WHILE BEFORE SHE truly earns their respect, and it takes looking the part—she still wears a concubine's tunic, but over her exposed thighs she wears leather greaves, braces over her arms, and a bronze choker from Priam's treasury around her neck. Some of the other Trojans remember how to braid her hair in the royal way; she pins the braids up and lets them frame her face like a Hittite painting, and darkens her eyes with kohl that used to live in Hecuba's jewellery box, and the ship itself, soon to be only one of many under her command, bears painted teeth under the name 'Astyanax'. One by one she captures the Achaean ships, Argive and Gerenian and Theban.

With them come the slaves, Ilion and Dardanian, Thracian and Phrygian and Miletian, mostly female with a few young and beautiful men. Some of the children are already with child. Those are the ships that Andromache burns and lets the men jump into the sea. It's not murder if she lets the gods sort them out.

The years pass and slowly, the past slips through her fingers. At first she misses it. She cries silently in the mornings, when the rosy-fingered dawn steals away names, faces, memories that used to be dearer than rubies. But they're replaced with new accomplishments, glory she could never have won as somebody's wife, somebody's daughter, somebody's mother. She could never have imagined inspiring fear, not before feeling it so deeply that it shattered her inside and out.

And soon, she locks the door behind her, and allows herself to be Andromache the Warlord, Andromache the Sword Queen. Phileas teaches her the sword. Epistor teaches her the bow. And the dark and inconstant and faithless ocean, that birthed Achilles and drowned his son, the ocean teaches her how to forget.

~9~

ALMOST TEN YEARS PASS SINCE the sack of Troy, and Andromache is invited—politely, with the air of those seeking safe passage through the waters she now owns—to the island of Scheria. She might be a vicious warlord, but she's known as a reasonable one, too, and so she goes in her finery, bronze armbands ringing her biceps and gems in her ears.

Step one of any negotiation, after all, is *presentation*.

She's welcomed into the hall of King Alcinous by young men clearly meant to appeal to her—and it's not that they *don't*, it's just that as much as her eyes stray, she's not interested beyond enjoying the view - and then she sits down for a meal in his hall.

"Queen Andromache," the King greets her with a smile, and invites her to sit by his side. There's another man with him, a man with cautious and cunning eyes, but he looks so wild that

Andromache dismisses him without another thought—almost. "I'm pleased you accepted my invitation."

"I'm pleased to be here. It was very gracious of you to invite me. I know outsiders are not favoured on Scheria."

Alcinous scoffs. "Men bring destruction in their wake. But you're no man, and I've heard of your ways." He smiles and raises a cup to her. "Liberator of slaves, and not a drop of blood shed except for those who drown themselves in terror - you are always welcome on Scheria."

It's flattery, but for all that, it's true. Andromache doesn't like the feeling of blood on her hands, for all that Neoptolemos never bled. She watched too much of it shed, for too little reason. "What do you want from me, Alcinous?"

"Oh, let's not. Let's have a song first." Then Alcinous turns to his companion, the man with the wild beard and the blanket wrapped around him. "This is my other guest, a stranger who washed up shipwrecked on our shores."

"What happened to men bringing destruction?"

"Destruction or not, I cannot in good faith turn away somebody who supplicated my queen and is in dire need of help. What would you like to hear, my friend?"

The man smiles, scratching his beard, then turns to the singer. "Anything you know of the exploits of the Achaeans."

Andromache's blood runs cold. She pushes her hands under the table, managing to keep herself calm by digging her fingernails into her knee as the blind singer begins to pick out a song on his lyre. It's a song about Odysseus and—who else?— Achilles. Achilles. Curse his name.

It's like the doors, once locked, are being thrown open from the inside.

The most horrifying part is looking up and seeing the nostalgic tears forming in the strange man's eyes. *I know you,* comes the unbidden thought. *I know you, and not for good reasons.*

The sense fades as the blind singer continues onto a different song, this one about Ares and Aphrodite. This time, Andromache can relax and attempt to eat, although her stomach is unsettled and tight.

I know you, comes the feeling again.

"Sing more about the Trojan War," bids the familiar voice again as the blind poet comes to an end, and Andromache's spine chills so cold she thinks it might break.

"I don't think that's necessary," she says quietly, but it's too late. The singer has started, and with a horrified, silent scream, she realizes he's singing — with *pride* — about the hollow horse that her countrymen had taken as a gift of surrender. The Trojan Horse, it's called now. A trick. A trap.

A victory, for the Achaeans — and for the man in front of her, so beaten, so worn down, but tearing up more and more with each word, almost *glowing* with mixed pride and sorrow, with skin and nose and hair she would never have seen in Troy.

"Why, my friend, what troubles you so?" Alcinous asks him. And with a dramatic flourish, the man opens his mouth, wiping his tears.

"I cannot hide my identity any longer. My name is —"

"Odysseus," she spits. The name is like a knife through the air. And nobody, *nobody* there, has reason to hate it but her.

But he knows. It takes him some time searching her face, but she can pinpoint the exact moment. His face blanches slightly, but he's at least a little heroic. He nods in understanding. He isn't going to pretend that she doesn't have *every* reason to want him dead.

"Andromache. The same of Troy, then."

"The very same." She gets to her feet, pulling the sword from her belt, and ignores Alcinous's gasp of horror. Everything is like it was yesterday, now—the sack of Troy, the smell of burning flesh, the bets placed on which of the women would crack first under pressure, the way Hecuba's eyes had rolled back in her head when she had lost her mind—

"You're far from home, Ithacan."

"And without a weapon, too. Unless you'd like to do me the honour?"

"You were happy to use your weapons on the women of Troy without allowing us to arm ourselves," Andromache scoffs. "Odysseus the Ithacan, suddenly so concerned with a fair fight. You murdered us in our beds. You raped us in front of our children. You pulled us from our altars and killed us in sight of all of the gods." She rounds the table, Scherians fleeing to the sides of the room and Odysseus backing away from the teeth and sword she's baring.

"War is *war*, Andromache—it was always going to end—"

"And how do you think it would have ended if we'd won, Odysseus?" She swings the sword at him, barely missing his torso and watching him flinch with a bitter enjoyment. "All we wanted was for you to *leave*. Paris was long dead by the time you rammed down our doors."

Odysseus takes another step back, and a look of panic flashes over his face as he realizes his back is against the wall. "We took a vow—"

"And isn't it convenient how much gold that vow made you?" Then she chuckles. "Well, how much gold it made everybody else. It doesn't seem to have done you much good." She leans in, the blade of her sword whispering over his throat. "Have you ever been helpless before, Odysseus? Have you ever been without the gods to help you? Have you ever been this close to a blade and not had anything between it and your skin?"

Odysseus doesn't respond, swallowing a lungful of nervous air.

"This is what you did to a whole city, you yellow-bellied, deceitful, pompous coward," Andromache spits. "To woman after woman. Child after child. And I want you to thank the gods and the stars, for the rest of your sorry life, that I am a better person than you will ever be."

And she steps back, sheaths her sword, and turns her back to leave. She waits for the footsteps to come after her — she wouldn't have doubted it of him. But when she casts a look over her shoulder, he's collapsed on his knees, rubbing the small cut on his throat, eyes fixed on her as she strides away.

~10~

SHE MAKES IT BACK TO the sea before she finally breaks down. Tears are a luxury as a pirate — any form of weakness is. But for a little while, she isn't a pirate anymore. She's a young woman losing everything all over again.

Andromache. It means "war of men," and she's been a victim of men's wars for too long.

She dips her hand into the water, and whispers, "You let me kill your grandson. Why?"

Perhaps it's her imagination that a hand slides into hers, and she certainly doesn't hear any voice in response. But she gives herself an answer anyway - that she's not the only one who doesn't care for violence and brutality as the only way to be, that hers is not the only family torn apart by war. That sometimes letting human action unfold is preferable to saving the life of somebody who will kill tens, dozens, hundreds more. That sometimes there is no right choice.

She boards her ship, watching her men lingering still on the shore, uncertain of what transpired inside. But there's no rush, not yet. She drags her fingers over the carved wood of each oar, over the strong pole of the mast, over the salt-soaked sides of her penteconter. *Astyanax.*

Time to sail — maybe back to Hypoplakia, finally, or back to Troy, or to everywhere and nowhere at all.

Rib of Man

BY GEONN CANNON

T HE NOOSE HUNG NEXT TO the door of her quarters, the rope stiff and hardened by the years since it was first tied. Henriette Talmadge often lay in bed and watched it sway with the movement of the ship. She still remembered very clearly the way it felt when the executioner slipped it over her head. The loop of hemp had an odd weight where it rested on her shoulders. She had been one of five scheduled to be executed that day, alongside a captain named MacManus. Henriette was barely sixteen, had only spent two months aboard a ship, and she accepted that her short life had reached its end with no gold, no glory, no name made for herself.

She was saved when MacManus' crew staged a rescue by disrupting the spectacle. Her freedom was an unintended consequence. She took full advantage of it when the constables paid more attention to MacManus and his crewmen than to her. She ran, hands still bound behind her back and noose — the rope broken a few inches above its bowknot by a man whose face she'd never even seen. Behind her was gunfire, shouting, the clatter of suddenly terrified people who had exulted at seeing animals so long as they remained in a cage.

Twelve years had gone by since that ancient day. Henriette truly believed she'd died on that morning, her life over and her soul reborn as this new creature. She kept the noose as a reminder of how far she'd come. These were captain's quarters, this was her vessel. The men and women she could hear shouting at each other on the deck were her crew. It was a far cry from the life she'd been told to expect when she was a child.

Henriette would have been content to remain in bed all morning, but her reverie was broken by a shout from the crow's nest. She swung her legs over the edge of her bed and pushed her hair out of her face, tying it back as she stepped outside. The sea air pushed against her like a solid wave as soon as she was on the deck. She took a moment to savor it and listen to the ship breathe. The rigging groaned, the sails moaned, and the entire ship seemed to vibrate with life.

Felicitas Caraveo, her quartermaster, had already investigated the lookout's cry. She crossed the deck with the gliding step of a dancer. She once claimed to have spent more of her life at sea than on land, saying, "I was born on the waves, and fates willing, I'll die there, too." Her skin was dark brown, her normally wild hair currently tamed against her skull in a series of intricate braids. She was barefoot and wearing a lightweight tan shirt and trousers rolled up above her slender ankles.

"Ship ripe for the taking, just this side of the horizon. We could change course and intercept. See if it has anything we might be interested in."

Henriette swept her hand across the lower part of her face as she considered the possibilities. The crew had gone some weeks without enriching themselves. Their morale seemed fine, but a victory would keep those spirits high until they were back in port. On the other hand, if they went to the effort of sacking a ship with an empty hold, she risked creating the very malaise she hoped to avoid. She didn't like attacking blind. Stumbling across a potential payday in the middle of the wide ocean could be Lady Luck grinning on them or it could be the Devil tempting their greedy souls.

She held out her hand. Caraveo filled it with the brass telescope she kept on her belt at all times. Henriette extended its length and brought the glass to her eye, squinting as she focused on the distant vessel. It would be prudent to continue on their way. But there was something about this other ship that made her feel as if it was worth the risk. The feeling was just a spark in her gut, a twinge she had trusted in the past, to great benefit.

"Riding very low," she noted.

"Heavy," Caraveo confirmed. Her hands were on her hips, chin up and shoulders squared.

It was clear what response she was hoping for, but Henriette knew she would abide by whatever choice the captain made. She was utterly loyal even when she disagreed. Henriette lowered the telescope and patted it against her palm as she weighed the risks and benefits. Finally, she handed it back and granted Caraveo a smile.

"Change course, Fel. We'll have some excitement today."

Caraveo showed her teeth with a feral smile. "Aye, Captain. I'll pass word."

As she hurried off, Henriette moved closer to the railing to get a look at their target with her naked eye. They weren't near any of the established shipping routes, which meant it wasn't likely to be carrying supplies. It could just be a merchant vessel, blown off course.

Or, as a ship traveling east from the Caribbean, it could have a hold full of human beings they intended to sell into slavery. Liberating those prisoners wouldn't do anything to help Henriette's crew or their coffers, but it would nevertheless be a prize worth the risks they were taking.

Beneath her feet she could feel the ship changing direction. She rested her hands on the railing and stared hard at their prey for a moment. Once they were underway, she turned and moved toward the quarterdeck with a confident stride. The crew had taken note of the new course and gave her their attention. She motioned for their silence and smiled down at them, the men and women who had chosen to follow her, their greedy eyes wide as they looked back at her.

"I hope you enjoyed your rest, crew, because we've got a prize ripe for the picking on the edge of the world. What do you say we go see what we can pluck from its vine?"

Their cheers rose as a single animalistic shout, loud enough that she feared it would carry across the water to alert the other ship they were coming. But it didn't matter. Let them know, let them fear what was to come. Henriette smiled and returned to her quarters.

ATTACKING ANOTHER SHIP WAS BY far the worst part of being a captain. There was the excitement, certainly. The firing of cannons made the entire ship quake underneath her feet, and the air quickly filled with the scent of burnt powder. Battles were quick and dirty affairs and never failed to make her blood churn. Unfortunately, she was less skilled with a blade than Caraveo, and they had an agreement that it would be best if

Henriette left the close-quarter fighting to those better suited to it. Caraveo planned the assaults and led the charge onto the other vessel. Henriette made the call when to show their colors—too early gave their prey time to flee or retaliate—then remained behind until the all clear had been sounded.

She had changed into her favorite silk shirt and striped trousers. She smeared paint around her eyes, the white clashing against her dark skin, and added a fiery red eyeliner to ensure she looked monstrous. When she heard the horn sound from the other ship, she placed a tricorn hat over her dark curls and left the safety of her quarters.

A plank was set out between the decks. Caraveo awaited her on the other side, hand resting on the hilt of her cutlass. It was always a good sign to see a sheathed cutlass with no blood-stains. Henriette crossed the short distance and paused after stepping off onto the captured ship, pretending to examine one cuff of her shirt as Caraveo leaned in close.

"Just a bit of scrapple," she muttered. "Fists and shouts, mostly. Been through worse at a tavern on payday."

Henriette nodded and walked on. Caraveo followed her to the main deck. The crew had been separated into three rows of ten each, kneeling and facing starboard so they could see the ship responsible for taking them. Henriette slowed so she could examine their faces as she passed. They were haggard but not starving. Some were unshaven and sunburnt, some scarred but others fresh as schoolboys. Their clothes were well mended. She reached the end of the row and spun on the ball of her foot.

"I am Captain Henriette Talmadge. That," she pointed, "is the *Rib of Man*. It's my vessel. I took it from the man who had it before me because he used it as a chariot for the selling and purchasing of human beings. I thought it deserved a more righteous destiny." She took slow steps forward as if marking distance. "I changed its name to *Rib of Man* because that, according to a certain book, is the origin of the female species.

"I don't know about you gentlemen, but I've always thought that story sounded rather savage. A man caught unaware. A bone ripped from his body. And not the bone of his arm, nor his leg, but a rib, curved and sharp, like a sword. A man's rib is a weapon, crafted while he lay naked and exposed." She smiled at Caraveo. "The women standing before you are descendants of that brutal moment. We are weapons who have been taught we are weak, fragile, helpless. The weaker sex."

"A bare fact," a man muttered.

Henriette couldn't tell who had spoken. "You believe it to be so? You call women weak because we are not as physically powerful as a man? Then it must also be true that a gorilla is mightier than a man or that men will bow down before a rhinoceros. You are simply a different sort of animal. You are aggressive and loud. You bellow and pound your chests to show you are unafraid while women plot, scheme or show mercy when it benefits us."

She stopped walking and looked at the kneeling men.

"I will show mercy today. My crew will take what we desire from this ship and then we will leave. We will leave it intact, and not one man aboard will be harmed. In the following weeks, one of two things will happen. Either every man aboard agrees to remain silent about what transpired, or they decide to talk. When you talk, you spread word that you were boarded by Captain Talmadge and the crew from the *Rib of Man*. Those stories shall include the fact we showed mercy in exchange for taking what we wanted. If you say nothing, this encounter remains between us, and our ships go their separate ways. Either way, it works well for me and mine."

A man in the middle row had lifted his head during her speech. She could see the defiance in his eye and knew exactly what he planned. He said, "Or perhaps you haven't the stomach to just take what you want. Lot of big talk just to —"

His head rocked back, his right eye replaced by a blackened bloom of blood and gore. He collapsed on the man next to him, who cringed and let the corpse tumble to the deck.

Caraveo holstered her gun and returned her attention to the water, no more bothered than if she had swatted a fly.

"I had a response," Henriette said.

"Was it as concise as mine?"

"Hm. No, not really." Henriette faced the crew again. "You want to live just a little bit more than I want to kill you. A ghost ship floating through these waters might be good for my reputation, but not if there are no survivors to tell the tale. Be smart, gentlemen. In a few hours, we will be miles away and considerably richer while you will be in Port Royal drowning your sorrows and ready to face another day."

She turned her back and walked toward the captain's quarters.

"Get these men off their knees," she called back to Caraveo. "Get them below decks, out of the sun. No reason for them to fry on deck."

"Aye, Captain," Caraveo said. "All right, you heard her! On your feet!"

THE CAPTAIN'S CABIN WAS MORE cluttered than her own. It clearly served as both living quarters and a center of operations, with an unmade bed against the far wall and a desk next to it. The windows were stained a dark yellow from years of pipe smoke, so the light filtering through gave the feeling of being submerged in murky water.

The desk was covered with a mountain of papers, books, maps, charts, and other detritus of commanding a ship. Seated behind it was Elias, a slender man with hunched shoulders and a pair of spectacles resting on the bump of his crooked nose. If he wore his hair down, it would have reached to his sharp cheekbones, but he shoved it up in wild tangles, only barely restrained by a bit of cord. He was currently skimming through a leather-bound book. He had not told her his last name, when he joined her crew five years ago, nor since.

"Love the speech," he said. "Always good when I get a chance to hear it."

"I could shorten it a bit. I could see the sacrificial lamb getting itchy about halfway through. If he'd decided to act before speaking, he might have caused others to make reckless decisions. Was the captain among the crowd I just addressed?"

"Nah. He was a little too rambunctious, so Caraveo took him down below. He's alive, just a bit less full of blood than he was this morning."

"Still have all his pieces?"

"Mm-hmm. He'll get a fine scar for his trouble."

Henriette settled on the edge of the desk and looked down at the pile. "Find anything of interest?"

"Not much we haven't gotten from other ships," he said. "The man who used to sit in this chair wasn't exactly a scholar, and he didn't keep updated records. But..." He held up a journal and tossed it into Henriette's hands. "Trade routes and nautical charts better than we have."

Henriette cooed as she thumbed through the yellow pages. "Spectacular."

"Ship is called the *Rebecca*, by the by."

She wrinkled her nose as if catching a bad smell. "Without fail. You give a man ownership of a thing, he immediately feminizes it. Women as possessions. What a way to see the world." She stood and tucked the journal under her belt. She would give it to Caraveo herself. "Let me know if you find anything else worth my attention."

He muttered some sort of assurance and she left him to his work.

Back in the sunlight, she squinted to watch the captive crew march obediently below deck. Caraveo was supervising, one hand on her sword and the other on her pistol, but she didn't seem overly concerned about a revolt. The dead crewman was still lying where he had fallen. She would leave the body for his crewmates to dispose of properly.

She walked to the railing on the seaward side of the ship, so she could look out over the water. The ocean felt different here. *Rebecca* didn't have the same personality as the *Rib of Man*. It was a smaller ship, heavier, and the water affected it differently. Being aboard it was like standing in a stranger's shoes, breathing with his lungs, wearing his skin.

"Ma'am."

The other woman had approached without a sound, and Henriette graced her with a smile. "You're a terror on those soft feet of yours."

Ofelia Solis tried to disguise how pleased she was at the praise. She held out a small book. "We got this off one of the crew. A woman. English, young."

"Is she with the rest of the crew?"

"Aye. Nearly took my head off when I grabbed the book from her, but she decided it was better to lose the book and keep her head than the other way 'round."

"Another scrappy one, hm? This crew seems to be full of them."

Henriette accepted the book and unwound the leather strap holding it closed. Ofelia remained where she stood since she hadn't been dismissed. Henriette anticipated the book would be nothing more than a journal full of some random girl's idle thoughts, written to keep her mind off the boredom of a long sea voyage. Such things might be useful in revealing new routes, new ports of call, or any number of things it might be useful to know, but she expected little. Instead, she was startled to find page after page of detailed charts.

"Well, hello..." She slowed her fingers and examined each drawing. Maps of the stars and the sea, with clearly marked distances and knots. "Ofelia, the girl you took this from, you said she's below with the rest of the crew?"

"Aye."

"Bring her to me."

Ofelia vanished below decks. Henriette ran her fingers over the page and thumbed to the back, then to the front. Every entry seemed to be written by the same hand with artistic representations of islands they had presumably passed. There were also a handful of portraits that were also very well done. Henriette ignored them for the time being and focused on the star charts. She didn't want to get her hopes up, but they were extraordinary if they were accurate.

This time Ofelia didn't bother to silence her approach. Her footsteps were echoed by that of her prisoner. Henriette waited until they stopped before she closed the book to give them her attention. The owner of the book was a slender woman with a man's haircut, a lock of ink black hair falling across her eyes. It was easy to see why she hadn't bothered to masquerade as a man; her lips were too full, her throat far too thin, to ever belong to a man. She might have tried passing as a lad if she wasn't so unusually tall. She was Henriette's height, lanky but definitely not a youth in the midst of a growth spurt. Her hands were bound in front of her with a rope so thick it made her wrists look impossibly frail.

"Do you have a name?"

The woman lifted her chin defiantly. "Not one I'll share with you."

Henriette smiled. "There's no need to be rude. I merely wish to compliment you on your work." She waved the notebook. "I assume this is how you bartered your passage on this ship. Many crews think women are bad luck at sea and refuse to have them on the boat. In my experience, women are only bad luck because men can't be trusted to act like human beings when a woman is involved. I'm sure many of the men aboard this ship had other thoughts about how you could earn your place among them."

"I never let a single one of them touch me."

"There'd be no shame in it if you did. We've only been aboard for a matter of minutes and the crew has proven difficult to control. Sometimes the easiest way out of a tight situation is to surrender."

"Never," the woman insisted.

Henriette looked at the woman's bound hands and saw the knuckles were bruised and marked with wounds both fresh and healed. She nodded slowly and opened the book again. "Then you're obviously a good fighter in addition to having a keen eye and a talented hand. I could take this book from you, but I doubt it would do me a lick of good without someone to decipher it. One thing the *Rib of Man* lacks is a trustworthy sailing master. Our previous one fell afoul of a cannon ball."

"You want to take me as your prisoner?"

"Of course not. How could you watch the sea and stars from the brig? I'm offering you a spot on my crew. You'd earn your keep by navigating, get your share of whatever we take from ships like this. Best part is, you'd be sailing with a crew well aware of the fact you'd earned your spot with your brain instead of lying on your back. Ofelia, tell her."

Ofelia said, "Mostly women on the crew. Some men, not one of 'em see a problem sharing the sea with us womenfolk. Captain Talmadge is fair and generous. Best captain I've ever sailed with."

"The only captain you've ever sailed with," Henriette acknowledged.

Ofelia grinned, showing her teeth. "Got lucky with my first, why would I risk trading down?"

"Good answer." Henriette stepped closer to the prisoner and held out the book. "Take it. Like I said, it's only useful to me if I have someone who can read the thing."

The woman brought up both tied hands to take the book back. She looked like she wanted to say something, but her lips remained pressed together.

"By my reckoning, we'll be aboard this ship until sundown." Henriette looked at the horizon and tilted her head to the side. "Maybe just past. You have that long to decide. If you want to come with us, tell Caraveo and she'll cut you free and bring you over with the rest of us. Or you can decide to stay. We don't conscript people onto our ship." She nodded to Ofelia. "Take her back below."

She had turned back to face the sea when the prisoner spoke again. "Genevalisse."

"What's that?"

"My name. My friends call me Lisse."

Henriette nodded. "You have a fine eye and a great talent, Lisse. I hope you decide to share it with someone who truly appreciates it."

"If I agree to go with you now, do I have to go back below with the others?"

"I don't see why you would." She looked at Lisse again. "Are you accepting my offer, then?"

Lisse pursed her lips and rolled her shoulders. "I've never really liked captains who name their ships after women."

Henriette's smile was wide and genuine. She touched two fingers to the brim of her hat and sketched a salute. "I think we'll get along fine, Genevalisse. Ofelia, cut her loose and help her pack up anything she wants to take with her. We'll find her permanent quarters once we're underway."

"Of course, Captain," Ofelia said.

"Glad to have you aboard, Sailing Master. Welcome to the *Rib of Man*."

IT WAS WELL AFTER DARK when her crew finished their inventory and began transferring goods to the *Rib of Man*. Henriette had ordered her cook to divvy up some bread from the *Rebecca*'s kitchen, since there was no sense in letting its people go hungry, and the remainder of their stores was packed and transferred to the *Rib of Man*'s galley. When Caraveo reported they were almost ready to leave, Henriette went below to speak with their captives once again. They were crammed into a single room, some men crouching against the walls while others were forced to sit on tabletops. Two of Henriette's sailors were standing by the door with hands resting on their weapons.

"I would like to thank you all for your hospitality," she said. "You will notice your ship is riding a little lighter than it was when the sun rose, but you're still alive. So I would consider today a victory for us all. Oh, and your crew will be smaller as well. Genevalisse is coming with us. So hopefully one of you has the navigational skills to get back to a safe harbor. I would make that my priority rather than pursuing us. I wish you well and share your hope that we never cross paths again. Fair winds and following seas, gentlemen."

They set sail again just after midnight. The Master Gunner kept a watch on the *Rebecca* for signs they intended to pursue, but no alarms were sounded and soon the victimized ship was out of sight. Henriette told Caraveo she could wait until morning to itemize what they'd taken, but the quartermaster insisted on doing it as soon as possible.

"My blood is still alive from all the excitement today. Sorting everything out will help calm me down enough to sleep."

"And the crew will probably appreciate knowing how much they earned from this fight. Let me know the shares when you're done. I'll probably be awake most of the night."

"Aye." Caraveo started toward the hold.

"You did excellent work today, Felicitas."

Caraveo saluted without turning around. "As did you, Captain. I was proud to be serving with you."

Henriette grinned and continued her stroll. The moonlight was filtered through a thick and roiling wall of slate-gray fog, leaving them just enough light to sail by. Most of the crew seemed to have spent themselves aboard the *Rebecca*. Those who hadn't made it back to their beds were strewn about the deck as if they were corpses. One man's arm was flung over the rail with a bottle of rum dangling precariously from his limp fingers. She saved the bottle from certain doom and wiped the mouth of it on her blouse before taking a swig. Not the best stuff, but certainly passable. She toasted the fog for aiding their escape.

When she reached her quarters, she paused at the door. She took another drink and then held the bottle toward the shadows.

"Care for a sip?"

Lisse stepped forward into the moonlight. "How'd you know I was there?"

"A woman and the captain of a pirate ship. Being either of those things makes you wary of people lurking in the shadows. You start to get a sense for it." She gestured with the bottle. "Go on. Consider it your first reward for signing on."

The younger woman hesitated a moment longer, then came forward and took it from the captain. She took a big mouthful, bigger than she was used to judging by the way her eyes squeezed shut when she swallowed, and nodded her thanks.

Henriette pushed open the door of her quarters and gestured for Lisse to go in ahead of her. "I don't suppose you were lurking here in the hopes of pinching my liquor. And I hope you're not here to tell me you regret your decision to come with us."

"No, not at all. From what I've seen so far, it seems clear I made the right choice." Lisse entered the room cautiously and slid her gaze across the desk, to the bed. She paused when she saw the noose but kept her expression neutral. She clasped her hands behind her back and faced Henriette. "I suppose I just wanted to officially thank you for the offer to come aboard."

"Wasn't pity." Henriette walked to her desk and perched on the edge of it. She crossed her arms over her chest. "You will be very useful to me. I don't have a navigator worth a damn. That book of yours is truly remarkable. I've never seen anything like it. If you can keep that up, you might become the most valuable member of this crew."

It was difficult to tell in the darkness, but Lisse may have blushed at the praise. "Captain Molloy never seemed to care much about quality."

"Molloy. The Captain of the *Rebecca*?"

"Yeah. Not the worst man, but..."

Henriette snorted. "People always say that like it's a badge of honor. You don't have to be the worst to still be plenty bad. I'll make you a promise, Genevalisse. You keep this ship sailing straight and true, and your skills won't ever be taken for granted. Do we have a bargain?"

Lisse said, "Sounds good to me, Captain Talmadge." She tilted her head to look past Henriette at the window. The fog swirled against the glass. "Although you might have to wait until tomorrow night for a true accounting of my skills."

Henriette laughed and looked at the floor. "Ah, yes, there are limits to even the most talented of us." Her gaze swept up Lisse's body, turned casually toward the bed, and finally drifted back to Lisse's face. "Did Quartermaster Caraveo manage to find you a place to sleep tonight given the short notice?"

The invitation was impossible to miss, and this time Lisse definitely blushed. "She did. It's a little space at the far end of the hold, but it's a lateral move from what I had on the *Rebecca*. It'll do nicely. For a little while, at least."

"Good," Henriette said. "Let me know if you ever desire something more comfortable. I'm sure we can find something for you."

Lisse bit her bottom lip. Henriette was certain the girl was considering the offer. "Thank you. It's nice knowing how, ah, amenable this ship can be."

Henriette raised an eyebrow. "You have no idea. Sleep well, Lisse. Tomorrow may be your first day aboard the ship, but you'll still be a full member of the crew. You'll be pulling your weight one way or another. Might have to put you in the galley if this fog doesn't lift."

"You might rethink that once you taste my stew."

"Maybe so. But we'll keep you busy."

Lisse nodded. She held out the bottle, but Henriette waved it off. "Enjoy the rest of it." Lisse went to the door but Henriette stopped her. "Did you hear my speech about the name of this vessel?"

"*Rib of Man*," Lisse said. "The origin of women. A violent birth. A weapon."

"Mm-hmm." She stood and closed the distance between them. She put her hand against Lisse's torso, just below her breast, and pressed gently through her shirt. "The ribs are also protection: a shield that is always with you, protecting your most vital organ, your heart. The brain might be good for strategy and the gut is superb for warning you of danger, but the heart is what truly guides a person. That is what this ship represents."

Lisse held eye contact as she put her hand on top of Henriette's. "Then I would say I've definitely found myself on the right ship." Her touch lingered until Henriette's hand became warm, and then the girl smiled and stepped away. "Pleasant dreams, Captain. You've earned it. I don't know exactly what the *Rebecca* was carrying, but I'm certain you came away with quite a treasure."

"More treasure than I expected," Henriette muttered once the other woman was gone. She rubbed her thumb against her fingertips, imagining she could still feel the material of Lisse's blouse under them, and went to her private stash to get a bottle of the best rum. It suddenly didn't matter much what Caraveo reported about their haul. The coin and liquor and whatever other bounty they made off with would be nice, but she had a feeling the true treasure wasn't down below.

Genevalisse was likely to prove her wealth in ways Henriette couldn't even fathom, and she could hardly wait to begin exploring.

A Smuggler's Pact

By Su Haddrell

F ROM THE BROW OF THE *Starling*, Maeve watched her crew loot
the beaten schooner. The vessel sat low in the water, its torn
sails flicking listlessly. It had the air of a fighter at the end of
a bout, barely able to stand, the splinters in its mast like cuts
drawn across its skin.

Captain Stuart appeared by her side and she wrinkled her
nose. He stank of blood and sweat and the four-day drinking
binge he'd returned from just in time to take the merchant ship.
They had intended to re-purpose and rename the schooner,
but the battle hadn't gone as cleanly as Stuart had planned.
The *Starling* had sailed in close and her carronades had torn
through most of the other vessel's hull while her guns had
reduced the sails to shreds. Now it would cost more to repair
the damn thing than it would to just dismantle it and use it for
parts. Maeve ran a hand through her mop of dark hair and then
retied her bandanna.

"A worthwhile battle!" said her captain, grinning with the thrill of it. Maeve scowled.

"We could have taken them with less aggression, sir. That pretty thing would have been a useful addition to the fleet. Now all we've got is a crew of dead merchants, a dozen guns and whatever they got stored in the hull. Not exactly profitable."

"Well, the men were itching for a fight," Captain Stuart said. "Least we didn't lose any of them and we'll still have plenty to trade at the port with a couple of good manifests to show off to the officials. All-in-all, a good days work!" He clapped her on the back but Maeve didn't react. The captain sighed.

"You'll get your chance at the next one that comes in," he said. "I know you want to have a crack at your own vessel, but I need you here right now." He sidled close and slid an arm around her waist. "C'mon, I'm sure I can order you to step away from first mate duties to join me for a little while..." His breath stank of alcohol and Maeve's temper snapped. She spun on her heel and raised a fist, but the captain was too quick. He gripped her forearm and had it pinned behind her back before she could even reach for her knife.

"Now then pet, no need to get your claws out. Our deal still stands." Maeve twisted her head and snapped her teeth at his nose but Captain Stuart wrenched her arm further and she moaned through her clenched jaw. "I could have you any time I want, kitten. Just you remember that. You serve at my pleasure y'hear?"

A young lad ran to them, looking harried and nervous. His skin was the colour of molasses and his thick hair was clipped close to his scalp. The captain released Maeve from his grasp and she relaxed and shrugged her shoulders, refusing to let him have the satisfaction of seeing her in pain.

"What is it, Henry?"

The lad bobbed his head at the captain and then the first mate. "We've got trouble, sir. The crew don't want to take the barges through the river route. They're scared."

Stuart huffed and slapped his hand against the bow of the ship. "What the devil they got to be scared of? They just took down one of the largest merchant vessels we've had passing through in months!"

Maeve nodded slightly at Henry to dismiss him. "I'll deal with this," she said, and the lad darted away like a rat among the corn sacks.

"I told you about this the other week," she said to Stuart. "Half the shipment we sent down the river route didn't show up at the auctioneers'. They weren't best pleased, as the spice merchants were in town to buy and the bulk load of madri wasn't there to sell."

"We lost a whole shipment of madri?" Stuart said in surprise. "When?"

"About eight nights ago. The barges disappeared. Now the crew's mad with rumours of magic and voodoo and half of them won't even go near the swamps. You were in your cups when it happened, I'd be surprised if you even knew what day it was."

Stuart chose to ignore the jibe and paced back and forth across the brow, his boots clipping sharply against the wood. "Bloody superstition and storytelling. That's what you get for taking on locals," he snapped, chastising himself more than her.

"Sir, we need that route—it's the best way of getting the goods into port under cover."

"I don't even know if it's worth it," Stuart argued. "It takes a week just to get through the damn bayou."

"The lads know it well enough though. It's the safest because it has the fewest patrols—you know that."

Stuart nodded, his earlier anger forgotten. "Aye," he said. "We need to keep that route open if we're going to be taking more ships. That's going to make us more of a target, but they'll be spread so thin, they still won't be able to hunt us down along the rivers."

"What do you want to do, sir?" Maeve asked, half knowing what was coming.

"Go with them. Escort the barges into St. Pascon see that the goods arrive safely. If the crew sees you're not afraid, they'll put their superstitions aside. The damned shipment probably got eaten by a bloody alligator, but the last thing I need is a crew who won't do as they're ordered."

Maeve sighed and looked up at her captain. Far be it for him to investigate and put himself in harm's way. At least she was disposable. She balled her fists and stared across the green water to the beaten schooner.

"Aye, sir."

THEY TOOK FIVE PIROQUES IN the end, three from the *Starling* and two from the fallen merchant ship. The crew sat two to a boat, with the cargo secured at their feet. They left in the early dawn, when the air was still cool and damp, and the humidity hadn't yet risen to stifling levels.

The fog rolled in from the sea, twisting and curling through the cypress trees. Green moss hung down from the low branches like horsehair and algae clung to the trunks, a carpet of green that smelled musty and ancient in the still air. The swamp was never silent. The insects and frogs chirped a song of their own and the burweed hissed constantly from the gentle tide of water that flowed through it. The piroques glided silently through the water, slicing through the field of duckweed like blades.

In truth, Maeve was relieved to step away from the *Starling* for a time. Her spats with Captain Stuart were growing more frequent and it was becoming harder by the day to resists his leering. When he was drunk, she could distract him with whores, but he had more of a temper when sober, and his advances were increasingly violent. She'd earned herself a decent enough reputation by siding with him at the beginning, but she was beginning to wonder if she'd be better off on her own.

They rowed gently through the river until midafternoon, the canopy of trees overhead casting the swamp into a dusky green. Shards of sunlight stabbed through the branches, accenting the wildflowers and lilies that floated on the cloudy river. They stayed silent for the most part, the thick miasma of the swamp cutting off any need for conversation. Voices carried easily through the marshland and they couldn't afford to be caught unawares by patrolling officials. The crew were nervous, but not about getting caught. The local authorities couldn't spare enough men to patrol the rivers and they knew it. But they were nervous about more supernatural terrors.

The heat thickened until the air was steaming and sweltering in the gloom. Maeve tugged at her shirt, finding it sticky with sweat. Their navigator, a dark wooden block of a man named Remy, changed direction and guided them though a thick swell of grasses, disturbing dragonflies into flight. Signs of civilisation began to appear like a fungus growing over rock. A hand painted sign nailed to a tree warned trespassers to beware. Lanterns hung from long poles dug deep into the marsh. Broken wooden jetties crumbled into the water.

They slowly pushed through until a building took shape in the murk, its lanterns flickering in its windows. The sound of a piano tinkled out through the thick forest and the spicy smell of hot stew carried on the muggy air. They tied the boats up against the jetty and headed into the crooked wooden inn. The hostel was empty save for a couple of local men who sat playing cards in a corner, a musician half-heartedly tapping at the piano keys, and an old man wiping down the ancient bar. Maeve's crew settled themselves quite happily and for the first time that day, the conversation picked up until they were laughing and joking easily in the hot tavern. Maeve ensured they were fed and watered and then went outside to sit on the porch and drink.

"Surprised to see you out in these parts," Cornelius Chenier appeared and sat down beside her. The old bench seat creaked beneath their combined weight and then settled. Cornelius had tended the bar from the day he had built it and he was as old as the cypress trees that grew around the place. His hair was thin and grey and hung long past his ears. He wore a floppy black hat low over his brow and his cotton shirt had holes at the elbows.

Maeve shrugged. "Didn't get a lot of choice in the matter. Crews gettin' scampy over damn ghosts."

Cornelius grinned. He shifted and pulled a pipe from his trouser pocket, fishing around the other pocket for his tobacco. He set about packing and lighting the pipe and then sucked and puffed with enthusiasm until he was satisfied. "Plenty o' ghosts in this here swamp," he said. "Won't do 'em no harm tho, just spirits wit' no home themselves."

Maeve snorted. "Don't you go telling that to them in there," she said. "They won't leave the place if you do!"

"Seems to me that'd be good for business then," Cornelius returned with good humour. Maeve grunted and sipped at her bottle. She leaned back in the seat and stretched her legs, crossing her feet at the ankles. "Well, you got us for the night, so you'll have enough coin from that," she said. "We'll be out of your hair by dawn."

They sat in companionable silence for a time, listening to the frogs and watching the mist swirl and twist across the wetlands. The night drew in and glowworms gently bobbed through the air, their eerie yellow lights casting soft patterns in the darkness. Maeve sighed in contentment. It was good to be off the ship. She felt at home in the swamps, surrounded by the thick green vines and the labyrinth of waterways. Part of her wanted to stay behind at the crooked inn, helping Cornelius cook his stews, tending bar when she was needed.

She smirked at herself. She knew she'd be bored stupid after a few days. She had a skill with a blade and a thirst for fire in her blood that was as bad as Captain Stuart himself and she knew she'd never be happy unless she was knee deep in trouble and winning the fight out of it. Once the run to St. Pascon was through, perhaps she'd need to find herself a new kind of trouble. The way they were going, it was only going to be another two days travel, all being well. She thought back onto the missing madri batch. It was unusual to lose cargo on the river routes.

"You heard of anything odd going on around these parts?" she said suddenly. Cornelius had dozed off and woke with a snort.

"Hngh?" he asked, searching around himself for his fallen pipe.

"We had a madri cargo disappear a few days back. Crews all spooked coz folk didn't come back. You know if anythin's going on?"

Cornelius shrugged. "Not seen any officials in these parts if that's what you mean. They can't navigate their cocks to their arses, let alone find their way around this place."

Maeve barked a laugh. "I meant anything with the stink of devilry about it. I love this place as much as you, but you know how it gets when folk start to get hot blooded."

Cornelius took a long suck from his pipe and looked out across the green waters.

"Mama Laveau said somethin' the other night. She been seein' more Will 'o the Wisp than normal, but it might just be the season," he mused. "She was out gathering herbs an' came across a big ol' dead patch of land. Pond water was as black as sin and still as the dead. Moss and vines all rotted and stinkin'."

"What did she do? Did she know what it was?" Maeve wanted to know.

"You know Mama—there's only so much occult voodoo she'll get involved in. She got out o' there and didn't look back. Whatever devilry be goin' on, it's best left alone." Cornelius rose to his feet and stretched his lanky frame. "You best get you and your crew some sleep, lassie, before they get themselves too half cut to be of any use to you."

Maeve grinned. "Aye, you're not wrong."

REMY LED THE CREW THROUGH the darkness back to the boats the following morning. They were sleepy and drink-fogged but followed orders without complaint. Maeve took the oars in the fifth boat to follow up the rear, feeling the need to exercise her muscles rather than sit placidly in the piroque for a further day. Henry sat up at the back of the boat, his eyes drooping with every sweep of the paddle.

The crew were subdued as they glided smoothly along the river in the early dawn, splashing gently through the water. The buzz of insects was hypnotic and Maeve had to wake herself on more than one occasion. The humid air was warm and soft rock of the boat was soothing. Maeve felt herself drifting...

A sharp cry rang out up ahead. Maeve's eyes snapped open and suddenly they were in the midst of a thick fog the colour of dead fish. She turned around but could barely see the barge behind her and the three further ahead had vanished entirely. She pulled hard on the oars, pressing the wood through the pea coloured water.

Another cry, strangled and suddenly cut off.

Then, a scream.

Maeve pulled hard and then handed the oars to Henry, whose eyes were wide and filled with fear. "Keep rowing!" she barked, when he swapped with her and then sat motionless on the bench. He snapped to attention and nodded, pulling against the water with fierce determination. Maeve stood up, balancing herself easily against the rocking of the vessel. She squinted through the thick mist, seeing nothing but grey. Something long and dark moved through the air up ahead. The piroque cut through the water and suddenly the mist cleared and Maeve saw...everything.

Several large tree roots rose up out of the brackish water, whipping at the fog and stirring up the water. The two remaining boats teetered back and forth on the turbulent swamp, their occupants clutching desperately at the sides. As the mist cleared further, Maeve gazed over the burweed and saw a huge tree. The thick trunk was blackened and twisted with knots like massive tumours growing across its bark. The branches were skeletal and crooked, reaching down towards the barges like scratching fingers. The vines at the base of the tree flexed and grew, stretching themselves across the water. A tendril of green caught against one of the oars and the men screamed, falling over themselves to cut it and throw it into the water. They were too slow. The vine thickened and more threads travelled along it, coiling tightly around the paddle until they grasped the side of the boat. The creeper knotted around the seats and pulled at the little piroque.

One of the men leapt into the water. Immediately a thick brown tree root snatched him up. He shrieked and the root squeezed, severing his body into two and cutting the sound off. The remaining man pulled out his knife and slashed wildly at the vines that were trailing around the little boat. They began to climb up his legs, knotting and entwining around his body, pulling his arms close and wrapping him tightly. His screams were cut off when the creeper enveloped his head and the vessel was pulled beneath the waves. The two men in the last remaining piroque frantically paddled in circles, their panicked cries carrying through the fog. The vines and roots slowly snaked through the green water towards the boat as though stalking their prey.

Maeve took in the entire scene with a calmness born of blood and fire. A shadow of movement caught her eye. "Take us nearer the tree!" she hissed to Henry, who stared at her blankly. "Do it!"

The lad pulled at the oars once more and the craft drifted towards the little island. A woman stood beside the disfigured old tree, her arms raised, her eyes blazing red with magic. Maeve drew her pistol and jumped into the shallows. She cocked the hammer and aimed. "I see you swamp witch!" she cried. "You let my crew go!"

The creature dropped her arms and turned to face Maeve. Her face creased into a wide grin and her teeth were blackened and sharp. "You have no power, girl. Who are you to order me so?"

"I am Maeve Chenier, first mate of the *Starling* and daughter of Cornelius Chenier! By the Laws of Arcadia, I command you to release my crew!"

The witched laughed, a deep cackle that cracked like dry wood. She raised her arms and the vines began their slow swim forward once more. "You have no command over me daughter of Chenier! These are my territories. Marked from here to the still pond and the Batreyu Island. You trespass on my domain and you pay with blood."

The vines grasped another one of the men and began to coil around his legs and arms. His companion pulled out his knife and began cutting furiously but the plant wound tighter and tighter.

"These territories were marked by Arcadia Decree," Maeve argued. She held her pistol steady, horribly aware that she only had one shot. The swamp witch scoffed.

"The Arcadia Decree is of no consequence. Its magicks are old and weak. This is *my* land now." Her eyes flashed with red once more and the crewmate screamed and died. Maeve cursed loudly. She turned to the man in the remaining boat and to Henry who was cowering in their own vessel.

"When I fire this shot, you get out of here as fast as you can. Go back the way you came, you hear me?"

"But Miss..." Henry stuttered.

"Go back the way you came. That's an order!" Maeve hissed. She spun on her heel, raised her pistol and fired the shot.

Her aim was true.

The swamp witch fell backwards, landing on the soft earth with a thump. The writhing brown roots and green vines dropped into the murky water with a splash.

"Go!" Maeve gestured, but didn't turn to see if they obeyed. The creature kicked out at the ground, her moans deep and guttural. Maeve walked over to where she lay and knelt beside her. The swamp witch squirmed, clutching fistfuls of grass beneath her. Maeve watched the steam rise from the wound in her chest. She was healing quickly.

Maeve opened her belt pouch and began to reload her pistol. "I grew up in these lands," she said calmly, as though sitting for a quiet drink again outside the inn. "I know the history. I know the magic. I know it's weakened." The witch moaned again and glared balefully up at Maeve. Her eyes flickered red, but she couldn't hold the spell and they settled back to muddy brown.

"I care not for your history, girl," she hissed.

Maeve shrugged. "What do you care for?" she asked.

The swamp witch seemed to hesitate. She was clearly unused to negotiation. She must have known only distrust for people—humans who fought and destroyed and used up everything around them until nothing was left. The wound in her chest sizzled and she wheezed uncomfortably. "I want my territory. I want to feed."

"Mmhmm," replied Maeve conversationally. She finished with her pouch, cocked the gun and held it to the swamp witch's head. "I am not in the habit of killing the inhabitants of these marshes unless they threaten me and mine," she said. "We both grew up here. You have a right to this land as much as I. I believe we should come to an accord."

The witch glanced along the barrel of the gun. "An accord?" she hissed. She had ceased twitching. The wound in her chest still smoked but had stopped sizzling.

Maeve nodded. "There are men who would take this land as their own. We use these swamps for our own ends, but there are men who try to stop us. In exchange for our crossing your lands, I propose we bring a sacrifice. You receive blood. We receive passage. What say you?"

The witch's eyes burned red for a long moment and Maeve felt the huge deformed tree beside her shift and move its roots. She heard the vines creeping up behind her, the soft hiss of the plant coiling around itself towards her. She didn't turn around, refusing to react. She kept her eyes steady on the swamp witch and tipped the pistol very slightly, preparing to fire. The magick left the witch's eyes. There was a thud behind Maeve as the huge vines dropped to the ground, sounding far too close for comfort.

"You got guts, girl," the witch hissed. She batted the pistol away from her head with a gnarled hand and sat up. "Get that thing away from me."

Maeve tucked the weapon back into her belt and rose to her feet, reaching out a hand to the swamp witch, which, after a moment of hesitation, she took. The creature was smaller than on first appearance. Her face was yellowed like a dying leaf and her hair was a nest of straw laced with grass and lichen. She wore a gown of sorts, woven from moss, and it hung over her shoulders like a thin blanket.

The witch stretched out her arm and opened her palm. Thin roots began to grow from its centre, knotting and twisting themselves over and over until they formed a small ornament in her hand. The knot was smooth and deep brown, the colour of swamp mud on a summer's day. It was quite beautiful. "Take it. Whoever you choose to cross these lands, have 'em bring my token. I will sense them. Bring token and blood. You will be allowed to travel."

"You have my gratitude, witch," Maeve said. The swamp witch grunted and began to shuffle away. The thick shrubs and vines opened up around her.

"Morag. Not witch. Morag," she said. Maeve gripped the token tightly and as the marsh swallowed Morag completely, she raised her hand in farewell

Maeve turned to leave, idly wondering how the hell she was going to get back to the *Starling*. Henry sat in their piroque just a few paces away. He quickly rose to his feet, his mouth hanging open in wonder.

"How...what...how...?" he stammered.

"I thought I ordered you to get out of here!" Maeve snapped. Henry closed his mouth and then shrugged.

"Couldn't leave you behind, Miss," he said shyly. Maeve raised her eyebrows and climbed into the boat.

"Your own damned fault if you'd been killed, then," she said.

Henry sat down and took the oars, but rested them in his lap, unwilling to move. "You must have powerful magicks Miss," he said with some awe.

Maeve shrugged. "Not really," she said. "Unless you count knowing all the lore around these parts."

Henry shook his head in wonder. "But how'd you stop her, Miss? She was going to kill you! When I saw all them creepers going after you..."

Maeve stared out across the bayou and watched the water slip back into stillness. Insects droned low over the water and she spotted the dark shadow of an alligator swimming purposefully towards the bodies of the dead. "Not everyone is the enemy, Henry," she said softly. "She was just defending her territory. Much like we defend our own."

"But Miss, she had magic!" Henry stared at her reverently.

Maeve dragged her eyes away from the beauty of bayou and scowled at the lad. "Was just nature," she snapped. " And we got ourselves a new ally, provided we got the blood to sacrifice for it."

"Powerful ally to have then, Miss, if she wants blood." Henry positioned the oars and then guided the boat out of the shallows and turned it around. "We going back to the *Starling*? What you going to say to Captain Stuart?"

Maeve gazed over at the deformed black tree and ran her fingers over the wooden knot she'd been gifted. They'd lost eight crew members, a dozen crates of supplies and would return back to the *Starling* empty-handed. Captain Stuart would likely lose his temper and she'd be under his thumb forever more. She suddenly felt very tired. Siding with Captain Stuart was no longer advantageous, she realised. If she'd gotten to the swamp witch sooner, she might have saved more of the crew. The guilt gnawed at her gut.

It was time she took on more responsibility. It wasn't just enough to look after herself. Most of the crew came from the wetlands — it was time she looked after them too. God knows Captain Stuart wasn't interested in doing so. While he still captained the *Starling,* whether it be from the deck or the local flophouse, none of the crew were getting a fair deal and it was about time that changed. Maeve grinned slightly. Maybe there *was* a way out from under his thumb.

"Everything alright, Miss?" said Henry, watching her carefully.

"I was just thinking on your question," she said. "What are we going to say to Captain Stuart?"

"He's going to be spittin' feathers when he sees us come back," Henry said nervously. "I ain't looking forward to it, that's for sure."

Maeve studied lad with more care. He was lean, but a couple of summers on the water had strengthened him. He was loyal and knew how to make himself useful.

"You don't like Captain Stuart much, do you Henry?" she asked gently. The lad looked away, but nodded slightly and carried on paddling slowly with long smooth strokes.

"None of the crew do, Miss," he said shyly. "He's too free with the whip and too stingy with the loot."

Maeve nodded slowly. "That he is." she agreed. She leaned forward on the bench, resting her elbows on her knees and toying with the wooden trinket between her fingers. "I was thinking it was about time the captain made one of these river route runs himself," she said, watching Henry carefully. "Maybe introduce him to our new ally." Henry was quiet for a moment, pulling on the oars as though he could do so for days.

"I don't think that he'd come all the way out here," he said, staring out over the water. Maeve waited, hoping she'd gauged the boy's loyalties correctly. "You'd need to give him a good reason to make the run himself," he said after a moment. He turned his dark eyes to Maeve and his gaze was steady. A smile twisted at the corner of his mouth. "Something that would convince him to make the expedition."

"Something like a decent hoard of gold that we happened upon?" Maeve said.

"I reckon you could convince him, Miss."

"I reckon I could too," she said. "And the crew?"

Henry thought carefully and then shrugged. "Half of them'll scarper and the other half would be loyal. What with you and your powerful magicks." He grinned impishly.

Maeve scowled again. "Weren't no magicks, I told you that!" she snapped.

"Well...they don't know that." Henry said. Maeve cast her eyes out across the bayou once more, a smile playing at her lips. The lad pulled on the oars and the wetlands swished softly against the hull.

"You know what, Henry?" she said after a while.

"What, Miss?"

"I think you'd make me a very good first mate."

"Um. Thank you, Miss."

Maeve pocketed the wood knot and sat back in the base of the vessel. A snake slid smoothly across a branch above them and up ahead, a heron took flight, its wide wings flapping lazily in the hot bayou air. The piroque cut smoothly through the marshes until the cypress trees and hanging moss engulfed them completely.

The Dead Pirate's Cave

By Soumya Sundar Mukherjee

Present: Waiting for the Dawn

THE DARK WAVES OF THE great Indian Ocean crashed at the bottom of our ship. I lay on the gently swaying deck and listened to the sound of water. At a distance, the darker silhouette of the island waited for us with a silent malice.

We were supposed to go there at sunrise, and, perhaps, never return.

Captain Natwar walked past me, eyeing my shivering body with compassionless eyes. Pawan crawled by my side and asked, "What do you think will happen tomorrow, Sima?"

Pawan's fate was even worse than mine. As I was the inventor's daughter, sometimes the crew members gave an extra bit of bread to me. But Pawan, a thin boy of my age, had to really earn his food by the sweat of his brow. And that was expected. Pirates were never noted for their hospitality.

I said, "The worst? We'll die."

"But do you really believe that the treasure's real?" he asked, his face glowing with excitement.

I smiled. "What could we do with it if it is? Both of us are probably going to die in that forest or in the cave - either at the hands of the wild things in the forest or in an explosion in the cave or at the hands of that monster."

"The monster!" Pawan mused. "When I was serving ale to the captain and the first mate this evening, they were talking about it. The captain said that it was far more ferocious than a Royal Bengal tiger. He was the first mate of the notorious Captain Dash, you know."

"And then Captain Dash sealed the entrance with explosive booby traps," I yawned. "Yeah, I know the story, boy. That's what's expected from a pirate to protect his treasure for the ages. I wish I could meet him for once."

"Meet Captain Dash?" Pawan stared at me as if he couldn't believe his ears. "He was not, you know, one of the friendliest people. He was cruel, bloodthirsty and clever as a fox. Besides, he is dead. Why do you have such a deadly wish?"

I looked at the dark island from our anchored ship. "I just want to ask him what exactly happened to my mom when they visited the island for the last time."

Past: Old Friends

THEY CAME WITH TWO REVOLVERS and one shotgun to our house and since Dad was incapable of moving, I had to open the door for the unwelcome guests. They replied in a civil manner by shoving a revolver on my face.

"Don't shout," one of them hissed.

"I won't, I promise," I said, trembling with fear.

They had a big wooden case, but there was no way to know what was inside it. They carried it in and placed it beside the door.

"Who's there, Sima?" Dad asked from his bed.

"Old friends, Alok," said the one with a scar on his right cheek.

Even from the door, I could see the shock in Dad's face. But he promptly regained control of himself and calmly said, "Yes, that's true, Natwar. Where's the dear Captain?"

Natwar gritted his teeth. "So eager to see old Captain Dash! Remember whom you buried in the island, Alok?"

My dad's eyes burnt with anger, but he kept silent in front of the three guns.

The tallest one said, "We need your help with something, Alok."

"You? Need my help?" Dad laughed. "After what you did to me, do you still expect me to humbly serve you pirates with a friendly smile? No, Vipin, time has changed. You killed Ratna, don't ever forget that."

"*We* didn't kill your wife," said the man with the shotgun. "Captain Dash took her to that cave. All of us were with you in the ship. Later, you recovered her corpse from outside the cave. Don't you remember that? We didn't kill your wife, man; Captain Dash did. You and Dash—both of you were mumbo-jumbo doers and the woman died because of your witchcraft."

Dad sighed. "It was not witchcraft, Satish. It's called 'science,' but leave it; you'll never understand."

"We do understand a little science, Alok, like you press a trigger and crack! You got a dead man. Enough for our business," Natwar pointed his revolver at me and gestured. "Hey girl! Come here and don't try to run, or your lame father here will take a bullet."

I came and sat beside Dad quietly, although my heart was beating very fast. *Mom was killed by a pirate? Why hasn't Dad told me anything about it?*

Dad could understand what was going inside my head. He put a hand on my shoulder, as if trying to say, "Don't worry, I'm still here."

"What help do you need, Natwar?" Dad asked. "Where's your captain?"

Natwar said, "The rumour is that Captain Dash is dead."

Dad laughed so loudly that I started, just like the three pirates. "That's why you've come to me, you greedy jackals. Now I understand it all. You want to visit the Cave of Treasures, don't you? And who'll be the new captain, Natwar? You?"

Nobody answered his questions, but their faces told me that Dad was correct every time.

Dad spoke again. "As you can see, old mates, I don't have legs. I can't go with you in your treasure hunt."

"We know that you can't," Vipin said. "We've decided to take a replacement."

All three of them stared at me and Dad shouted, "No!"

Vipin smiled like a wolf, knowing that he had hit Dad in his weakest spot.

I hated to give them the satisfaction of seeing my fear. I said, "Don't worry, Dad. I'll go."

Dad's eyes were full of tears. I knew that he was afraid of losing me, but I had to do this. I couldn't let them get an upper hand on Dad.

Natwar said, "Do you remember, Alok, what gifts you gave to your friend?"

Dad's face darkened. "I know that I had friends whom I should never have trusted."

Natwar smiled and gestured to Vipin who started unpacking the big wooden case they had brought with them. The metallic right hand came out first, and then the torso. I could see the horror of recognition in Dad's eyes.

"What's this, Dad?" I asked.

"One of my greatest mistakes," Dad replied.

Shotgun Satish reverently said, "A dangerous piece of witchcraft—this thing, I say."

"Who's this friend of yours?" I asked again, still looking at the unboxing of this strange thing.

"Oh, you don't know!" Natwar laughed like a demon. "Perhaps your father forgot to tell you about him. Why don't you tell her his name, Alok?"

I stared at Dad. His jaws tightened as he lowered his eyes and said, "Yes, Sima, Captain Dash was my friend."

Present: To the Island

MORNING ARRIVED WITH THE SQUAWKING of seagulls. The eastern horizon poured bright blood over the waves as the red sun gradually started moving upwards. On the deck, the sailors were getting ready. Captain Natwar and Vipin came to the place where I was standing with Pawan. Natwar said, "Pawan, this'll be your test. If you fail..." He made a gesture of slicing his own throat.

Pawan nodded. "I know."

Pawan had told me the story he had told to these pirates. The infamous Captain Dash spent his last days in his house. Captain Dash, a paying guest in Pawan's household, had been suffering from a high fever and passed away recently. The little dagger-locket on the gold chain on Pawan's neck had belonged to Captain Dash, every one of the pirates confirmed that. "The last gift on his deathbed," Pawan said, "along with the directions to the cave."

Vipin said, "If you can't lead us to the Cave of Treasures, boy, I myself will take the responsibility of flaying you alive."

Vipin was known for his unique ideas of torturing people. One of the crewmates once told me never to enrage him, for he enjoyed doing bad things to people.

Pawan smiled and said, "I know what you're capable of, Vipin."

I liked his courage in the face of imminent danger. Pawan smiled recklessly at me, and I could see the twinkle of mischief in his eyes. *It's good to have a friend who can keep a cool head in time of need.* The thought gave me a little hope as I looked around us. The blue waves of the Indian Ocean were streaked with ever-changing white lines of foam. The morning air seemed so cold on the deck that I rubbed my hands together to keep myself warm.

"Lower the boats," Natwar ordered.

Satish came over with his shotgun and nudged us from behind. "Get in the boats."

The two motorboats sped over the water to the island. The green of the island was very soothing to the eyes against the dazzling blue of the sea-waves in the bright morning. The sun was comfortably warm upon my skin. The whirring sound of the motorboat, the seagulls overhead and the waves under the boat—all of it made the journey quite pleasant, even though I knew that it was going to be just the opposite of 'pleasant' once we set foot on the island.

"They say that the treasure consists of kilos of gold coins and jewellery," Pawan whispered in my ear, the dagger-locket dangling from his neck as he leaned over. "All the loot that Captain Dash hid. Can you imagine how big that is?"

Perhaps Pawan doesn't know that a pirate's gold is always stained with blood. The thought reminded me of Dad and I tried not to cry.

Shotgun Satish came a little forward, probably to listen to what we were talking about.

I said, "You know, Pawan, I've no interest in the treasure. All I know is that my father lost his legs and my mother lost her life because of this cursed treasure. I'll be the happiest person on Earth if this whole thing goes to hell for good."

"A little girl on the ship is already a bad thing," Shotgun Satish growled. "Don't bring more bad omens by speaking ill of the treasure, I warn you." He pointed his shotgun at me.

Superstitious pirate! My heart was beating faster as we neared the shore. From here, we could see the yellow shoreline and the greenery behind it. At a distance, we could see the topmost portion of a brown hill with green patches that stood like a giant from fairy tales.

Somewhere near that hill, Dad had buried Mom's body.

Natwar jumped on the low water and waded to the beach. Vipin went after him, an AK-47 slung around his shoulder. Shotgun Satish ordered us to follow, "Move, you two."

There was another man named Rahul with us. He was a short, bearded man with a long sword in his hand. Satish had told us that he was one of the finest swordsmen in all Southwest Asia. I wondered why they needed the swordsman when they had all the guns, but I didn't ask.

The beach was full of soft yellow sand. The forest waited for us beyond a mile from the beach. We could see the grey outline of the hill from here. *In this forest, my Dad placed two...* But I had no time to finish the thought.

As we gathered on the beach, Natwar said, "Now, Pawan, show us the map again."

Pawan hesitated for a moment. Natwar said, "I don't have all day, boy. When I tell you to show it to me, you show it to me. Remember, I can easily cut your hand from your shoulder and use it as my portable guide to the treasure." He gestured at the naked sword in Rahul's hand, dazzling in the morning light.

Pawan rolled up his shirtsleeve and for the first time, I could see the map tattooed on his forearm. The pirates surrounded him like dung-beetles over a fresh heap of cow dung. He looked at me and said, "Captain Dash drew it himself a few days before his death. He gave me a gold coin for the pain of making the tattoo and made me promise to always wear full-sleeve shirts."

Shotgun Satish added, "Captain Dash never trusted any one of us."

For good reason.

"And you," Natwar turned to me, "You need to keep our journey through the jungle and the cave safe. What your father gave to that damned captain is your responsibility now. If you fail, you know what will happen to your father." He showed me the satellite phone bulging in his pocket. "I just need to send one voice command."

"Don't do anything to Dad," I said. "Please. I'll do what I can, I promise."

"Good," Natwar said. "Now Satish, you and Rahul will be at the front of the line. The kids will be at the middle and Vipin and I'll cover the rear. Let's move, guys. The treasure of Captain Dash is waiting for us."

"Yay!" Vipin and Satish yelled together. Rahul only smiled. He was not very fond of speaking, I had noticed.

Just then, there was a little tremor in the ground. Earthquake? Or something else? Satish and Rahul started walking toward the forest anyway, as if they didn't feel it. Pawan mouthed at me, "Let's go."

I sighed. My dad had created some monsters and let them roam free in the forest. Now it was my job to stop them. Somehow.

Past: Dad's Story

THEY UNPACKED THE ROBOT AND activated it. The red lights in its eye-sockets sparked with life. "Do you remember him, creator?" Vipin asked.

"I remember every mistake of my life, Vipin," Dad said. "With much regret."

"The personal bodyguard you once made for Dash will be your jailor now," Natwar clarified. "If your daughter disobeys us, she'll be killed, you know that. But she must know that if she takes some reckless step like fleeing from us, I only need to give the jailor a voice command over the sat phone and her father's head will be separated from his body."

The jailor robot stood like a statue. I looked at Dad's face and knew at once that Natwar was not bluffing. The robot could really do what he just told us.

"Why do you want to take her?" Dad asked, though I sensed that he already knew the answer.

The three pirates laughed. Natwar said, "Don't you know why, old buddy? The beautiful things Captain Dash made you release in the forest, they smell humans. They know yours and Dash's smells as the only friendly ones. Dash is already dead and you are a legless and useless man. But your daughter will serve the purpose. Those things will smell you in her and thus we can go safely to the cave. If possible, we can also kill those things with a little help from her."

"What if they can't smell Dad in me?" I asked suddenly.

"Then I promise we'll give your dead body a fine burial," Vipin said, showing his uneven teeth. "At least what'll be left of it."

Dad said, "Just do me a little favour, Natwar."

Natwar said, "A favour? From me? Just ask for it, dear scientist."

"I need some time with my daughter. Alone."

The three pirates looked at each other and I could see them decide that it was a harmless enough request. Natwar said, "Well, your wish is granted, old friend. We're leaving for now. One hour, max. The jailor will be here to keep an eye on both of you, of course."

Dad nodded. The three of them left while the jailor's red eyes stared at us from its lidless sockets. As soon as they went out of sight, the expression on Dad's face changed. He straightened his body and said in an urgent tone of voice, "Listen carefully, Sima. We don't have much time."

I listened with rapt attention as Dad began his story:

In your life, you meet a lot of people. Some of them are good, some are bad, and some are very, very bad. Captain Dash belonged to this last group.

He was a scientist — at least that's how I knew him at first. He was a biochemist preoccupied with the search for an element that could prolong a man's life indefinitely. He wanted to find the mythical elixir of life and he believed that he would one day be able to make it.

When I first heard that idea from him, I dismissed it as the ravings of a crazy man.

As a scientist, my own field was robotics. I had a theory that I could make a robot more human-like by extracting memories from a living person and uploading them into the brain of the robot. But my research needed a lot of funding, and nobody was willing to invest so much money in a project so fantastic in nature. One of the leading scientists in my field even called my project "visionary, but impossible."

Imagine my state of mind. I was married to your mother, she was pregnant and my dream project was just dismissed by the Einstein of Robotics. I didn't have enough money to support my family. I was in such a mess.

Just then my old friend appeared almost out of the blue. One day he came to my door and asked, "Remember me, Alok?"

I could, not by his face, which had changed quite a lot in the past few years since I had seen him last, but by the golden dagger-locket that dangled above the second button-hole of his shirt. I invited him in. I didn't know then that I was inviting the devil himself to my house.

He knew all about my financial condition. He said that he had himself faced the same problem but he had overcome it. He proposed a high paying job to me. My head started spinning when he told me the amount. "What would I have to do?" I asked.

"You're good at handling artificial-intelligence, aren't you?" he said. "I just want to use your talent in that field. You need to build me a few machines according to my specifications."

I at once agreed.

"There's another condition," he said.

"What?"

"Both of you need to come with me to the island where you'll activate the things I want you to make."

At first I disagreed, but I had no other way to convince him. I asked Ratna and she, too, agreed, because the money Dash was willing to pay was so big that we could never have earned it in our lifetime.

Dash said, "Take your time, Alok. I need to make preparations myself for the journey. I'm paying you in advance to make things easy for you. I will need at least two years to become fully prepared."

"Prepared for what?" I asked.

He smiled mysteriously and said, "To complete my own research work."

The money he gave us solved every problem we were in. He gave me detailed instructions of what kind of robots he wanted. It turned out that he wanted two ferocious machine-beasts that would kill anything that come into their territory. I started building those beasts and ended up with a wolf and a tiger; both of these could smell humans and they would kill anybody except Dash or me. They recognized the smell of our blood as the only friendly ones. Dash also made me write a manual for transferring intelligence into a robot in writing with charts and diagrams.

After that, Dash took me and Ratna in his ship, and only then we realised that we were in the middle of a crew of modern day pirates. And I was helpless in the hands of the villain who used me to build dangerous murderous weapons. Once he became angry with a crew member and just threw him to the wolf on the ship. Then he enjoyed his screams from outside the closed doors. Later we recovered the bloody corpse of the man and caged the beast again.

I knew that I had made the mistake of my life by making a deal with this devil.

He also instructed me to build another robot — the one that Natwar and others referred to as 'the monster.' It was by far the most dangerous and most sophisticated thing I had ever built. It was placed inside the Cave of Treasure.

That afternoon he ordered Ratna to go with him to the island. I was locked into a room while the pirates enjoyed my shouts. Captain Dash came back to the ship after almost three hours and Ratna was not with him when he came to my room. I asked him where the hell my wife was and he just said, "Dead."

I pushed past him and jumped in a boat and rowed madly to the island.

"Don't go," the captain shouted from behind, but I was in no mood to listen to him. The wolf and the tiger did nothing to me as I ran past them. In front of the sealed entrance of the Cave of Treasures, I found her lying dead, her body as cold as ice, but without a mark from a single wound. I couldn't believe my eyes.

You know, Sima, I still think that it was a punishment from God for my greed. I buried her there, crying. I thought of killing myself, but then I remembered your face and I came back to the ship.

The pirates surrounded me and started beating me. Captain Dash laughed and said, "You disobeyed a direct order, Alok, and rowed away me. Break his legs, boys."

And those bloody pirates started beating me with yells of joy. I lost consciousness. When I woke up, I couldn't feel my legs.

I'm glad that the villain is gone for good. I know that now I've no other alternative to letting you go with them, but this is my final advice to you, my girl: NEVER trust anyone on that ship. Remember what your father paid for believing one who came as a friend.

Present: Wild Metal

WE SAW THE WOLF FIRST.

Or perhaps *it* saw us first.

It was waiting for us behind a tree. The forest was dense enough to prevent us from going in a straight line to the hill where a dead pirate's treasure waited for us. I could see the excitement in the men's faces. I was feeling a little excited, too, although I'd never admit it to Pawan, who seemed to think that gold was the most intoxicating thing in the whole world.

Rahul cut the creepers and little branches with the ruthless swiftness of his sword. We moved forward, treading upon the freshly-cut vegetation and leaving a plant-scented trail of destruction behind.

Bloody pirates! Leaving a trail of destruction wherever they went!

Suddenly, Rahul stopped.

"Captain! I think I saw one of them," said Shotgun Satish.

Before Natwar could reply, the beast came out in the open. I couldn't take my eyes off my Dad's creation—so dangerous and so beautiful!

Sunlight dazzled on its silver skin, while its red eyes glared at us, trying to find a weak spot in the group. "Go ahead, girl," Vipin ordered.

"Yes, go ahead," Natwar echoed.

Pawan said, "Don't worry, it'll smell your father in you, and think that the whole group is friendly."

I swallowed a lump in my throat and felt my heart beating faster than usual. The beast stared at me as I slowly walked towards it. It sniffed the air and started retreating. The red glare in its eyes softened.

"Now, Rahul!" Natwar roared from behind me.

Rahul jumped upon the beast and in a flash severed its head from its metallic body. "One gone!" Vipin exclaimed.

I didn't know why tears came to my eyes. I knew that it was not a living animal, but still my whole being wanted to protest against this barbarism. But I could see the bloodlust in their eyes and controlled myself.

"Good job, mate!" Satish patted Rahul's shoulder.

I looked at Pawan to see his expression and found him gazing at the map on his arm with a stony face, as if he was totally unaware of what just happened. Sometimes I really didn't understand him.

We walked as Pawan directed the way. The forest seemed to be getting a bit thinner as we progressed.

"The tiger's behind us," Vipin shouted.

But thanks to the timely warning, the men were ready. The animal was just as clever as the real Royal Bengal tiger; I never heard it coming. No rustle of paws on leaves, no sound of footsteps, nothing. We could only see its metallic body jumping like a flash of silver lightning under the bright sunlight, missing Natwar by an inch or two as he ducked just in time. It stood firmly on the ground, eyeing us, waiting for our next move.

Intelligent machine! *What did you do, Dad?*

Something fell from Natwar's pocket, and I quickly hid it.

Rahul again came bravely forward to face this beast, but this time the machine won. As soon as he jumped with his sword, the tiger promptly moved and hit him on the neck with one powerful paw.

The swordsman fell on the ground and never moved again.

Vipin only said, "Good. One less share for the treasure."

"It's your turn, girl," Natwar said. "Rahul should have waited."

I moved forward. Although I just saw what it did to Rahul, I was not afraid this time. The animal hesitated as it saw me approach. As I came near it, it sniffed the air, just like the wolf had, and started retreating. "Kill it!" Natwar ordered.

Shotgun Satish and Vipin both fired their weapons. The bright tiger collapsed on the dark green forest floor.

Vipin said, "Look, girl, both of your father's creations are done for."

"Great achievement!" I muttered under my breath.

"The monster is still in that cave," Natwar reminded.

Pawan said, "We're not very far from it. Look."

We could see the hill from this part of the forest where the trees were thinner. Before us was a grassland from which the hill was just a short walk away. I had secretly named it Mother's Home, and the hope of finding some trace of her there made me want to walk faster.

"At last!" Natwar heaved a sigh of relief. "Captain Dash! Your treasure will be mine!"

"Ours!" Vipin reminded him.

"Yes, ours!" Natwar quickly corrected himself.

Present: Mother's Home

"NOBODY'S GOING INSIDE THE CAVE except you two," Natwar said.

Pawan and I looked at each other. We were standing in front of the hill, a mound of brownish rock, but here and there were patches of moss that made it look like an alien panther.

We knew that the pirates wouldn't risk their lives, but still when they told us to go, I realised that the last moment of my life had come. *I'll miss you, Dad.*

Pawan, on the other hand, looked excited. "Why so tense, Sima? We're going to find the treasure of Captain Dash, can you imagine?"

"We're *doing* it, you fool!" I said. "We don't need to *imagine* it. It's not just the monster; this cave is booby-trapped with explosives. How are we going to survive that?"

"Leave that to me. Captain Dash told me *everything*," he laughed as if this was the greatest joke he made in his entire life.

Vipin aimed his AK-47 at us. "Now get going, kids."

We started climbing the hill. Pawan said, "Take that right; we need to move to the other side of the hill to find the entrance."

I climbed according to his instructions. It was not very steep, so the climbing was not very exhausting. We took the right turn and the three pirates vanished from our sight.

Inside this hill the monster we all fear is waiting for us. It was harder to climb after I thought about that.

"Come here, Sima," Pawan called. "I think I've got it." A giant boulder blocked the end of the path. We had to push it aside with all the strength we could manage and even then, it moved only enough to let us in. The inside of the cave seemed to be pitch dark at first.

"Wait a minute," Pawan whispered.

We waited until our pupils adjusted to the darkness inside. After a few minutes, we realised that it was not completely dark and could see that the walls of the cave were rough. The tunnel we were in led to a broader space inside. The monster wasn't visible yet but I prepared myself for anything.

The cave shook with another earthquake. "Come on," I said, regaining my balance. We had to get this over with.

Pawan followed me closely as we walked over the uneven stones of the tunnel. The large open space inside had several low mounds on its floor. On one of which rested…

Six great iron chests! Captain Dash's treasure!

"That's it!" Pawan shouted.

"Shush!" I warned him. "Have you lost it? Do you want to invite the monster or what?"

Pawan grabbed my hand and went to stand in the middle of the cave where the boxes had waited for the touch of human beings for years. "Come on, girl! Let's have a look at the gold!"

The inside of the cave was silent except for our voices. *Where the hell is the guardian monster of this treasure?* But instead I asked a different question. "Where are the explosive booby traps, Pawan?" I asked.

Pawan stiffened. "Those were just stories to prevent people from searching for the treasure. Captain Dash was a great liar, you know."

I know.

"And what about the guardian monster? Is that a legend, too?"

Pawan smiled. "No. That's very real. In fact, you're standing on it. Now, I have to kill you, Sima. And all others, too."

Suddenly it seemed like time had stopped; my head started spinning as the eyes of the thin boy in front of me glowed with an almost unearthly wickedness. "Wake up, Princess!" Pawan's voice-command echoed from the cave walls.

Then the stones shook under my feet and from under one mound, the monster stood up. It was not very tall, perhaps only six feet, but it had talons like an eagle. Its whole body was made of a white metal, and its eyes were flashing red, just like the tiger and the wolf. It was a robot built to kill. Its long, extremely powerful metallic arms, I thought, could strangle even a horse. The tiger and the wolf would have seemed tame before this monstrosity.

Oh Dad! What've you done?

Pawan opened one of the chests and fished out a handful of gold coins. "My gold! After so many years!" He kissed the coins and let them cascade back to the chest.

The monster robot advanced upon me, but Pawan called from behind. "Wait, Princess."

The walking death halted. I stared at him and said, "Who are you?"

"I am," Pawan bowed, "the one and only Captain Dash."

Present: Bloody Pirates

"I NEEDED YOU TO MAKE sure that the wolf and the tiger can be crossed safely," Pawan said. "I was not sure that they would recognise me in this new form with their lower capacity for smell recognition. To create them, I gave your father the brain of a dying tiger and a dying wolf, and he uploaded their memory in those machines. But you know, they were just beasts! They needed to be tested continuously. That's why I suggested to Natwar and Vipin to fetch you from your father for this journey."

"You suggested that!"

"Yes. I came to Natwar and my ex-first mate didn't even recognise me. I told them that I was there at the deathbed of Captain Dash and that he had told me how to find the treasure. And they fell for everything I've told them since then"

The monster stood like a statue. Looking at it, I suddenly had an impossible thought. I tried to reject it the moment it came to me. *No, that's crazy! That can't be!*

"Your dad once called my idea of preparing an elixir of life a delirium. I never forgot that insult and vowed revenge upon him, which, I must say, has been sweet. But, as you can see, I successfully created the elixir. What's the secret of long life, Sima? Continuing to live in the same body? No, that's where everybody got it wrong. My elixir gave birth to new cells and destroyed the old ones. It gave me a new body of a teenager.

Captain Dash is back in a new container, but with the same old spirit." He scratched his neck with the dagger-locket.

"What did you do my mom?" My voice trembled.

Captain Dash laughed. "That bit of information I'm not going to share even with you, because you're intelligent enough to use it against me." He looked at the robot and ordered, "Kill her, Princess."

The robot's metallic hand grabbed my throat.

No time! Do it, you crazy girl! I must be right, or why did Dash want the brain-uploading manual from Dad?

Before it could crush my windpipe, I screamed, "MOM! IT'S ME, SIMA!"

Two things happened at the same time: Captain Dash shouted "No, no, no!" and the robot woman's grip on my throat loosened as it looked into my eyes with a twinkle of sudden recognition and as much wonder as a machine was capable of displaying. I hugged her metallic body tightly and began crying like a child.

The robot turned to the thin boy trying to hide behind his chests of gold. In a thundering voice, she said, "You traitor! You promised me that you'd spare my husband and my girl in exchange for my life!"

The infamous pirate Captain Dash tried to run, but he was powerless against the machine. Mom caught him by the neck; I could see the anger radiating from the reddish glow of her eyes. I said, "Don't kill him, Mom!"

The red in her eyes softened as she lowered him on the ground. She walked us out of the cave into the sun, still holding Pawan by the back of his neck, and I followed them.

But there were still people outside who wanted to kill us. The entrance of the cave was surrounded by the three pirates, all pointing their weapons at us. "Good job, kids," Natwar said. "The monster looks harmless enough. You've done well. Now comrades," He looked at the other two pirates, "kill them all!"

Mom spoke and the three pirates froze. "You need to leave this island. Now. Or you'll die." Mom shoved Pawan to the ground.

"You're in no position to threaten us, junk-lady!" Vipin said.

"Don't talk about death, you witch!" Satish shouted.

"Kill them!" Natwar demanded again.

Mom did a thing that I never expected her to do. She shouted "Come on, Sima", and grabbed me by the waist as she rocketed into the air, and there we were: a flying robot-lady with a little girl, going to the seashore. Jets of long, white smoke came from the exhaust pipe from her metal backpack.

It must have been a sight for those sky-watching pirates! "To the ship!" I said. We landed on the boat and rowed quickly to the almost empty ship. The two or three pirates still on the ship were no problem for Mom.

Epilogue

"YOUR FATHER INVENTED AN EARTHQUAKE predictor," she said. "You experienced a few quakes on the island, didn't you? I detected radon emission from the rocks underneath it. The island had been gradually sinking into the sea for years; my robotic sensors were telling me so. They're not going to make it. It will be gone within two days."

I had bought a hat, overcoat, sunglasses and trousers for Mom. As we walked to our house, I showed her Natwar's sat phone. I had stolen it when they were busy fighting the tiger.

She made a noise like a laugh and said, "your dad's genius was inherited."

The morning sun felt refreshingly warm after so many days in the sea. I knocked on our door. The jailor didn't get a chance to make a noise. Its severed head flew like a golf ball to the ceiling.

"Who's there?" Dad called from his bed. "Sima, is that you?"

"Yes, Dad," I announced. "I've brought someone with me."

Even from this distance, I knew that Dad had recognized who it was. The teardrops on his cheeks were unmistakable.

Rosa, the Dimension Pirate

By Matisse Mozer

Rosa didn't learn how to pilot the ship until she was twelve, and even then, she wasn't allowed to fly until her fifteenth birthday. Now it was two years later, and Captain Don Schaeder was trying to shoot her down.

"Hold on!" Rosa yelled, heaving her whole body sideways and taking the ship into a corkscrew spin. She stood on the bridge, hands interfacing with the holographic controls. Two lime-green torpedoes wove through the wings of her small ship and kept going, passing through white clouds and disappearing in the blue sky. "Goose? Goose, what's our fuel look like?"

Goose Mackenzie sat at the navigation computer behind her. Four computer screens, six tablets, and two holographic displays all blinked rapidly, but Goose's thin fingers whipped away at her six keyboards. "It's about as it good as it was when we took off," she said.

"We're not empty yet."

"Not yet, because we maybe have... And I do mean, maybe..."

"Goose, just give it to me!"

"We've got about five minutes of fuel left."

Rosa swore.

Don Schaeder's ship came into view overhead.

"They're activating tractor beams, Cap," Goose continued. "I can try to hack their navigator's equipment, but without fuel, we're gonna fall."

Rosa took her hands off of the holographic controls and let her worn arms hang limp. The ship was meant to be piloted by a grown man with typical pirate muscles, not a teenager who never had enough to eat.

She weighed her options.

"Let them tractor us," Rosa said.

Goose smiled. "I'm guessing that means you have a plan."

"That's a word for it."

The ship buckled. Goose's displays went dark.

They had seconds before the ship was in docking range.

Rosa ran, pulling Goose with her as she went, leaving the bridge behind, then running down the short hallway past the mess hall to the cargo load. The rest of her crew — two older men and one man from a dimension that hadn't developed spoken language — all looked at the cargo bay door with unease.

"Goose," Rosa said, "I need the smallest tablet you have."

The ship gave a final rumble. The cold, recycled air was suffocating in Rosa's lungs.

There was a *BANG* against the cargo door, and another, and another. Goose passed Rosa a small tablet, busted up at the edges but still functional.

Rosa turned the small screen to the program she needed, then placed it in her hip pocket.

The locks released with a gentle click, and the doors pulled to the sides. There were familiar faces on the other side: Barnes, the young man who towered over everyone and Jameson, with his dark skin, long gray beard, and piercing blue eyes.

Barnes and Jameson entered the cargo room and aimed their handguns at Rosa's crew. Barnes glanced at the defiant Rosa and Goose. He smirked.

"That went on long enough," came another low, gravelly voice from behind them. "Did you work out your little tantrum yet, Rosa?"

He came through the doors just as he usually did: with a long-barreled gun in one hand and a cigar in the other. His height, his powerful arms, his thick mustache and even the snarl on his face intimidated his foes, but they weren't his calling card. Don Schaeder's remaining human eye had died long ago and calcified, but it had been left in the socket for no good reason other than that it looked terrifying. His other eye, the bronze metal one had a black hole and green dot for a sensor; it darted in his skull as he surveyed the room.

"Don't get me wrong," he continued, "I'm proud, if anything. Stealing my map to the Treasure, taking a cruiser, even getting a crew—it's all good stuff. You're a lot like your old man."

He was not Rosa's father but he liked to think that kidnapping someone earned him the title.

"The only problem here," Don Schaeder said, "is that you recruited a crew from prisoners." He clicked his tongue, then turned to Rosa's crew. "You all could have had lives when we returned home. You all blew it."

"Slavery," said the oldest crewman. "Slavery is not a life."

"Sorry you feel that way," Don Schaeder remarked.

He aimed his gun and pulled the trigger.

The bullet caught the crewman between the eyes. The man fell backwards with the gunshot, his eyes still open.

Rosa's agonized scream echoed around them.

Don Schaeder turned his weapon to the younger man. Rosa understood his grunts and panicked gestures. Any human being would have. But Schaeder didn't care. He fired.

Rosa closed her eyes. Counted the seconds. She could still get away. She had to get off this ship and make it to the Treasure. She just had to wait...

The final crewman's final word was a curse. Then he, too, was gone with a blast.

She'd failed them. Good men, all of them. But Rosa's plan was almost complete...

Then Goose screamed.

Rosa opened her eyes. Don Schaeder had Goose's head in his gigantic hand, gun at his side.

"Those idiots betrayed my kindness," he said. "But you, kid?" He nodded at Rosa. "You need to learn a lesson for all this, I think."

He aimed the gun at Goose's head.

Rosa took a quick breath and tapped the button on her tablet.

The ship's lights went out. It was pitch-black now, save for the *BANG* of the next gunshot, but Rosa had tackled Goose, and the two girls fell to the ground unharmed. Goose opened her mouth and struggled to breathe, but the life support was out, along with everything else. Barnes and Jameson began choking.

Rosa got up and ran like hell.

She got to the bridge and activated the holographic displays. She hit the ignition on the ship. Everything came back on, but the life support wouldn't turn on again until they were well out of range.

She made sure the cargo bay was still wide open, then she flipped the engines to overdrive.

The tractor beam was good, but not that good. Rosa's cruiser tore away from its captor. She dared to look behind her: the cargo bay was empty, bodies and inhabitants shifted and thrown by the chaos. Goose would be okay, Rosa told herself. Goose *had* to be okay.

She swallowed the pit in her throat.

Goose would forgive her. She hoped.

The holographic displays flickered on and off. Goose had been right: they were out of power. Rosa set the steering to autopilot and went to the navigator desk, feeling herself go weightless as the gravity went offline. She saw the one device she needed and caught the small glass mechanism in her anxious hands.

Only thing left to do: get into an escape pod. Outside, the ground got clearer and clearer. Buildings, trees, even roads. She wasn't going to make it.

JACK HURWITZ WAS LIVING THROUGH the worst summer of his life.

Okay, so maybe he was exaggerating. He'd failed his classes, sure, and he wasn't going to a four-year college right away, but what did that matter? He would go to community college, move out, get a job, live like everybody else.

The future would *suck*. It didn't mean he had to hate the present, too.

Jack sat in the backyard of his stepmother's home. After his grades came back, he'd gotten the cold shoulder for two weeks straight. Jack wondered how people managed to be pissed off at someone 24/7. Didn't that get exhausting?

At any rate, he wasn't going to get bored. A stolen beer from his father's stash and a view of the afternoon sky told him that much.

And even better, there was a plane with one of those smoke trail things, probably about to write something in the sky. That was Colorado for you: a beer and an artist in a plane, and you were good.

Except the plane wasn't changing direction. It was heading straight down, at a ninety-degree angle, as if his trigonometry teacher had drawn the damn thing. It caught fire and accelerated, landing past the town's main street and clear west of the Thompsons' property.

Another piece of the — what, maybe a satellite? — broke off, this one curving and shooting upward first, then coming back down with a vengeance. Jack stood up, cold beer freezing his hand.

It was coming right for his backyard.

Jack ran into the back porch. He put the beer on the windowsill and clapped his hands over his ears.

The impact shook his world. Laundry fell off the machines, plates fell from the kitchen cabinets and shattered, pictures in the living room dropped and exploded into glass shards. His parents were *definitely* gonna kill him now.

Jack lay on the linoleum tile of the back porch and watched the smoke trail rise up. He got to his hands and knees slowly. He glanced out the window. The satellite piece had formed a straight-up smoking crater where the tool shed used to be.

A loud banging noise came from inside the crater. *BANG. BANG.*

Satellites didn't usually have people fighting to get out, right? Jack's mind went to the first thing he could think of. It was an alien. Definitely.

He knew that aliens probably could do better than attacking Beaton, Colorado on their first invasion, but still. He had to see it. Jack took his beer from the windowsill, took a deep breath to give himself courage, and went to the smoking ruins.

A final *BANG* and a blue-and-green metal door fell off of the very-probably-alien-ship.

If they said, "Take me to your leader," Jack was *totally* going to say he was the President.

The alien emerged. The alien looked an awful lot like a teenage girl.

"Holy shit," Jack said. "You're like a kid, aren't you?"

She held a hand to her head and she was staggering as she walked out of the crater. Her skin was a tanned honey color, and she had a jet-black ponytail of thick curls. Jack didn't know what he expected at this point, but her chubby cheeks and short, round legs weren't part of it. And what the hell was she wearing? They looked like tattered rags.

She opened her mouth to speak.

The words that came out were the fastest, fiercest gibberish he'd ever heard.

"Sorry, I can't understand you," Jack said. He pointed at his mouth. "Are you an alien?"

The girl's brow furrowed.

"You're on Earth," Jack said. "This is my parent's house."

"Earth," the girl said. "Earth."

That was a start. "I'm Jack," he said. "Jack Hurwitz."

The girl pointed to herself. "Rosa." She held up a finger, like she wanted him to wait where he was, before going back to the crater.

The alien girl — Rosa — came back with a flat piece of glass in one hand, and a small black tablet in the other. *Like an iPhone*, Jack thought.

Rosa pressed a few buttons on the tablet's screen. A piece of it detached, and when she removed it, it looked an awful lot like one of those micro earbuds. She offered it to Jack.

He mulled it over for about two seconds, then stuffed it in his right ear.

"Can you understand me?" Rosa asked, in clear-as-day English.

Jack nodded. "Sure. Welcome to Colorado. Is that your ship?"

She pulled a huge, long-barreled gun out of her back pocket and aimed it at his chest.

Jack dropped the beer.

"Is Don Schaeder with you? Is he here?" she asked.

"Don what? Is that a drink, or something?"

"Is he with you?" Rosa looked past him, at the house, back at the rubble, then up at the sky. Jack could basically feel her anxiety in the air. "Does he have the Treasure?"

"Treasure? What the hell are you talking about?"

Jack did a mental back-up. If this was a smaller ship that came from a crashing one, it was probably an escape pod. She had a gun, she had worn-out clothes, and now she was asking about treasure.

"Are you like, an alien pirate or something?"

Rosa kept the gun trained at him, but her features relaxed. She finally took a breath, then the gun lowered. "Where is this?" she asked.

"Colorado. It's like, in the middle of the USA? Part of North America?" But then, when she showed no reaction, added, "You have no idea what those are, do you?"

"Colorado's supposed to be by the waterfront."

"No, I guarantee you, there's no beaches around here. I mean, if there were, rent would be so crazy...I mean, I have a cousin out in Cali? That rent is insane, and you're not listening to me, are you?"

She had the flat glass thing held up to the sun now. "Tell me something. Do you have wireless computation on in this reality?"

Jack tilted his head. "You mean like the Internet? You're from another planet and you're asking about the Internet?"

"I'm not from another planet. I'm not going to ask for your leader, Jack. I need an AC adapter."

Jack snapped his fingers. "I have that! That, I do have." He started toward the house, but stopped and said, "Come inside. I have, like, six phone chargers."

This summer was going to be *awesome*.

THIS WAS GOING *HORRIBLY*.

She had landed fine, but her ship was lost somewhere out in the forest of an alternate Earth, one where the states and geography didn't match up with what she remembered from this version of Earth. Her escape pod was busted beyond recognition. Her crew was dead.

But at least Jack Hurwitz seemed nice enough.

Jack led her through a hallway to a room cluttered with manuals, vaguely recognizable circuit boards, and multiple computer towers. Jack tiptoed through the mess to a table in the back and waved her through. "Be careful," he said. "My dad sort of likes his mess where it is."

He fished through the jumble of wires on the desk and held up a squid-like cable. It had a port to connect to the wall—Rosa recognized the AC out—and six different kinds of tablet interface dongles. "See if any of these work," Jack said. "I mean, it's probably like, stone-age-y compared to what you've got from wherever you're from."

Rosa looked at him. Jack was a pretty disheveled looking guy, now that she thought about it. Bushy brown hair in need of a cut, a shirt that was too baggy, pants with holes in the knees and calves. He had none of Don Schaeder's intentionally terrifying look. There didn't seem to be anything intentional about Jack at all.

But he helped her find an outlet and plug in her glass screen. It blinked gold, on and off. When it showed a solid gold color, Rosa ran her finger along the glass, then flicked it up into the center of the room. The map exploded all around them. It was a wirework—no buildings or specific locations—of the general area, with X and Y-axis coordinates on the edges. Jack spun around, watching the wirework rotate and calibrate itself to the size of the room.

Rosa held her hands out and twisted them. The map responded, spinning with her movements and soon there were three silver dots hovering in the air.

"This one is us," Rosa explained, pointing to the one furthest from the other two. Then at another dot: "This is the Treasure I was tracking, so this one..."

"That's your ship, right?"

"Right." Rosa touched the point for the ship. Coordinates wrote themselves into the map. "You need to take me there."

"Hold on. Nobody said anything about driving you around."

Great. Now she had to actually be a pirate.

Rosa closed the map. "Here's the deal, Jack. I'm from an alternate Earth," she started. "Don Schaeder is the captain of the ship I was on. Pirates like us travel to different realities and steal the core of territories scattered around the planet's surface. That's the treasure. We keep taking more territory cores until the planet is drained. Then we go back to *our* Earth and sell them to the highest bidder, and half the time, they end up destroying the treasure to make something else. That means the dimension that treasure is from *dies*. If you don't take me to my ship, right now, Don Schaeder will kill everything you know. I won't let him do it, but I need you to work with me."

Jack didn't fall over. He didn't even react. In fact, for such an easygoing guy, his silence was worrying.

"Fine. Do it your way, then." Rosa reached for her weapon.

That seemed to wake him up. Jack rolled his eyes and held a hand up. "I'll take you, don't trip out. Jeez. Let a guy process dimension pirates for a second, would you?" He put his hands in his pockets and shrugged. "I mean...that's a pretty neat story."

"It's not a story."

"Yeah, yeah, I heard you and I saw the map and everything. Let me get my dad's keys. Just tell me where to turn, yeah?"

JACK'S PARENTS' CAR WAS OLD enough that the stereo didn't have an aux port, but at least the engine went fast. He pulled out of the driveway and started for the highway. Rosa directed him out past civilization and to the forest.

"Hey," Jack asked. "Question."

"Ask it."

"When I get you to your ship, what happens then?"

"We'll find a way to jump-start the ship, and then I'll fly to the treasure's coordinates."

"See, that right there. That's what bugs me. You're still gonna take the...what were you calling it, treasure? Won't that kill everyone here, anyway?"

"I don't plan to sell it. Or let it be harmed in any way."

"So...you're just going to hide it?"

"Protect it, actually."

Jack clicked his tongue. "Huh."

"You don't trust me, do you?"

"Not in the forty-five minutes since you crash-landed in my parent's backyard, not really."

Rosa spoke slowly. "There are a lot of Earths, but this one is mine. It's my responsibility."

"How does a pirate have a responsibility? Unless piracy is like, a completely different thing than what I'm thinking," Jack said. "Swashbuckling and all that."

Rosa relaxed back in her seat with a shrug and changed the subject. "Things look a lot different from the last time I was here," she said. "Everything's...greener. I'll give it that."

They pulled out of the main road and came into a clearing. The downed ship had left a lot of burned branches and foliage in its wake. Jack just followed the trail.

The ship had crashed in a ditch. Jack had clearly imagined something grander than what he was seeing: an inter-dimensional car wreck, with chunks of metal flung off and stuck in trees, and long plates of steel standing upright in the dirt. He parked the car before the ditch started to slope.

"Wanna check out your ship?" he asked.

They got out of the car and approached the wreck slowly. The ship was maybe four times larger than the escape pod with the same purple hull and same kind of thrusters.

The back area—what would be the trunk in a car—was wide open. It was dark inside.

They walked into the interior of the ship, Rosa feeling for handholds and a walkway, and Jack doing his best not to stumble and fall.

"Just keep going straight back," Rosa said confidently. The air smelled like smoke and iron. "I think it's...it should be this button here," she said.

The cruiser came alive. Jack watched as the overhead lights came on to reveal a chair surrounded by computers and a large, open space in the frontmost part of the room. Holograms flickered, and Rosa stood in the middle of them, effortlessly touching the floating diagrams.

"The ship is working," Rosa said. There was an accusing tone. "It was dead before I used the escape pod. Someone must have done something to it. I should check the ship's logs."

"I know what those are!" Jack shot a finger in the air. "Do you guys have a holodeck, too?"

"A what?"

He sighed. "Never mind."

Jack sat in the chair by the computers. He spun the chair once, just for kicks, then froze. There was another pirate in the doorway.

"Holy shit," Jack said.

The pirate was taller and older than both of them. He was leaning on the doorframe, his gun trained at Rosa but his hand shook as he tried to keep it pointed at her. He must have taken a blow to the head, judging from all the blood on the hand he pressed to it.

"You're not going anywhere," the pirate said.

Rosa regarded him with a shrug. "Hello, Barnes. I see you survived. Did you want a bandage?"

"Betrayin' the Cap is a capital offense. You'll be hanged for your actions, you hear me? And you're giving me that map," Barnes said.

"We both know you can't touch the treasure without Schaeder's equipment unless you're originally from its dimension. It'll blow you apart," Rosa said. "But go find the treasure yourself anyway. Have fun with that."

Barnes' gaze darted to Jack.

He changed targets. Jack's hands went up and his body went stiff with fear.

"He dies," Barnes said. "The boy dies, or you give me that map." The demand lingered in the still air. None one of them moved.

"Suit yourself," Barnes said.

There was a gunshot and Barnes fell forward, lifeless as his blood poured onto the floor. Behind him stood another teenager, this one with her hair in a conservative ponytail, wearing thick glasses, and holding a gun in her hand.

Rosa's hug was more of a tackle. "Goose!"

"I'm alive," Goose said, gasping . Rosa's arms were around the girl's neck, tight. "Though if you don't let me go, I'm gonna get knocked out again."

"What happened? Tell me everything."

"I hid in the cargo load and sealed myself in a locker so I wouldn't fly out the back when you did that nosedive thing," Goose said. She held the gun out with her index finger and thumb and placed it on the ground gingerly. "At least, I think that's what I did. Blacking out from choking sorta does a one-two on your memory."

Rosa winced. "Sorry," she mumbled.

"Can I get a 'sorry' too?" Jack asked. "For, I don't know, almost being shot?"

Goose glanced over Rosa's shoulder at Jack. "Is he from this Earth?" she asked.

"I'm Jack," he said, "and yeah, I'm from here."

"This is Goose," Rosa told him. "She's my navigator and first mate. Plus, she's the finest mechanic I've ever met."

"She's only exaggerating a little bit," Goose added.

Then, the two girls' excitement faded. They leaned against the doorway edges.

"So," Goose said. "We've got the map to the treasure and I found some reserves to let the ship fly for another hour, at most. I mean, then the engine will have to be nearly rebuilt, but that's the best I can get you...oh, and there's an escape pod. For if we wanna run away again."

"I have a plan," Rosa said. She added, "But I hate my plans."

"Most people do," Goose said, then added, "but I'm not most people."

Rosa exhaled and ran her hands down her face. "We can't just go get the treasure," Rosa said. "Don Schaeder is waiting for us to lift off. He'll follow me until I have it, and then...but he won't shoot us down until we land because he doesn't want me dead, and he won't *know* we're landing at the treasure point." Rosa snapped her fingers once, twice, and then she turned to Jack, the urgency in her eyes threatening to electrify him. "How quickly can you drive?"

WHEN JACK FIRST HEARD ABOUT treasure, he figured it would be something grand. Maybe a literal pot of gold, but also possibly an ancient crystal, or a magical key, or hell, a magical credit card, for all Jack knew. It was gonna be amazing.

Sitting in a Starbucks on Main Street wasn't what he had in mind. He sipped his grande coffee and did some math: three hours of his time, five bucks for the coffee, and some likely-PTSD-inducing run-ins with weapons. In exchange, he was helping a cute girl save the world.

Not a bad deal, really.

The clock on the wall struck the top of the hour, and right on time, Rosa and Goose kicked in the door and pointed their guns at everyone. "Stay where you are, and nobody gets a bullet," Rosa announced. "I'm not here for money. Stay still."

Goose stayed near the door, her weapon trained on the manager. Rosa walked through the tables. "I need a volunteer." A woman with her child on her lap let out a frightened sob. Rosa pointed the gun at Jack. "You. Up, on your feet. Now."

Jack was no actor — his F in Drama confirmed that — but he did his best to have a shaky walk, shifting eyes, and a trembling lower lip. "What do you want from me?" he asked.

Rosa jabbed the gun in his back and they kept moving, walking behind the barista's counter. The two college-aged employees backed away, their hands in the air. Rosa and Jack stopped in front of the register. Rosa took out the map screen and pressed it with her thumb. Instead of opening the wire-work of coordinates, it sent up one beam of golden light, first to the ceiling, then shooting straight through the glass and down into the ground.

The building shook, gently at first, then with a decided rumble. Porcelain mugs, thermoses, and displays hit the ground and shattered. The tile at Jack and Rosa's feet cracked from the inside, lifting up like a welt, and finally shattering through the ground entirely. The gold beam lifted up a small gold object from the hole and held it hovering in the air.

"That's it," Rosa sounded awed. But only for a moment.

She prodded Jack with the gun. He took the flat golden treasure from the beam and held the warm metal in his hand.

"Let's move," Rosa called. Goose nodded, still brandishing her weapon at the customers, as Rosa led Jack to the doors. He went outside first, followed by Rosa, and finally Goose went behind them.

There were no cars in the intersection, thankfully because this needed to be dramatic.

Goose turned her gun on Rosa.

"Fork it over," Goose said. Rosa kept her weapon at Jack but focused her attention on Goose. "Give it back now, and you get to live."

"Goose?" Rosa asked. She was a pretty lousy actor, too. "What the hell are you doing?"

"That doesn't belong to you. The map belongs to Don Schaeder. If you ask me, so does the treasure."

Rosa lowered her gun, eyes wide and arms open. "You're not doing this. Tell me you're not. Please."

"I will kill you, Rosa. Give it to me."

Goose could definitely sell it, Jack thought.

"Goose, you're not from this Earth," Rosa said. "You can't even touch it."

"No, but *he* can." Goose nodded to Jack. "Give him to me."

"This is my home," Rosa said. "Don't let Don Schaeder destroy it. Not this dimension."

Goose did not relent. "Give it to me, or I'll kill you, Rosa. I swear to God."

This was the part that Jack sincerely disagreed with.

Rosa pointed her own gun at Jack's head and pulled the trigger.

Then Rosa's gun burst and shards of the wooden hilt and metal barrel flew, one chunk catching Jack in the eye and sending him to the ground howling in agony. Rosa fell beside him, cradling her hand and crying from the pain.

Pain had *not* been part of the plan.

The road behind them blurred, then re-focused. The purple ship of Don Schaeder, in its massive glory, hovered directly overhead. A shuttlecraft had landed in the street, its doors open.

Standing in front of Jameson and another man who Rosa did not recognize, was none other than the captain himself, smoking gun in one hand, cigar in the other. His mechanical eyeball watched the scene, emotionless. "Ain't this a sight for sore eyes," Don Schaeder said. "Just the one. Ha!"

Lifeless laughter from the crewmen filled the silence

"Gwendolyn, dear," he said. Goose cringed. "Staying loyal to her captain over his renegade daughter. I'm impressed."

"Thank you," Goose said.

"You'll be rewarded soon enough," he added. "Now, about that treasure." He motioned for Jameson. The older man pulled Jack to his feet and dragged the bleeding boy to his feet. "Open your hand, boy," Don Schaeder said.

"Not on your life."

Don Schaeder sighed. "Young people these days."

He snapped his fingers. Jameson and the other crewmate took Jack by both arms and dragged him toward Don Schaeder. Jack's legs scrambled and skidded on the pavement while his face dripped blood. Jameson took Jack's hand and held it out, but he kept his fist closed.

Jameson twisted Jack's arm, not hard enough to break it, but enough to force Jack's hand open. The Treasure fell from his palm and landed on the ground.

"I'll grab it, Cap," Jameson said.

Don Schaeder yelled, "You blithering idiot, don't touch it—"

It was too late. Jameson knelt down. The instant his hand touched the smooth surface of the gold piece, his body shone with the same golden light as the map, his skin illuminated from the inside.

For an instant, it was beautiful. Then his body turned in on itself. A golden black hole pulled his arms and legs and screaming mouth into itself and shut, just as fast as it had appeared. Then, he was gone.

"I tried to tell him," Don Schaeder remarked. He knelt down and studied the treasure for a moment. Then he picked it up, flipped it in the air with his thumb, and caught it in his grip.

"That's impossible," Rosa said, her words slurring as her jaw hung. "You can't be from here...you can't."

"I'm just like you, dearest daughter of mine. I'm from this dimension, too."

"Stop."

"You never wondered *why* a pirate would kidnap you? Let me tell you, I like my job, but it gets lonely every once in a while. You want someone to talk to, and children are so young and impressionable." Don Schaeder stared at her, making sure she felt the weight of his presence. "Someone took me away, too, you know. Showed me what the world—what all the worlds—had to offer. I like to think I did you a favor, raising you myself."

"I had a family!"

"And I gave you who you are."

Rosa had a speech ready for the day when this happened. Things she had wanted to scream at him since she was a little girl. A lot of 'how could you,' maybe a 'why *this* world,' that sort of thing. But today, she could settle for brevity. "I am going to kill you."

Don Schaeder pursed his lips. "Good luck," he said.

Rosa pushed the button on the tablet hidden in her pocket.

"That reminds me," Don Schaeder said. He clicked the hammer back on his gun. "Gwendolyn? You've been a great friend to my daughter. Shame you thought betraying her would make me happy. A traitor only gets one reward, you know."

He took aim at Goose.

Sudden strong winds kicked up around them, dizzying Don Schaeder's crewman and blowing his robes up into his face. He lowered his gun and covered his face with his arm.

Overhead, his ship exploded. Orange flames doused the violet craft, submerging the blue sky in jet-black smoke.

"What the *hell* happened?" Don Schaeder barked, his booming voice almost lost in the noise of falling metal. He dropped a hand to his right side. His artificial eye changed color, shifting from the standard green to the same purple as his former ship. "Readouts...we were hit by an *escape pod*? What in hell's name?!"

Rosa moved. She crossed the short intersection and went into a slide, her hand reaching for Jameson's handgun as she dove forward. But she wasn't fast enough, even with the debris and cacophony of the exploding ship, and Don Schaeder pointed his weapon at Rosa before she could aim—

Then, he staggered back, clothes and flesh and blood flying from his shoulder. "Gwendolyn," Don Schaeder snarled. Rosa caught Goose in the corner of her eye, ducking for cover after taking the shot. His wound bled like a waterfall and he sank to one knee. When he tried standing again, his leg gave out, and he landed on his back.

Rosa stood above him, gun pointed at his head, looking him right in his robot eye.

"A lot like your old man. Watching 'em squirm," Don Schaeder growled. "You made a mistake, though."

"You will not belittle me. *Ever* again—"

"Turn around, kid."

Rosa didn't trust him as far as she could chuck his stupid robot eye. But Don Schaeder gave her the same semi-gentle smile he'd used on her for all these years, and she glanced to her right. The crewman she didn't recognize still had his weapon. Jack Hurwitz was standing, cradling his bloody head with both hands, and the crewman stood behind him, gun to his back.

"Looks to me like you've got a choice," Don Schaeder said. "Your old man or the treasure?"

"You planned this."

"Don't look at me! It was all you. And it wasn't a bad plan. I'm not even mad, except for...that," he said, pointing limply at his burning ship. "You made me proud, Rosa. You're a bona-fide pirate's daughter."

Civilians hovered around the intersection. Most of them were looking up, pointing and screaming and taking photos. Sirens wailed in the distance.

She had to make a choice, like it or not.

"I want Jack," Rosa said. "I want him. And the treasure. And I never want to see your face again."

"You sure you won't kill me? You won't get this chance again."

Don Schaeder searched her face for any weakness, any crack in a facade of bravery.

Rosa was damn sure he wouldn't find anything.

Don Schaeder signaled to his crewman. The other pirate lowered his weapon. Goose approached Jack and the crewman, her gun aimed but shaking. The crewman backed away from Jack and the boy stood for a moment before falling. Goose was there to catch him before he hit the ground.

The shuttlecraft lifted into the air behind Schaeder and his remaining ally. Once it was directly overhead, a green light shone on the two men, and when it vanished, so did they.

The ship took off for parts unknown.

Rosa had let him live. She thought about that for a minute.

The infamous Don Schaeder, retreating as he bled, without his treasure and without most of his crew, disgraced and defeated by the girl he kidnapped. A killer would have done him in.

Rosa liked her way better.

Jack Hurwitz's parents almost killed him. Their Infinity had been crushed under parts of the ship that had exploded over Beaton, Colorado. Their backyard and tool shed were left looking like imitations of the Grand Canyon. And to add to that, Jack would never see again out of his right eye.

He had to wear bandages for his first few weeks out of the hospital and then the doctors had him in an eyepatch until they were ready to operate. If his afternoons at home had been boring and lonely before, now he was a full-blown untouchable. Was he even going to go to community college anymore? It was a realistic question.

And did any of that really matter, when he knew about alternate dimensions and pirates and girls with chubby cheeks and guns?

Jack doubted that he would ever see Rosa again. But he hoped. And waited.

And on one autumn afternoon, months later, as a one-eyed Jack sat in the backyard counting the seconds, a purple cruiser materialized above the backyard crater. Jack finished his drink first this time.

The ship landed in the crater and the cargo doors opened. Rosa hadn't changed a bit: her clothes were still ratty and full of holes, and she still had those stubby legs. She walked down the landing ramp and stared at him, her expression suggesting that she was waiting. Calculating.

"Question," Jack asked.

"Ask it."

"You're not gonna pull out a gun and shoot me, are you? You guys do that a lot."

Rosa looked away. "I need to give you something."

"Is it a bullet?"

Rosa held out her hand. In it was the treasure, shining like the sun.

"It's yours," Jack said. "We had a deal. You saved the world, you keep the treasure. Just don't destroy it, right?"

"That's all okay," Rosa said. She bit her lip, tilted her head. "But it turns out, you need more than two people to run a ship. And the next Earth over is sort of deadly."

"...so, Goose is doing okay? Speaking of your crew."

Rosa furrowed her brow.

"Okay, okay," Jack relented. He knew what she was getting at. It was just fun watching her squirm a bit. "If I'm gonna be a pirate, I have a few demands."

"You don't get demands."

"One? And I've only got one. I don't wanna see this Colorado ever again."

"That's doable," Rosa said. "I can't promise you won't get shot eventually. Or get blown apart by shrapnel again."

"Whatever," Jack said. "Besides, what are the odds I lose *two* eyes and need an evil robot one?"

He started up the cargo bay ramp. Rosa followed him. "That's it? Leaving your old life, just like that?"

"Rosa, my life is boring," Jack said, pointing to his parents' home. "The way I see it, it's the pirate's life for me. I've got nothing to lose. What do you think?"

"It's not for everyone," Rosa said, fighting a smile. "You can probably handle it, though."

The ship's door closed behind them. It rose up over Beaton, Colorado, and right as Jack's home became another blip on the horizon, the ship blasted off for the next dimension.

A Crooked Road Home

By Caroline Sciriha

Five jumps to Xanta

ONCE YOU TOUCH THE DEPTHS, the only way is up. Jesson flicked on his music bank and leaned back in his chair, his whisky glass gripped between his hands. The liquid sound of pipes filled the tiny cabin. He closed his eyes, letting the melody fill his mind with other places, other thoughts, and wash away the lingering memory of those last moments on board the colonists' starship.

The haunting sounds and the fiery fluid loosened his neck muscles. He gulped down the last of the whisky and poured himself some more, then glanced at the monitor imbedded in the console before him. The starship had floated to the edge of the screen, looking like a silver octopus in a black sea.

He toggled to map mode, and the image faded to be replaced by grid lines and a couple of pinpricks of flashing light. This sector of space was devoid of traffic; it was why he'd chosen it.

The sliding doors behind him swished open and First Mate Stee, a miniscule female with a greyish complexion, stepped into the cabin. "Captain, the booty inventory." Stee placed a translucent sheet on the console.

"Thanks." He ran a fingernail down the list. The starship's control chips would fetch a goodish price on the black market. As for the rest, there was nothing unusual, mostly the colonists' personal cards plump with galaxy credits, as well as jewellery items and some gadgets — nothing that would excite the big traders. He hadn't expected anything else, just an easy board and raid to cover his next loan payment.

But nothing ever came easy.

His finger's downward slide stopped at item 43: the ship's destination chip.

"Shadow would be interested in that," Stee said.

"Hmm." According to the information on the chip, the newly discovered planet was fertile, and its mass and distance from the sun promised moderate temperatures. The Galactic Federation protected these discoveries with the highest security. Which meant Shadow, the richest crime ring in the galaxy, would pay well for the chip — finding premium land for their hallucinatory crops had become a priority. And patrols would be practically non-existent so far out of the normal trade routes. "Seventy-one percent water is a lot of sea, but still leaves a sizable area for Shadow to play with. I'll send an encrypted message to my father."

Stee cocked her head. "I thought you already had. The communication schematics recorded a fluctuation just before I left the bridge."

"Have the Knight Hawk run a system's test." A malfunction would be disastrous at this point. Every galaxy credit he netted from this heist had to go into paying back his debt and accrued interest. His beloved father hadn't offered reduced terms. *Never let family interfere with business, if you want to succeed,* Father had told him when he protested. Still, this latest heist might enable him to finally break away from Father's control over him and the ship.

"I'll let my father know that we'll be auctioning the chip to the highest bidder."

Stee's eyebrows rose.

"Other crime lords might gang up to outbid Shadow," Jesson said. "That could put the price up." He was his father's son after all.

"Shadow won't like it. And they would expect more loyalty from Lord Jesson's son."

"I've not taken the oath." One master was one too many. But for now, he needed to keep Father happy. The remaining whisky in the glass trembled. The Knight Hawk had fired the thrusters and would soon make the jump.

"Set the coordinates for Xanta," Jesson said. "My father'll take the loot off us. For his usual cut, of course."

Stee picked the inventory sheet and left to oversee the jump. Jesson leaned back in his chair and steepled his fingers. With a bit of luck, the destination chip would enable him to pay all that he still owed for the Knight Hawk and the technology he'd installed to make it the fastest ship in the galaxy. The extra expense had been worth it. The Knight Hawk could outrun any galactic patrol. It was what had kept him alive and out of custody these past ten years.

Jesson removed the patch of artificial skin which covered one of his eyes and rubbed the scar. It itched each time he felt stressed, and even more so when he had to deal with his father. He switched off the music. Pipes and flutes weren't going to help him today.

A light on the console blinked. He brushed his finger over it and Cargo Master Vincente's voice crackled out of the speaker. "A freight ship and a patrol answered the colonists' distress signal. They're heading here."

"How long?"

"The Patrol's the closest. Four jumps away."

"The colonists might not be alive by then." Which meant more deaths tallied against him.

"And we'll be long gone," Vincente said.

Jesson grunted, then cut the connection. Had he caught a hint of disapproval in Vincente's tone? Unbidden, a picture of gas-dazed and sobbing colonists rose in Jesson's mind, but if he grew soft each time a child cried, he should have remained on Xanta. Besides, crying only used up the colonists' air reserves. And with the control chips in his possession, they wouldn't be able to generate more. However, if they were very lucky—and had a smart captain—the Patrol might reach them just before their air ran out.

The heist should have been just a routine raid—board; fire the gas; cripple the ship; bag all that was portable. His crew knew the drill. But one of the females hadn't been as disorientated by the gas as the others. These ten years had taught Jesson to never underestimate those with nothing to lose. Unfortunately, his youngest crew member hadn't been as vigilant.

The life of a skinny boy for a loan payment. Plus the lives of the starship's crew and passengers. Perhaps.

He'd need to let the boy's family know, but it would have to wait. More essential business beckoned. Jesson emptied his tumbler, then tapped into the encryptor to reach his father.

Two jumps to Xanta

The Knight Hawk drifted towards the waiting cruiser. The airspace was crowded this close to Xanta, but if anyone cared to check, their ships' designations declared that the Knight Hawk was trading in gems and jewellery, while the cruiser was a rich man's toy, a means of shuttling the pleasure-loving from one hot entertainment spot to another.

The airlocks kissed. Jesson straightened his closefitting jacket and ran his hand over his short hair. As his father had always drummed into his sons, appearance was half a sale.

The cruiser airlock opened with a hiss of warm air. The Shadow lord preferred his ship's temperatures to be high, it seemed, at least higher than Jesson allowed on his. But then Shadow had a bottomless supply of galaxy credits. Unlike the Knight Hawk.

It was also Shadow's way of showing who had the greater muscle.

A plump man stepped into the opening. "Jesson's little bastard."

Jesson tensed, but this was not the time to take offense. If Shadow thought they could rattle him with an old insult, they did not know the man he'd become.

"Lord Teir." He'd often seen the drug lord at his father's house. Jesson schooled his face not to show disappointment— he'd hoped to reach someone higher.

The man's gaze swept over Jesson from the flesh-coloured eyepatch to the tip of his scuffed boots. Jesson felt warmth rise in his neck. The needier he appeared, the lower the offer would be.

"I see you've inherited your father's eye for business, if nothing else," Teir said.

Jesson's fingers tightened into a fist. Teir probably knew that he'd lost his eye at his father's house, and that Lord Jesson hadn't bothered to pay for regenerative surgery. "You honour me," he said.

The Shadow section leader did not advance to offer the customary arm grip. So be it. Teir had called him bastard after all. And there was no hiding the tawny tinge in Jesson's skin that broadcasted his Ma'attan blood. Taking offense would damage the negotiations before they even started.

"We've verified the information you sent Lord Jesson," Teir said. "Shadow will buy the chip. There will be no auction."

The hell there won't. He'd take the slights and the attitude, but no one dictated what he could do with his booty. He opened his mouth to tell Teir just what he thought of that, but the fat man put his hand up. "Our records show that we hold IOUs in your name for the amount of 3 million galaxy credits."

What! It was the amount he still owed his father. He'd paid back 7 million, plus interest already. And it had taken him ten years and every credit he could spare.

"Lord Jesson was glad to recoup the amount early. Which means, of course, that we own the Knight Hawk. One point five million units is a fair price for the planet's coordinates."

He'd hoped for more, much more. "It's worth three point five." Enough to pay the rest of the loan and tidy him till the next heist.

"It's worth nothing without a buyer." The man's eyes bore into him. "Or if you're dead."

Sweat trickled down to the small of Jesson's back. In the tiny space, the bigger man had the advantage. But who was he kidding? A Shadow crew member would be monitoring their conversation, and Jesson would be incapacitated with gas before he took a single step toward Teir.

"Good, I see we understand each other," Teir said. "Lord Jesson is authorised to receive the chip. One more condition. We have a cargo we need delivered to Xanta. Once it and the chip reach your father, we'll cancel your IOUs for the amount of 1.5 million."

Jesson shook his head. "The ship's weight has already been registered with the port authorities. They'll know I have illegal cargo if I add anything."

"Credit Shadow with some intelligence. You've lost a crew member. The cargo will be the equivalent weight of one sniveling boy."

How the hell did Shadow know about that? "Then you'll have to pay passage."

"Get it through customs and your little bird will be fuelled and serviced at our expense. That should cover it. You're more useful off Xanta."

Teir would look charming with a knife scar running down his fat face. "What's the cargo?"

"Nothing to worry about. Just feed and water it and deliver it alive."

What! "Now wait a minute…"

Teir spoke into his wrist mike. The airlock behind him parted and the fat man ducked through it. Jesson took a step after him, but a uniformed crew member filled the space where Teir had stood. He wheeled a square plastic box, the height of Jesson's hip, through the airlock, then stepped back into the cruiser, leaving the box behind.

The cruiser airlock closed behind him.

How was he going to hide a box that size? It would certainly not fit in any of the secret compartments. The muscle at the side of his jaw jittering, Jesson pulled the box through his side of the airlock and locked the hatch shut.

"What have you there?" As expected, Stee was waiting for him. She eyed the tubes jutting out of the container—one for liquid, one for dried food pellets. The furrows on her brow deepened.

"I don't know. Some animal or other."

"We don't do animals."

"Yes, well, I wasn't given much of a choice."

"We always have a choice."

"Not when they hold your IOUs." He'd find a way to pay the old man back for selling him to Shadow. One day.

One jump to Xanta

"NE MAJEY GE…

> *Old is the land of the people.*
> *Fertile and ripe are our wombs.*
> *All are father and mother*
> *Blessed by the two moons."*

Ma crooned the Ma'attan lament as her thin arms held him, turning his sobs to sniffs. He was safe here in her embrace. She would protect him from the big man's fists. *"Ne majey ge…"*

A slap, and he slammed onto the floor, his shrieks mingling with Ma's. Pain lanced down his cheek, burnt his eye. Pain as he'd never felt. He couldn't see, and warm liquid cascaded down his face, into his mouth.

The tang and taste of salt and iron mingled with his tears.

Thud. Fists on flesh. The flash of Father's ring.

Moans.

The silence was worse.

Jesson struggled against the constricting webbing—he had to save Ma. He had to hide from Father. The rhythmic throb of the Knight Hawk stilled his limbs.

He hadn't had that dream in years. Snapping open the webbing, he swung his legs off the sleeping pad and buried his head in his hands. His encounter with Teir must have triggered the memories he preferred to keep locked away. He was a ship's captain now, not a frightened boy. And that planet, that land of peace and beauty that his mother had sung about, no longer existed. Singing, or dreaming about it, wouldn't bring it back.

He folded the sleeping pad back against the wall to pull down the flap of his console and the swivel chair that transformed his sleeping quarters into his office. Space on the Knight Hawk was limited, but at least he was master here.

Passing his thumb over the console, lights flickered on, and the Knight Hawk's trajectory and current position appeared on the screen. The Knight Hawk had started the countdown to the last jump before the final run to its home planet, Xanta. That planet had stopped being home the day Father drove his fist once too hard into Ma's face. But Father and Shadow had ensured he hadn't escaped his fetters, yet. Saddling him with a caged creature that was probably the size of a well-fed canine was proof enough.

If Shadow, or his father, wanted to get him arrested on entering Xantian airspace, they couldn't have found a better way.

He thumbed in the link to the cargo bay.

"Captain?" Vincente's bald head filled the screen.

"Has the creature eaten?"

"It's taken water but left the dried meat pellets."

Not a predator, then. Damn Teir for not giving him any information about what was in the box. "Give it vegetable pellets."

"Did so already. It would be better if we know what we've got."

"I'll come down later."

"Ne majey ge…"

Jesson whirled round, for a crazy moment expecting to see Ma behind him. Nothing but blank walls and folded bed pad. His cabin was too small to hide a desert rat, let alone a mortal. Yet someone was singing.

Cutting Vincente off, he searched his room for some hidden device. Nothing.

"Ne majey ge…"

His empty eye socket twitched and itched. The voice sounded young, anxious. Could one of the crew be playing a joke on him? Yet who knew Ma'attan?

He strode out of the cabin, the voice continuing to cocoon him in its embrace. It was everywhere, and nowhere, filling the spaces of the Knight Hawk with sound—which no one else heard.

Of course they didn't. Ma had no reason to haunt them. Only him. He'd failed her.

He was going mad.

The singing continued. Songs about Ma'att, songs about freedom, songs about love, songs about loss.

Stee took to following him with her eyes, her gaze a silent question. She knew something was amiss. She'd been with him since his first voyage, when he was a mere youth who'd barely known how to program the Knight Hawk and get the ship in the air. But he couldn't tell her his mother's phantom had decided to take up residence in his head.

The voice piped on.

Why had Ma waited twenty-six years to curse him? The death of the boy must have been the chaff that tipped the scales. The Ma'attan valued life above all. The boy had been part of his crew, his responsibility. He had betrayed his Ma'attan heritage, and all that Ma had taught him.

He'd become just like his father.

Off Xanta

JESSON WOKE UP DRENCHED. FATHER was angry with him for going into his office. He whipped him, then he whipped Ma for not keeping him close, out of sight.

"*Ne majey ge…*" *Old is the land of the people.* The land was Ma'att, and Ma'att meant both homeland and Mother.

"*Farem'ije toa…*" *A mother's love is infinite, eternal.*

"Stop it," he yelled.

The voice faltered, then halted, as if the phantom paused to watch him unravel.

"*Ajeni!*" Help me.

Jesson groaned. "Help me," she'd screamed then, too. But he hadn't been Ma'attan enough to stop his father. Just as he hadn't stood up to Teir and demanded what that chip was really worth.

"*Ajeni, toimoi'd.*"

Jesson shuddered. The voice sounded frightened, but hopeful, too. Ma had always been strong—like all Ma'attan. At least she'd stopped singing.

His heart banging against his ribs, Jesson sat up, his gaze darting round the cabin. He hardly remembered what Ma had looked like; he only remembered long black hair, and green eyes the colour of wet grass.

"*Ajeni, toimoi'd.*"

Toimoi'd. Male — not son. "*Who are you?*"

"*Ye'ma.*" Girl.

Jesson crashed off his bed, swept out of his cabin and lunged for the descent pole that would take him down to the lower levels of the Knight Hawk. Not bothering to latch on the safety strap, he plummeted down and his boots slammed onto the cargo bay. Rounding the shuttle, he gazed around the space as if he'd never seen it before. Every square inch had a function: food storage; flares; weapons rack; off world clothing; space-suits; one square box.

Teir's container stood in the middle of the floor.

"Captain?"

"Leave."

Vincente snorted, but did as he was told, shimming up the pole as agile as any of Xanta's primates.

We're all animals after all.

Jesson ran his hands over the container. He didn't have the codes to open it.

Father would.

"*Ye'ma? Ye'ma?*" He hadn't communicated through thought since he'd been three years old. With Ma.

"*Toimoi'd?*"

"*Stay low, as low as you can get.*" Jesson strode to the weapons rack and took down a laser gun.

Shadow would not be pleased. They might even renege on the payment.

How had they expected him to get a box that size through customs? Of course they knew he'd have to open it, break it up. And Shadow needed that chip. He'd be made to pay a price for the loss of a containment box, but they wouldn't back out of their agreement.

He set the intensity of the laser to its lowest setting and fired.

Plastic blackened, dissolved, and one of the locks fragmented. The jagged hole grew around the ruined lock, and a stench of sweat and fear exploded out of the breach. Jesson enlarged the opening, then took his finger off the trigger. Large green eyes below a fringe the colour of the void peered out of the opening. Skin more golden than his. A pure Ma'attan, one of the few still alive.

"Close your eyes. Don't look."

The girl lowered her head and shut her eyes. He pressed the trigger again to destroy the second lock. The child did not whimper or move as the laser continued to melt her prison. She was Ma'attan—strong and resilient. Just as Ma had been.

"You can come out now," he said. He pulled up the lid and reached in, but the girl flinched and backed away.

Long moments passed. Jesson felt the girl touch his mind, like a feather across his thoughts. Her rapid breathing slowed. She shuffled within the box, then thin fingers gripped the side of the container, the girl's disheveled hair appeared above the rim, then her dirt streaked brow and her eyes, the exact shade of grass after the first rains.

She couldn't be older than ten.

Father liked them young. Ma had been young too, he'd just never realised how young.

Jesson reached for one of the landside jackets hanging behind him. He chose the smallest one—the boy wouldn't be missing it—and draped it round the girl's shoulders. "We have a spare cabin you can use."

XANTA'S GREY ORB FILLED THE console's screen. Jesson shut it off, then, pocketing a gas pistol, he strode out of his cabin and slid down the pole. He found the Ma'attan girl and Vincente in the galley, one floor up from the cargo bay. The girl was seated by a fold-down table, playing with one of the toy gadgets they'd lifted off the starship, while Vincente monitored the two food portions he was heating.

The girl looked up and her contentment faded.

Of course she knew what he intended. The Ma'attans could read minds. Even his half-breed one.

Vincente switched off the heater and straightened. "Have you thought about how we're going to explain Eja?"

Eja? If even a stone-faced Xantian cared enough to learn the child's name, the quicker she was off the ship the better.

The cargo master placed one of the food cartons next to the girl. "Careful, it's hot." He mimed touching and pain.

"We'll drug her and say she's a crew member who drank too much. We can't have her questioned by customs."

"Her parents were killed by Shadow." Vincente's gaze shifted behind Jesson as Stee joined them. The tiny galley had become decidedly too crowded.

"How do you know? Ma'attans are dumb," Stee said.

Jesson stifled a bark of laughter. Silent to others, perhaps. But not to Ma'attans. Eja hadn't stopped prattling and singing these two days.

Stee eased past Vincente and filled a cup with water. She dropped a sleeping tablet into the water and pushed it towards the girl. "Drink." She mimicked the action.

Eja's gaze swung to Vincente, then Jesson.

Her fear lanced him. Fear had darkened the colour of Ma's eyes, too, whenever she knew she'd displeased Father.

He'd lose his ship, perhaps even his life, if he didn't deliver the girl.

"Help me," she'd cried in her box. Just as Ma had screamed, before Father had silenced her forever.

Eja must have been terrified in the dark, locked in a box, but she hadn't cried. She'd face worse horrors at Lord Jesson's house.

She'd survive — she was Ma'attan.

And he...he was not. A man without dignity has nothing. No race, no motherland. Not even song. His mother had been wrenched from her home, her family, her planet, but she had not stopped singing.

The girl had sung in her cage, too.

Ma would have been ashamed to call him son. And Father never called him son, either.

Once you touch the depths, the only way is up. That's what Ma used to say after each beating.

He had the fastest ship in the galaxy and the coordinates to an unknown world. He couldn't give Ma the homeland she'd lost, but he could give it to one little girl. And shield her as he couldn't shield his mother from Father's fists.

"Don't drink it," he told Eja.

"Don't be a fool," Stee said. "She's not worth it."

"Behind you," Eja cried.

Jesson whirled, sheathing the girl with his bulk and drawing his pistol. Vincente had drawn a weapon, too. Heat seared Jesson's cheek, stunning him. Eja cried out and, behind him, a pistol clanged to the floor.

Stee reeled and crumpled to the ground.

Jesson gaped at Vincente and tightened his grip on his pistol. "You're a Shadow man." He should have known. Vincente was Xantian after all. Shadow, or his father, must have arranged to have Vincente meet him, just when his previous cargo master had decided — or been induced — not to return on board.

The fluctuations in the communication schematics now made sense. "You sent encrypted messages. Who do you report to? My father? Teir?"

Vincente's eyebrow twitched. "Drop that." He jerked his chin at the pistol in Jesson's hand.

"After you."

"That's not going to happen. A gas pistol's no match against a laser."

"You wouldn't have fired it inside a ship unless it's at its lowest setting." He had to bank on Vincente not wanting to blow them all to smithereens. *Get down, Eja.*

The girl slid under the flimsy protection of the table. It would have to do. "I want you off my ship," he told Vincente. "You can take the shuttle to Xanta."

"You'll need a cargo master to get through customs."

"I'm not going to Xanta. You can tell my father he's not getting Eja. He's destroyed one Ma'attan too many; he won't hurt another."

Vincente smiled. "I'm not Shadow, Stee was. I'm Patrol."

What?

"Drop your pistol, you'll only get us all killed."

There was a reason why lasers were locked away on board spacecraft. The little girl gazed up at them. She still clutched her toy and a tiny frown scrunched up her face.

"Don't be frightened," he said.

She shook her head. *"You're Ma'attan. And Vincente's a good man."*

If Vincente was a good man, what did that make him?

He could fire his pistol, the gas would disorientate Vincente. And with a bit of luck, the patrolman's laser wouldn't hit anything too vital before that happened.

What then? He could bundle Vincente into the shuttle and set its coordinates for Xanta. Then he'd load the Knight Hawk with the colonists' destination chip and race away from this system. He'd be on the run from Shadow. And on the run from the Patrol — but that had been his life these last ten years.

It was no life for a little girl.

She'd love that watery planet.

He couldn't go there. The Patrol knew he had the coordinates. They'd follow them. And Eja deserved better than a life on the run. Just as Ma had deserved better than a life as a slave. And she shouldn't have died so young.

Just as the boy shouldn't have died.

And nor should the colonists have died, and so many others like them. So many lives lost because of his wrong decisions. *A mother's love is infinite, eternal,* Eja had sung. Perhaps he could deserve that love and honour Ma's sacrifice. Jesson let the pistol drop from his hand.

Vincente kicked the weapon away. "Captain Jesson, you are under arrest for piracy. You will be locked in your cabin till I hand you over."

"Trusting of you. Will that be before or after you inject me with paralysing serum?"

"You were ready to give it all up for the girl. I don't think I need to incapacitate you. Yet." Vincente slid a location bracelet over Jesson's wrist. "I'll see the colonists get back what you took off them."

"So they're alive?"

"Of course. A Patrol was waiting a jump away. I beamed the information as soon as you decided on your target."

And rigged the schematics. "When you return the destination chip, perhaps the colonists could take Eja with them. She'd like that planet."

Vincente smiled at the girl, and she scrambled up and slipped her hand into Jesson's. Her delicate fingers radiated warmth into his palm.

He should be comforting her, not the other way round.

Would the colonists think her dumb, too? He coughed to ease the tightness in his throat and looked at Vincente. "Why did Patrol plant you on me? I'm nobody."

"You're Lord Jesson's son. We hoped to get to him through you." Vincente thumbed his credentials into the console by the exit hatch, then input a string of digits. "I've denied you access to the Knight Hawk's control."

"Of course." He'd lost the one good thing he'd called his own.

"Trafficking in Ma'attans will earn your father a few years on a penitentiary planet. But if you testify against him, we could ensure he'll never be able to hurt another child again."

Jesson rubbed his destroyed eye. It always itched in times of stress. He hadn't been able to defend Ma when he was three. Perhaps he could see that she got justice. He was Ma'attan, after all, just like the girl. Solid as the land. Fluid as the rivers that no longer ran in that lost world. He had needed to be, to survive. Perhaps one day he'd be allowed to board a colonists' ship and join Eja. He'd sing the songs with her and make Ma proud.

When you reach the depths, the only way is up.

After the Deluge

By Peter Golubock

"SHOULDN'T WE HOIST THE BLACK flag?" asked the first mate. They'd been shadowing the merchantman for more than an hour in the East Channel, edging closer by dribs and drabs, acting the part of a lowly water taxi ferrying tired servants from the island back to the main as the day came to a close.

The captain adjusted her eyepatch. "Not quite yet, I think," she said. She didn't speak loudly, but then again, she didn't have to. The crew hung on her every word. Now she reached in her pocket for a stale crust of bread, offering it to the pigeon perched on her shoulder. It regarded the morsel for a moment, then cooed appreciatively and snatched the crust from the captain's hand. "Whaddaya think, Bloombito?" said the captain to her bird. "Is it time?"

It wasn't an easy question to answer, and Bloombito the pigeon would have been well advised to think before responding. Hoisting the Jolly Roger too soon would give the merchie time to run and sound the alarm. But every second they waited was another opportunity for a sharp pair of eyes aboard that fat merchie to sweep over the seemingly innocent water taxi a few points windward and to see the concealed gun ports and then to turn tail and run, screaming for help from the navy as they fled.

The Captain's reverie was interrupted by the second mate's arrival on the quarterdeck. "Avast, Cap'n," he said, doffing his battered ball cap by way of greeting.

"Avast and ahoy, Roberto," replied the skipper. "What's the word?"

"The boys and girls are eager, Cap'n," he said, tugging one of the plaits in his matted black beard for emphasis. "It's been, what, near three weeks now since we caught that pleasure-yacht in the Central Lagoon?"

"And what's the latest on the fuel situation?" It was this problem more than any other that had gnawed at the captain this past hour, as they'd crept up on their unwitting quarry.

"Clemenza says we've got ten minutes at full speed."

The captain produced a spyglass from one of the innumerable pockets that adorned her battered blue pea coat, putting it to her remaining eye. It was dusk, and the wind was starting to pick up a bit from the southeast. The garbage-choked waters of the East Channel slapped the ship's hull. The air smelled like mud and seagull shit. It was time.

She turned to the first mate, who'd been silent since being rebuffed not five minutes ago. *Was it really just five minutes ago?* thought the captain. *It feels like a year.* "Beat to quarters and hoist the black flag, Aki," she said. "It's time to start slitting throats."

The first mate smiled, which would have been kind of cute were her teeth not filed into points. "About time, Cap'n," she said, and then she swept down the stairs from the quarterdeck.

"Battle stations! Look hearty, you scurvy dogs!" she screamed to roars from the crew.

Not to be outdone, the second mate had been pulling down the yellow, white and black tricolor of the Water-Taxi and Limousine Commission. The ship had burst to life and was now a swarm of activity, as the pirate crew ran out the guns and the Jolly Roger crawled its way to the top of the flagpole.

From another pocket of the captain's coat came an antique red and white megaphone, which she thumbed on and directed at her prey. "Ahoy, there, merchie!" she yelled at the ungainly, slate-grey ship — *more a bathtub than a boat,* thought the captain with a sneer — that was now only a couple hundred yards off her starboard bow. She lifted the megaphone to her lips again. "This is the *Pizza Rat!*" she said, and her crew pounded the gunwales with the butts of their guns and shrieked. "You've heard of us, and what we've done. Now heave to and prepare to be boarded, or we'll have your guts for garters!"

A few months ago, after a merchantman had refused to strike the colors, leading the *Pizza Rat* on a lengthy chase and then resisting the boarding party tooth-and-nail to boot, Aki had actually tried to turn the offending captain's guts into garters. It hadn't worked out very well, and indeed, it was days like that one which made the captain wonder if perhaps she hadn't gotten herself into the wrong line of work. She banished that stray thought from her mind as she grabbed the fire pole that went from the quarterdeck to the bridge and shinnied down.

Unlike the quarterdeck, the bridge was enclosed from the elements by a set of spectacularly grimy floor to ceiling windows. It was empty save for Fouad, the helmsman, a per-petually rumpled middle-aged man with curly greying hair and a walrus mustache. Fouad's grandfather had driven taxis on land; his father had driven them on water. "Driving is in the blood," is what Fouad himself said whenever he'd had one too many and was feeling ruminative. He turned and sketched a mock salute as the captain arrived on the bridge.

"Ready for action, Fouad?"

He snorted, sending the ends of his mustache skyward for a moment. "Action? What action?" He motioned at the merchie. "We've caught them with their pants down and ass hanging out."

There were a few other ships in hailing distance and each and every one of which had bugged out the instant the Jolly Roger made its appearance. That left only the *Pizza Rat*'s prize, floundering pathetically in the water dead ahead. The captain didn't even need her spyglass now. She was close enough to see the tub's name — the *O'Melveny*, whatever the hell that was — and its crew, scurrying around like ants whose colony had just been smashed by a vengeful giant.

"They put about on the port tack when we raised the black flag," said Fouad, "then changed their damn minds and went hard a-starboard. Now they're caught up in stays, and not a motor to be seen."

It was just then that the *O'Melveny* struck the colors. The captain smirked. "And we didn't even need to fire a warning shot," she said. "Oh, well. Suppose it's about time everything went right for once."

Fouad frowned. "Look over there, Cap'n," he said, pointing starboard and astern. "One of the other ships is turning around."

This did indeed call for the spyglass, which made an encore appearance. The captain frowned into the lens. One ship had, indeed, turned around, and was headed back directly towards the *Pizza Rat* and the merchie. It was going fast, too, a sleek little blue number with some contraption mounted on the bow.

The captain put down the spyglass, turned to Fouad, and said, "I don't know what in hells they think they're playing—"

She would have said "at" next, but then there was a loud explosion. Bloombito squawked, flew directly into the ceiling, and landed in a heap of feathers on the tiller. A massive gout of water shot into the air uncomfortably close to the starboard beam.

"It's NYPN!" shouted Fouad, pointing at the advancing blue ship.

"Disengage, and do it now," said the captain, fighting to keep a note of hysteria from creeping into her voice. "Set a course for LaGuardia Bay, and fire up the motor. Full speed ahead, Fouad."

She didn't even wait for him to confirm her orders before hauling herself hand over hand back up the fire pole to the quarterdeck. *We've got to put in a set of stairs*, the captain thought for the hundredth time, wondering as she did if it would be the last. The only greeting she received on the quarterdeck was a shell that shrieked overhead, clipping lines of rigging and barely missing the mizzenmast. The *Pizza Rat* was starting to pull away from the *O'Melveny*, whose captain was surely kissing the deck and thanking whatever set of gods she worshiped. The sun was a rapidly disappearing disc of orange in the west.

Aki ran onto the quarterdeck, gun in hand and eyes wild. "Why are we running?" she asked, gesturing with her rifle at the approaching police cutter. "We're bigger than they are. We should stand and fight!"

A kettle of tension deep within the captain boiled over at that moment, and she took three quick strides across the deck, grabbing Aki's gun with one hand, tossing it overboard, while holding onto her first mate's throat very tightly with the other. Aki opened her mouth to speak, but the captain squeezed. A hoarse squawk was all that emerged.

"Shut the fuck up," said the captain conversationally. "We're pirates, you idiot, not soldiers. We slug it out with them, and we wind up with a boat full of holes and half the crew dead. And that's if we're lucky. Now where's the profit in that, I ask you?"

Her grip loosened and Aki once more attempted to speak, only for the captain's grip to tighten again just as suddenly, resulting in a slightly more truncated squawk. Bloombito cooed in response from his perch on the captain's shoulder. "Again, shut the fuck up," said the captain. "I wasn't actually asking you."

The *Pizza Rat* had turned away and accelerated south, giving them a chance to open fire on their pursuer. The ripping sound of machine-gun fire filled the air. Then there was a short sharp smashing sound, and the ship shuddered. The police cutter had scored a hit, punching a hole in the *Pizza Rat*'s hull just above the waterline amidships on the port side. A few scattered screams added their voices to the cawing of gulls overhead.

"Now go do your fucking job," the captain snarled, "and be a good little girl, or I'll cut off your fucking tongue and feed it to the fish." She pushed Aki away towards the damaged area of the ship. The first mate stumbled, opened her mouth as if to say something, then thought better of it and ran.

"That was a bit dramatic, no?" Roberto had somehow managed to appear on the quarterdeck unnoticed. He was surprisingly good at sneaking around for a man who was the size of a small bear.

"What's the damage?" asked the captain, waving towards the smoking hole amidships. Another shell sailed overhead, detonating harmlessly about fifty yards astern.

"We'll live, for the moment." The *Pizza Rat's* guns continued to tear away, though from the looks of it they weren't doing much.

"That's comforting," said the captain. "You always did have a way of putting me at ease, Roberto. It's probably why you got the second mate gig."

"We'll live," repeated Roberto, "for about six more minutes, after which we'll run out of fuel, at which point they will proceed to run circles around us until we are dead."

"That's not so comforting."

"They'll also definitely have called for backup by now." There was a crash and an unearthly screech as a shell smacked into the foremast, turning it into an assortment of bent metal shards. Four of the crew were pulped across the deck.

"You know, maybe you should just shut up." The only thing they had going for them, the captain thought, was that night was rapidly approaching. Oh, and that they were leading the police into a trap. Couldn't forget that.

The *Pizza Rat's* gunners finally scored a hit of their own. There was a muffled blast. Smoke started pouring from the pursuer's stern.

"That'll slow them down a bit," the captain said. "Now if we can just—"

"You know what I said about how they'll have called for backup by now?"

"Didn't I just tell you to shut up?"

"At your nine o'clock, amidships," said Roberto, flinging an arm in the offending direction. "Another of the little buggers."

"Hold the course!" shouted the Captain to Roberto, and Fouad at the helm, and really to everyone. It was too late to do anything else at this point anyway, with only a few minutes of fuel left. Hopefully, a few minutes would be all they needed. Their original pursuer was lagging noticeably now. Dusk was changing to dark, and if they could shake this newest tail and get out of open water they'd be as good as invisible.

The *Pizza Rat* juddered through the choppy waters of LaGuardia Bay. A salvo of rockets shrieked overhead, as the second police cutter tried to gauge the range and sight in. The *Rat*'s gunners returned fire, but their broadside didn't trouble the enemy. Fouad had opened the throttle as far as the old engine could go. It whined and retched as the ship skipped over the waves. Their pursuer matched the *Pizza Rat's* acceleration with an almost contemptuous ease. It was edging closer and closer, though gunnery on both sides was hampered by the encroaching darkness.

A blast from their pursuer's horn hailed the pirate ship, as the chase continued. "Now hear this," blared a disembodied voice. "Attention unidentified criminal watercraft. You are hereby required to heave to at once, by express and lawful order of the New York Police Navy. Failure to comply may result in the use of lethal force against your vessel. Again, this . . ."

The recording continued, but the captain had heard enough. She sputtered in indignation. "Failure to comply may result in the use of lethal force! What the fuck have they been shooting at us for the past twenty minutes, party favors?"

Roberto sighed, shaking his head mournfully. "I swear," he said, "their standards just keep on dropping. Give it a few years and they'll be grunting at us."

"We're coming up on it, Captain!" shouted Fouad, from below. "Just a minute now!"

The smell of smoke and blood filled the air. It was all too familiar. "All right, Fouad," the captain said. "Execute when ready. Let's give these bastards a little gift from the Old City!"

A few seconds later the ship twitched a point to port, so imperceptibly that one could be forgiven for not noticing it, and then slid back to resume its previous course. All of a sudden, there was a terrible mangled screech, the sound of metal clashing on metal from behind them. Their pursuer had collided with some object beneath the waterline and run aground. It listed over on the starboard side, hull belly-up in surrender. LaGuardia Airport may have been long gone, but its air traffic control tower was not. Lurking beneath the waves, just inches beneath the surface, it waited to ensnare careless travelers. It was easy enough to avoid, of course. You just needed to know exactly where it was.

As the crew cheered and burst into song, the captain heard a cackle waft up from the helmsman below. "Fugheddaboutit!" shouted Fouad, triumphantly, as the *Pizza Rat* and its pirate crew slipped away into the murky nighttime streets of Jackson Heights.

IT WASN'T A BIG SURPRISE when New York sank beneath the waves. The surprise was that everyone stayed. Life went on much as it always had. There were a few minor alterations to people's daily lives, of course; boats replaced cars, food carts became food canoes, and no one lived on the ground floor anymore. But there was no mass exodus from the five boroughs, no long snaking line of refugees wending its way deep into flyover country. New Yorkers stayed. They built up, and kept on building. Great swathes of Brooklyn were brownstones underwater as far as the second floor, with ramshackle additions welded onto roofs.

Labyrinthine passages were strung between the skyscrapers of Manhattan, a spider web of streets hundreds of feet above the water. Most New Yorkers lived their entire lives without ever setting foot on land. The city sank, and rose again.

Everything about this new New York, an ungainly Venice on stilts, was outsized; both the virtues and flaws of the old New York were magnified in the newer version. Denizens of the Old City who battled rats, cockroaches and bedbugs would doubtless have been pleased that they shuffled off this mortal coil early enough to avoid the sharks, crocodiles, and poisonous jellyfish of the New City. Traffic choked the main water-streets and thoroughfares at all hours. Hapless crossing guards in rickety dinghies tweeted whistles and waved stop signs as every imaginable make and model of watercraft jostled for tiny scraps of space.

Inequality, that yawning chasm that separated the fortunate from everyone else, had grown by leaps and bounds, the two sides of the chasm moving farther away from each other. The rich lived in opulence on verdant islands dotted amid the waters of the city. The super-rich lived on dry land, a concept beyond the ken of ninety-nine percent of those who scratched and scraped and drifted through the streets. It should come as no surprise that some of those ninety-nine percent, the dispossessed and desperate, forsook the law and took to the waves with ill intent. Like the old stories of Robin Hood, the pirates of New York stole from the rich. They were rather less enthusiastic about giving to the poor, though.

The Floating Conclave was supposed to take place, by ancient and hoary tradition, on the first Thursday of every month. There was no explanation for this. In point of fact, the Floating Conclave took place whenever the most powerful pirate captains of the Five Boroughs had enough free time to sit down and do some day planning. It was thus a rare and momentous occasion.

Even so, there is one tonight, and we are invited. Let us go, then, to the old Statue of Liberty, the chosen site for this edition of the Conclave, convenient enough for all the great captains yet out-of-the-way enough to, hopefully, not catch the wandering eye of the New York Police Navy. The captains need not fear. The NYPN knows in vague and general terms about the Conclave. It may even know where it will meet. But the NYPN will do nothing due to the bitter certainty that it could arrest every pirate captain in New York and a day later there would be a brand new crop, possibly even more bloodthirsty than the current lot and definitely less predictable. Better the devil you know than the deep blue sea.

Enter Roberto Garcia-Rosenberg, second mate of the good ship *Pizza Rat*, a toasted everything bagel in one hand and his hole cards in the other. He is losing at poker and has been for some time now, but the bagel is delicious and a sweet young thing from the *Hedge Funder's Bane* has been making cow eyes at him all night, so this particular Conclave is by no means a total loss.

"Are you going to fold, or what?" Copper Gourd asked. He was in a hurry because he was winning. Ride your luck while it lasts, he'd said not two minutes ago, waxed mustaches quivering with glee.

"Call," said Roberto, tossing a pile of chips into the center of the table. His father had had a set of mustaches like that, back when he and Mom still owned the family artisanal pickle factory in Williamsburg.

"Fold," said Madam Mercury. She turned to Roberto. "Heard you and the *Rat* got in a bit of a scrap the other evening."

"That we did," acknowledged Roberto with a nod, as The Mop raised the pot. "But the captain saw us through it."

"You talk about her like she's got a magic wand stuffed up her ass," said Copper Gourd. He called The Mop's raise.

"Who's to say she doesn't?" asked Roberto. He folded and stretched, taking in the view. Dozens of pirate ships were tied to the spikes of the old statue's crown. There were a couple of look-outs perched on the torch, scanning the horizon for intruders. Salesmen and touts flitted to and fro on the periphery hawking their wares. The bold and desperate hoping to earn a place on a pirate crew circulated through the crowd, trying to catch a captain's eye. They had quite a bit of competition.

The captain was talking to a spy. One thing that the rich of every era have had in abundance is employees. Invariably, some become disgruntled. Like any other pirate commander worth her salt, the captain maintained a network of informants throughout the city. They fed her morsels of information and were repaid with morsels of cash. While the information was generally idle gossip and stray rumors, every once in a while one of those morsels of information had a bit more meat on it.

"So, you're saying it won't have a guard escort?" The captain frowned dubiously and scratched her nose. This sounded a bit too good to be true, and after the debacle last time out, she was scrutinizing each and every gift horse with care.

"No guards," said the contact with a definitive shake of her head, sending blonde curls flying every which way. "They said it would attract too much attention."

"And the cargo is…fancy plates? What the fuck am I supposed to do with those?"

The contact flounced and stamped her feet. "You're not listening! It's china, it's silver, it's art, it's everything! All going to their beach house in Vermont before the summer season starts.

It's worth, God, I can't even imagine how much! And you're just going to sit there?"

The captain didn't actually doubt the contact. She'd worked for the House of Greenstone for a few years now. The contact always demurred when the subject of why she was so keen to sell out her employer came up, and the captain had never felt it wise to press the issue. The *Pizza Rat* had made more than one score thanks to information she'd provided, and the contact had made a fair bit of coin for her trouble. It had been a mutually profitable relationship. So why did the captain feel like she was being played?

"I didn't say I'd just sit there," said the captain, "though, frankly, I'm not sure what your problem with sitting there is. I find sitting to be quite an enjoyable activity." She waved at the scenery surrounding the two of them, as they sipped tea at one of the tables that had been placed on the Statue of Liberty's head.

The contact started to splutter and pout, then thought better of it. She smoothed her sea-green dress and took a deep breath. "I thought you'd be over the moon when you heard about this one," she said. "I don't get it. You need money, I definitely need money, and there's a barge that's begging to be robbed. What's the issue?"

"A smash-and-grab job right smack in the middle of downtown is a tall fucking order, whether the boat is guarded or not." The captain took a deep breath and played with her eyepatch. It'd start to fray at this rate, what with all the worrying away at it she'd been doing.

The contact tossed her arms in the air, then let them fall back onto the tea table. Saucers, spoons and teacups clinked and rattled. "It's dangerous?" she asked. "So what? You're pirates! Violent, amoral, adrenaline-crazed lunatics! Am I right?"

"You're not wrong."

Oh, to hell with it, the captain thought. *In for a penny, in for a pound.* She smoothed out her napkin and fed Bloombito an oyster cracker before focusing on the contact. "So, where did you say the best place to intercept the shipment was?"

THE FIRST ORDER OF BUSINESS was to disguise the ship. That was easy enough. Hack off the figurehead and stow it in the hold, slap a new coat of paint on the old rust bucket, hide all the guns, make sure everything was spick and span, then call it a job well done. The second order of business was to disguise the crew, which somehow turned out to be more time-consuming. Most pirates tended to look as though the contents of a thrift shop had exploded all over them. Then there was the business of the false body parts several of the crew were sporting, which were entirely too noticeable. That led to the bold tonsorial and facial hair styling that was the fashion among pirates, and was most certainly not the fashion among contracted merchant seamen.

Even the captain herself was not immune. The eyepatch was gone for this mission, replaced by a glass eye and a pair of over-sized sunglasses. It didn't feel right at all.

"The target is late."

This from Aki, who had been subdued since her dressing-down on the *Pizza Rat's* previous adventure. The ship slowly punted up Lexington Avenue, moving in time with the traffic, looking like nothing more than yet another tramp steamer hauling a load of who-knows-what to who-cares-where.

"Yes, it's terribly unsporting of them. If they're going to be late they should have the decency to call ahead and let us know, so we can get a coffee before robbing and murdering them."

Roberto always did tend to get snappish when he was nervous. It was quite endearing. Sometimes the captain felt like a parent mediating between two siblings.

"We may not know where they are now, but we know where they're going, right? Right?" asked the captain. Her reward was a pair of strained nods from her bickering underlings, which she took as a signal to continue. "They'll take 58th out to open water, then make for Connecticut Bay. We'll just keep loitering until they show up."

It was a boiling hot midsummer day, which didn't help anyone's mood. Every now and then the faintest puff of a breeze blew in from the east. The air was so humid that you could almost cut it into slices and spread it on a piece of bread, thought the captain. It should have been lunchtime, but the crew watched and waited for their quarry to emerge.

And then, all of a sudden, it did. Aki claimed the honor of first eyes on the prize. "I think that's it," she said, pointing ahead. "Orange hull, two masts, double motors at the stern?" she asked, but it really wasn't a question. The whole crew had memorized the vital details of the ship they were hunting.

Off went the sunglasses and out came the spyglass. The captain held it to her good eye, squinted, and then slammed it shut and started barking orders. "That's it, all right," she said, a note of excitement creeping into her voice. "Add sail, get the sculls working, and start the engines! We've got to cut them off before they get to open water or they'll outrun us with those big motors for sure."

The *Pizza Rat* started to pick up speed. It swerved into oncoming traffic for a beat, edged past a few slowpokes, then slid back into its lane just in time to avoid a collision.

"Turn east on 56th!" the captain shouted down to Fouad at the helm. It was narrower than 58th, but there wouldn't be nearly as much crosstown traffic. They turned hard a-starboard on 56th Street, which thankfully was quiet. Only a few personal canoes and kayaks plied the quiet residential way. Their passage was rudely interrupted by the *Pizza Rat*, which roared down the street, leaving a trail of whitecaps in its wake.

"Left on 2nd Avenue!" roared the captain, caught up in the thrill of the hunt. "Clear for action!"

Second Avenue was much busier, and the traffic was heavy. They were still about two-thirds of a block shy of 58th when the captain saw the target starting to negotiate the intersection ahead. She wasn't the only one to notice. A muffled groan was audible from bow to stern.

"They're going to get away," warned Roberto.

"Not if we blow our cover," said Aki. "How about it, Captain?"

She pretended to consider the situation for a moment, though of course she'd already decided what to do. The *Pizza Rat* would have had to announce its presence soon enough anyway. It was time to start the dance.

"Raise the Jolly Roger," she said, "and run out the guns. Fire a warning burst at those sluggards ahead of us. That should speed them along a bit."

The staccato rat-a-tat-tat of gunfire punctured the drone of motors and horns. Chaos reigned in the street, as the traffic struggled to process the situation. Some boats fled to port, others to starboard. Still others opened their throttles in an attempt to flee. The result was total gridlock.

"Keep firing!" said the captain. "They'll move out of our way, or we'll move them to their graves!"

The pirates plowed through the wreckage of the morning traffic, guns firing as they approached the cargo barge. It had gotten stuck in a knot of ships trying to escape the scene, all tangled into a crazy quilt of desperation at the corner of 2nd and 58th. Horns and screams sounded in a crashing wail as the *Pizza Rat* bore down.

The captain was an island of calm in the storm. She thumbed on her megaphone and said to the crew, "All hands, prepare for boarding. We'll only have about five or ten minutes before the cops show, so don't play around. Find the valuables, take them, and get the hell out. If anyone looks at you funny, kill the bastard, but be quick about it. You're on the clock."

They'd slowed down now as they approached the target and there was a hiss-whistle of grappling hooks, lashing out and binding the two ships together. There were a few crewmen scuttling around on the deck of the barge, milling about in confused circles like lemmings that couldn't find a cliff to leap off. *So few,* thought the captain. *Why not more? Where's their crew?*

The pirate crew started to jump from the *Pizza Rat* to their prey now, guns and axes held aloft, singing dreadful sea shanties as they leaped. They plunged onto the deck, swiftly clearing it of resistance. The demolition crew was preparing to blast the hatches open and roust the leftovers from their hiding places when someone started screaming. This was not an uncommon happening on board the *Pizza Rat,* and the captain didn't really pay it any mind until it dawned on her that it was the lookout in the topmast who was screaming. Then there was a smash and a bang, and all of a sudden she was lying on the deck.

The captain levered herself up with one hand to a sitting position and wiped the blood off her face. Three undercover Police Navy gunboats, which had been hidden away somewhere in the traffic, were raking the *Rat's* stern with controlled bursts of machine-gun fire. On the barge, supposedly as helpless as a beached whale, the hatches had burst open and a full platoon of action troopers had flooded forth onto the deck. The boarding party was being quickly and efficiently slaughtered.

It was a trap. The contact had sold them out. She'd been played.

She took a deep breath, opened her mouth to issue the orders that would set everything right, and then stopped short. The bridge was on fire now. Thick clouds of smoke were pouring from the engine room as the gunboats continued to tear at the *Pizza Rat,* hungry predators satiating themselves on wounded prey. The troopers were mopping things up on the barge. There was only the captain and what was left of Roberto on the quarterdeck.

It was already over. Everything ends so fast.

All of a sudden, she remembered the beginning, back when she wasn't the captain, with a brace of pistols, an eyepatch, a pigeon on her shoulder, and a ship at her command. In the beginning she had been Teresa, or Ms. Cheng, to her supervisor at the fulfillment center to which she'd been subcontracted. They all dreamed of running away and joining a pirate crew, all the young drones processing orders and taking gigs, but Teresa was the only one who'd actually done it.

She'd signed on to the *Credit-Default Swap,* a sturdy barque that sailed out of Red Hook Cove, and old Captain Queenie had taken a shine to her. She was a great grey slab of a woman with a nose that looked like it'd been carved out of granite. Teresa hadn't been with the *Swap* long before they made a big score running down a merchie crammed to the gills with product in Jamaica Bay. That night they made anchor in the bay and celebrated. It was almost dawn, when the sky shifts from black to grey, and everyone was passed out round the embers of the bonfire except for Teresa, still savoring every moment of this strange new world she had fallen in to. Then Old Queenie had appeared, as if from nowhere. She looked at Teresa and said, "This life is short and sharp and beautiful. Enjoy it while you can."

The captain pulled herself up. Everything stank of blood. She fitted two pistols carefully into her hands. The troopers were starting to come over to the *Rat* now, wiping up the last scattered pockets of resistance. She couldn't help but wondering, in a little corner of her mind, here at the end, how they'd remember the ship and her. Would they tell stories about the fights she'd won, the treasures she'd stolen, the lovers she'd had, or the escapes she'd made? Would they even sing songs? The captain thought about it, just for a moment.

Then, with a shout, she launched herself into the fray.

Tenari

BY MICHAEL MERRIAM

T HE THING THAT SURPRISED CAPTAIN Kathleen Reed the
most about commanding a pirate ship was the amount of
paperwork it involved.

She set her data pad on her grey metal desk and closed her
eyes. Pain was starting to set in behind and between her eyes,
the kind of pain that only the master of a marauding space
vessel knew. Too much paperwork, not enough plunder, that
was the problem. If only she had stayed sober, she would never
have gotten into this mess.

The ship's intercom buzzed on her desk. She barely recognized the voice over the static. She thought it might be her
executive officer, and he might have said, "Captain to the
bridge," which was reason enough for her to leave the ship's
accounts unfinished. Captain Reed stepped from her ready
room onto the bridge of her ship, *The Black Manta*.

She looked at her executive officer. Roger Baldry was
well into his seventies. Most thought him far too old for this

life—and he *did* have grandchildren back on Pegasus—but she knew Roger Baldry could out-fight, out think, and out-drink any two of her crew.

"What have we got?" she asked.

"Civilian bulk freighter," Baldry said. "An old Savros, probably a second series model three."

She raised an eyebrow. "All the way out here and all alone?"

A throat cleared. Captain Reed turned to her chief of gunnery and ex-wife. "Yes, Janet?"

"It's a trap, Captain. That's a Melpomene cruiser disguised as a freighter. There's no other explanation."

Captain Reed nodded. Janet Sobrinski thought everything was a trap, up to and including the food served in the mess. The annoying thing was, sometimes Janet was right.

"Orders, Captain?" Baldry asked.

Reed looked out her window at the freighter. "Fire a laser burst and transmit an order to cut their engines and prepare to be boarded. Tell them if they cooperate, no one gets hurt."

"Aye, ma'am," Janet said.

Captain Reed felt the low hum of her ship's cannon powering up. The lights on the bridge dimmed and the ship gave a slight shudder as the weapon discharged.

The engines on the big freighter glowed white-blue and the ship turned starboard and down.

"They're running," Baldry said.

"So it seems," Reed sighed. "Match their speed and course. Stay with them, Helm."

"Aye, ma'am," her helmsman said. "They won't get away."

Captain Reed wasn't worried about her quarry escaping. Old her ship might be, but there was no way a freighter would be able to best *The Black Manta*'s speed and maneuverability.

"XO, get the boarding party together and down to the air-lock, I'll join you after we've docked," Captain Reed ordered. "And Roger, tell everyone we're going to be extra careful over there. They might be smugglers, this far away from normal shipping lanes."

Baldry nodded. "Yes, ma'am," he said.

Reed turned to her gunner. "Target their engines. Use a missile. I want them to know we mean business."

There was a metallic clank from deep in the ship, and *The Black Manta* rocked.

"Missile away," Janet reported.

Captain Reed watched the chemically propelled weapon close rapidly on the target. She was surprised at the lack of any counter-measures by the freighter. The warhead on the missile exploded before impact, sending a shockwave into the back of the big ship. The old freighter's engines dimmed. "Helm, take us in."

"Yes, ma'am."

Captain Reed sat in her chair and grabbed the armrests. Roberts, her helmsman, made the landings hard and noisy to frighten the occupants of the ship they were raiding. She watched the freighter fill her view screen.

There was a jolt and a series of loud clangs as *The Black Manta*'s landing gear slammed into the hull of the freighter and gripped it magnetically. There was a second loud thump.

"Lock and seal," Roberts said.

Reed stood. "Good. Mr. Roberts, you have the bridge. Janet, you're with me."

Captain Reed smiled as she rode the lift to the lower decks. This was exactly what she needed to take her mind off her troubles. Two minutes later she was standing among a dozen members of her crew, her pistol drawn, preparing to board the freighter. "Open it," Reed commanded.

A pair of crew members stepped forward: Jeffers, a young blonde man carrying a small electronic device and Tilly, a brown-haired woman nearly as old as the captain, holding a large wrench. The young crewman placed his piece of equipment near the joined airlock and started punching buttons. After a minute the lights on the device and the airlock control both turned green.

"Ready, Captain."

Reed looked at Tilly and nodded. The woman jammed the wrench handle through the airlock turn-wheel and, with a grunt, gave it a tug. There was a hiss of air and she withdrew the wrench and spun the airlock mechanism. The hatch opened. The smell of stale air and food past its prime filled their noses, and no one was shooting at them. This came as a pleasant surprise to Captain Reed.

"Go!" Reed shouted.

Janet Sobrinski charged into the vessel, screaming at the top of her lungs. Behind her a dozen of the crew followed, each brandishing their weapons and yelling a battle-cry.

Baldry snorted and stepped through the airlock onto the freighter. "Janet likes doing that entirely too much."

Reed laughed. "All the youngsters do, too."

"No sound of gunfire. Maybe this will go off clean after all."

"One can hope. So, what do we have on the chief's wish list this time?" Reed asked.

Baldry pulled the pad from the pocket of his flight suit. He poked at it a couple of times, shook it, and then slapped its side. The pad whined and gurgled and made a noise like a hissing cat.

"Induction couplers and coils. Targeting sensors. Circuit boards of any kind. Soldering wire. Copper tubing, fresh water, and yeast—"

Reed smiled at the last. "So that's what he plans to do with all that wheat grain he's been hiding in the engine access tubes."

"It's supposed to be a secret." Baldry paused. "Smithwick will brew up something that won't kill the crew or make them go blind, unlike some other idiots we have aboard."

The captain's reply was cut off by screaming ahead of them. Drawing her pistol, she set off at a jog toward the voices. She turned a corner and pounded down a metal staircase toward a narrow corridor as the young blond technician started up it.

"Report!" she barked.

"Captain, there's...well, I think you'd best see for yourself, ma'am."

"What is it, Jeffers?"

"Children."

The captain looked up at the sound of her gunnery officer's voice. Janet stepped around a corner and into the corridor. A brown-haired girl, no more than ten years old, clutched Janet's hand as if it were a lifeline. The girl's face was flush from crying and she stood slightly behind Janet, barefoot and shivering in her faded floral dress.

"There's nothing but children on this ship," Janet said.

Captain Reed holstered her weapon. She squatted down and looked at the little girl and smiled. "Can you tell me where all the grown-ups are?"

"The Tenari took them."

Jeffers snorted. "There's no such thing as Tenari. The shadow-stalkers are a bedtime story spacers and colonists tell their children to scare them into line."

Kathleen Reed stood and drew her pistol in one swift motion. "No," she whispered. "The Tenari are real."

She made eye contact with Baldry, who swallowed, sweat breaking out on his bald head. If the girl was telling the truth, they were well and truly screwed.

They had met the Tenari, Reed and Baldry, and done battle with them in the one encounter between the two species decades ago. They knew the myth for its ugly reality.

In those days, the *Black Manta* was just the *Manta*, a fast attack interceptor of the Colonial Defense Forces protecting the far-flung outer colonies. Lt. Commander Baldry was the ship's chief navigator and second officer, Reed a senior lieutenant.

By the time they escaped the colony planet of Iago II with the children left behind from the Tenari raid, half the landing party was lost to the shadowy, lightning-quick creatures, and The *Manta*, her captain killed in action, had fled the sector at best speed, their hold filled with frightened, orphaned children. It was the last time humans and Tenari had interacted for nearly thirty years. Until this raid.

"How many kids are on the ship?" Reed asked.

"At least fifty."

"When they came, the adults loaded us all on the ship and we ran, but they found us," the girl whispered in a tiny voice.

"Captain?" Baldry asked.

"Round the children up and transfer them to the *Manta*. We get them safe and we run. Keep the crew in teams of three or —"

"Ma'am!" a voice cracked and hissed into her ear. "We have incoming ships! Two minutes to intercept! I don't know where they came from, captain. They must have been running silent."

"Seal the airlock and undock!" she shouted into her comm-link. Her ship was helpless attached to the hull of the freighter.

"Ma'am?" Robert's voice crackled.

"That's an order, Mister Roberts. Undock and send a distress call."

There was gunfire, a sound like ripping cloth, and a man's short scream echoed down the corridor. The lights on the freighter flickered and died as the wail of terrified children filled the air. The comm-link in her ear went silent. Baldry and Janet produced emergency lights from their belts, filling the corridor with flickering, washed out illumination.

Captain Reed gripped her weapon tighter and licked her lips. Her crew had gathered around her, a gaggle of dirty and underfed children mixed into the lot. "All right, Baldry and Jeffers come with me to the Bridge. Janet, take the others. Round up the children and get them to Engineering. Barricade yourselves in and try to get this tub working."

She turned to the woman at her side. "Tilly, you're the closest thing to an engineer we have in this party. I'm counting on you to get this ship moving. We need power and propulsion, and we need it yesterday."

Janet took a deep breath and turned to the rest of the crew. "You heard the captain! Form a circle around the young'uns and stay sharp. Who's got more lights? Get them out! Move, people!" With a sloppy salute to Reed, Sobrinski took point of her little party, and the whole mess moved out.

Reed watched them for a moment before turning to the two men with her. "Let's go."

"Captain? What's the plan?" Jeffers asked.

"Draw the enemy off. Try to gain control of the ship at the bridge," Baldry answered. He looked at the younger man. "You ready for some close-up action?"

Jeffers nodded his head yes, his face pale in Baldry's emergency light.

They moved around a gentle curve in the corridor and found the first casualty. Baldry frowned. "Levy, God help him."

"No one can help him now," Reed said. "We trust to speed. Don't worry about noise. We want to draw them away from Janet and the children."

Baldry nodded. "I'll lead."

Reed gave him the go-ahead and the older man set out down the dim-lit corridor, Reed in the middle of the formation, with Jeffers bringing up the rear.

"How far to the bridge?" Reed gasped out between breaths. She was not familiar with many of the older ships still in service.

"It should be just another twenty yards or so, then up two levels. Shouldn't—"

"Drop!" Reed yelled, raising her pistol. Baldry dived toward the deck and twisted, bringing his own weapon into play.

It shimmered from the darkness, a long, sinuous shadow, six-limbed, the barest hint of wedge-shaped head on a long neck.

Reed fired wildly as the thing moved along the ceiling. The pistol roared and echoed in the enclosed space, bullets rang off the steel walls. Jeffers ducked as Reed fired over his head. As quickly as the creature appeared, it was gone.

And so was Jeffers.

Katherine Reed stared into the darkness that had seemed to consume the man. Just like that, silent as the grave, one of her crew was no more. "Jeffers!" she called.

"He's gone," Baldry said, grabbing her arm. "We have to get to the Bridge. Captain!" Baldry barked in his best parade ground voice when she failed to move.

Reed jerked her arm out of Baldry's grip and pushed a fresh magazine into her pistol. "Lead on, Mr. Baldry." Reed kept glancing over her shoulder, looking for any sign of the Tenari. She had *remembered* how hard they were to fight, but one of her crew was snatched away while only a handful of feet from her and that brought it all back. She was so busy watching behind them, she ran into Baldry when he stopped at the ladder leading up to the bridge.

Baldry pointed his weapon upward. The light he carried shone silver against the polished steel of the tube. "They could be in there, waiting for us. It's what I'd do."

Reed peered over his shoulder up the tube. "Is there any other way up?" she asked.

"Yes, but this is the most direct route."

"Let's go."

Baldry holstered his weapon and started climbing, scrambling up the ladder with the grace of a monkey, despite his advanced years.

Reed gave the corridor a last glance and then followed until Baldry called a stop. Reed looked back down the dark tube, one hand holding a ladder rung, the other aiming her pistol into the darkness. Above her, Baldry worked the hatch, his light rod gripped between his teeth. It unlocked with a clang. Baldry pushed the hatch open and scrambled over the edge, Reed hard on his heels.

Nothing attacked them. Reed closed the hatch and spun the locking mechanism. She stayed crouching, ready to fight, and swept her gaze around the Bridge.

Several of the control consoles were lit up and the navigation station was giving off a gentle beep. "There's emergency power," Baldry said, flipping some of the switches. The lights flared to life. Reed holstered her weapon and stepped up to the helm and navigation controls.

"Can you get me internal sensors?" she asked.

"There aren't any, but I *can* get the comm working."

Reed glanced out the port window. Large pieces of wreckage floated past. "Roger?" she called.

Baldry looked up. "Not ours," he said after a few seconds.

Reed nodded. "Looks like Roberts gave them a good beating. I hope he got away."

Neither needed to say what they thought. They were trapped, surrounded, and all alone. The soft rustle of movement reached her ears. She turned and drew her pistol. To her left, Baldry had done the same. He pointed at an access panel under the damage control station. Reed nodded, reached down with one hand and snapped the panel open. Baldry reached inside and yanked out the occupant. The small, twisting mass pulled away from Baldry's grip and backed away from the two pirates. It was a young woman. Her brown hair was ratty, her clothes wrinkled and torn. Like the other children, she looked underfed.

The captain held up her hands. "Easy girl. We're not going to harm you."

The young woman gave each of the adults a quick look. "Who are you?" she demanded.

Reed decided on honesty. "Well, we're the ones who disabled your ship, truth be told. I'm Katherine Reed, captain of the *Black Manta*."

The girl frowned. "You're a pirate?"

"Yes, but we're not going to harm you. We don't rob children. You got a name?"

"Mira. Mira Morgan. You shot us."

Reed shrugged. "I didn't know it was a ship full of kids running from the Tenari."

"How did you avoid getting snatched?" Baldry asked. "You look old enough for them to take."

"I hid. They didn't find me."

Captain Katherine Reed cursed herself. She had fired on a ship loaded with defenseless children. Reed swore that if she somehow survived this encounter, she would give up pirating. If someone else wanted to take the *Manta* and continue pirating, fine. She was done.

When she and the others had stolen the *Manta* from the salvage yard, they were recently decommissioned officers of the Colonial Navy, cast aside after the war with Earth. Their beloved ship, well past its prime and no longer needed by the service, was towed to the salvage yard to await scrapping. They had gotten drunk, and Janet had suggested they steal the ship and go rogue. Reed, several cups past sober, had agreed to be their commander. They captured the ship with no resistance and robbed a remote weapons depot. From that point on, it was all raiding and running from the Colonial Navy. That had been nearly seven years ago. Now here she was, shooting at children.

"I've got Janet on the comm," Baldry said.

"Sobrinski, this is the captain. Report!"

"We've made it to the engine room. Tilly says she can get you about one-quarter speed in maybe ten minutes. Captain, I lost a couple of crew along the way. Travers and Burke are gone."

Reed grimaced. "We lost Jeffers, too. I want you to sit tight, barricade the doors, make sure there's no way into the room."

"Captain," Janet's voice sounded strained, "these creatures, how do we fight them if they get inside?"

"The best thing to do is set up a hail of bullets."

"I've got external sensors," Baldry said. "There's a ship approaching."

"Ours or theirs?" Reed asked as Mira started to shiver and whimper.

"Ours. We'll have to wait until she docks and use your radio."

Reed looked to her long-time friend and executive officer. "Recommendations?"

He frowned. "Go back to the original plan. Get the kids on the *Manta* and run like the devil is on our heels."

Reed nodded. Speed was their best bet. She looked at the girl. "That's my ship coming in. Once she lands, we're going to make a run for the airlock. I want you to stay between me and Mr. Baldry. We'll get you to safety." After Mira nodded her understanding, Reed tapped the ship's internal communication control. "Janet, are you all right down there?"

"We're still here, Captain."

"Roberts is bringing the *Manta*. As soon as he lands, I'll give you the all-clear. I want you to move your group to the airlock."

Janet chuckled. "And we just got settled in."

The hull reverberated as the ships docked. Reed opened a channel on her personal radio. "Reed to *Manta*. Report, Mr. Roberts."

"Two hostile ships attacked. We destroyed one. The other fled, trailing atmosphere. We've sent a distress call, but long-range sensors show three more hostiles approaching, twenty minutes out." He paused. "We took some damage, Captain. I don't know how much fight the ship has left in her."

"Very well, Mr. Roberts. Sit tight and wait for orders." She turned to Baldry. The XO was frowning.

"We might be able to evacuate everyone in that time if everything goes smoothly," he said.

Reed nodded in agreement. It was time to modify the plan. "Janet, how close were you to having the engines running?"

"Tilly says any second."

"Get them running and then head for the airlock on the run."

"Captain," another female voice broke in, "I'll need to baby-sit the engines if you want them to keep running."

Reed growled. "How long will they work on their own?"

"A couple of minutes at most," Tilly said.

"What are you thinking?" Baldry asked.

Reed settled into the helm chair. She touched the controls on her headset. "If we start moving away, even at a limp, we could buy ourselves a little extra time. Mr. Roberts, give me a heading away from our friends."

"Make your heading two-one-eight mark six, ma'am."

Reed punched in the course and gave the old freighter all the power it had. They started a slow turn and acceleration.

"Mr. Baldry, take our friend and meet Janet at the airlock."

"No, ma'am," Baldry replied, stepping up to her.

"Roger, I don't have time to argue this."

"Captain, the crew needs you to organize the evacuation." He smiled at her. "They need their captain if they're going to get out of this alive."

"Roger, whoever stays here—"

"Probably doesn't make it. But I'll seal the bridge, and once you've got most of the crew and the kids on the *Manta* or the engines stop working, I'll try to join you. Those Tenari ships are coming, and the Manta needs her captain. "

Reed turned on the comm. "Janet, tell Tilly it's her choice if she wants to volunteer to stay, but the rest of you need to move out."

Reed relinquished her chair to Baldry and grabbed Mira by the upper arm. "Come on."

She stepped to the floor hatch, spun the lock, lifted the hatch, and pointed her pistol through the opening. Nothing swarmed up from the darkness to attack them.

She looked back to Baldry. "Roger —"

"Get 'em to safety, Captain. I'll join you soon enough."

Reed nodded. "Good luck," she said and started down the ladder. She heard Mira climbing down above her and the sound of the hatch closing. They both hit the bottom deck within seconds. Reed looked at the ragged teenaged girl.

"If you *think* you see anything, scream and point."

The girl nodded, her eyes wide with fright.

As they approached the soft curve where Reed's party was attacked previously, they heard distant sounds of shouts and weapons firing. Reed quickened her pace, dragging Mira along toward the apex of the curve.

It rushed toward them. The Tenari's narrow, furred face on its wedge-shaped head looked surprised in the dim light. There was a dark fluid running down the front of its clothing and into the fur along its slim frame. It bunched its four back legs and leapt at her, extending the dagger-like blades it wore on its hands.

Reed stepped into the middle of the corridor and fired, getting off three rounds before it slammed into her body. She jabbed her weapon into its belly and fired again, even as it stabbed her in the shoulder. Reed pulled the trigger on her pistol again as the Tenari withdrew its blades and slashed her across the face, opening a cut on her cheek. The creature pulled itself up, trying to disengage. She grabbed its clothing, holding it fast and fired into its chest again. The alien gave a low whine, and slumped back down onto her, dead.

Reed pushed the body off and rose to her knees, bleeding from her shoulder and face. She stumbled forward, moving to where she hoped her gunnery officer was evacuating the rest of the crew off the ship. A light touch on her arm made her jerk away and raise her pistol.

Mira jumped back, shrieking.

"Sorry," Reed gasped, leaning against the wall. She felt the young woman move toward her, settling under Reed's good arm and taking her weight.

"Come on," Mira said. "I'll help you."

The two limped down the corridor to the airlock. They found most of the Manta's crew forming a defensive perimeter around the airlock as Janet and the others ushered the last of the children on to the pirate vessel.

"Janet?" Reed called out.

"Captain, we just need another couple of minutes."

Reed nodded. "Finish up here. Baldry's still on the bridge trying to buy us some time."

Janet nodded. "Tilly's down in the engine room as well."

"Captain," a younger voice said. She turned to face her helmsman, who was standing guard in the airlock. "Four ships are on intercept. The one that got away is coming back with friends, ma'am"

"How long until they get here, Mr. Roberts?"

"Five minutes at most."

The freighter shuddered, and a low hum started up. Reed looked around the area for a comm panel.

"Help me over there," she said to Mira, who was still supporting her weight. The two women hobbled to the unit. Reed toggled the switch. "Roger?"

"We're accelerating," came the static-riddled reply. "I can get us a couple more minutes at this pace."

"Roger, you and Tilly need to come here. We're out of time!"

"Yes, ma'am."

"You too, Captain," Janet said. "I'll take care of this."

Reed nodded in agreement. She was starting to get dizzy from blood loss, and she would not be doing her crew any good if she was passed out on the deck. She let Mira help her all the way to the bridge. Reed settled in the command chair. "Mr. Grisham," she said.

The man turned in the helmsman chair. "Hostiles will be here in two minutes. Gunny Sobrinski reports that all the children and crew are aboard except Commander Baldry and Ms. Horn.

Captain Reed sighed. She couldn't wait any longer for Baldry or Tilly. They were on their own. "Mr. Grisham, secure the airlock and begin the launch sequence."

"Yes, ma'am." She felt someone press a bandage onto her shoulder. Reed looked to find Mira, who had pulled the first-aid kit from the wall.

Janet Sobrinski dashed onto the bridge, followed closely by Roberts and the rest of her bridge crew. Roberts slipped into the chair Grisham vacated. "The kids are in the hold," Janet said. "The Tenari are thirty-seconds out."

"Ready for launch," Roberts reported.

"Get us free, Mr. Roberts." Reed held the arms of her chair as her ship shuddered and powered up, pulling away from the freighter. "Janet?" Reed asked.

"Laser cannon powered and ready. Missiles loaded."

"Mr. Roberts, turn us toward the enemy. Janet, fire a full spread. Given 'em a punch in the nose." A series of deep thuds sounded in the ship, and four missiles raced toward the Tenari. Reed decided it would be enough to cover their retreat. "Turnabout. Best speed toward the nearest friendly warship or outpost." *I'm sorry*, she thought to her crew still on the freighter.

The Manta shuddered and rocked, its lights dimming. Sparks flew from several control stations, and anyone not sitting or holding tight to something was thrown to the floor.

"We're hit!" Janet cried over the alarms. "Near the engines."

"Damage?" Reed called.

"We're losing power."

"Captain!" Roberts said.

Reed looked out the window to see three of the large, predatory-looking ships, each the size of a cruiser, closing on her damaged craft.

"Missiles!"

"Loaders are jammed," Janet replied.

"Laser cannon, Mr. Roberts."

The cannon fired. Its deep hum and discharge left the Bridge nearly dark. The beam caught one of the hostiles, slicing it in half. Debris tumbled through space. The remaining Tenari ships fired their slow moving-missiles at the wounded *Manta*.

"Evasive maneuvers! Engage counter-measures!" Reed felt her ship turn as she heard the soft clang of the chaff-launcher engaging. One of the missiles exploded harmlessly to starboard. The other passed over the *Manta* and detonated, setting off a fresh round of fires and alarms. The ship decelerated and the hum in the deck plating stopped. The *Black Manta* was dead in space. Reed looked out the window.

The two remaining Tenari vessels had formed up together and were closing on them.

"Are they going to board us?" Roberts asked from his useless helm controls.

Reed sighed and blinked back nausea and light-headedness. "No. I think they just want to be sure of their shot."

Reed watched quietly as the two alien vessels closed the distance. "Janet, transmit the log to the nearest colonial base." She paused, took a deep breath. "It's been a pleasure to serve with all of you," she said to her bridge crew.

"Likewise, ma'am," Janet said. Her weapons station was dark and smoldering. "I think the *Manta* gave a good accounting of herself today."

Reed nodded agreement. "Our little attack ship took out most of what looks like a cruiser battle group. The *Manta* did good."

"Look!" Mira yelled, pointing at the edge of the window.

The Savros freighter, her fusion engines burning bright white in the darkness of space, slammed in the formation of smaller Tenari ships. The first of the crafts disintegrated on impact. The second Tenari vessel started to turn away, but the lumbering freighter's crumpled bow caught it as well, sending it spinning as all three ships broke apart in space from the force of the collision.

"Goddamn it, Baldry," Reed whispered, trying not to cry. "You crazy old bastard." Reed slumped back in her chair and closed her eyes. Her adrenaline crashed, and the blood loss finally overwhelmed her. She blacked out.

REED LOOKED AROUND THE BRIDGE of her new ship. She ran her hand over the control console. It was clean and shiny.

"Admiral Weston on the comm!" Janet Sobrinski called out.

Reed turned and looked at her view screen. An older woman looked back at her, seated from the office on the space station they had just left.

"Ready to go into harm's way, Captain?" she asked.

Reed nodded. She liked the fleet admiral, had served with her during her first tour out of the academy, when Weston was the executive officer on the battle-cruiser *Nairobi*. "Yes, ma'am. The *Black Manta* and crew are ready for action." Reed paused for a moment before giving the flag officer a salute. "Admiral, I just wanted to thank you again for advocating for my crew. Without your voice in the High Command, we'd all be breaking rocks on Freyr or something."

Admiral Weston snorted. "You're the only commanding officer to ever fight the Tenari twice and live. We need you in the captain's chair of a warship, Kathleen, not rotting in a prison cell. A blanket pardon for you and your crew in exchange for accepting a letter of marque to raid Tenari commerce and scout their border was a good comprise for everyone." The admiral frowned at her. "Find out what you can as quickly as possible, Captain. We need facts about the Tenari, not space-tales. Good-luck to all of you."

Reed nodded. "Yes, ma'am," she said. The admiral nodded and signed off.

Captain Kathleen Reed settled in her comfortable new command chair and punched up her letter of marque on the data pad resting on the chair's arm. The Colonial Assembly didn't want to send a Navy task force yet, wasn't ready to commit to war with an enemy they knew almost nothing about. The Colonial Navy, however, was happy to send a flagless freelance-warship to the border, armed to the teeth.

"Mr. Roberts?" she said.

"We have permission to depart the system," her executive officer reported.

"Ms. Sobrinski?"

"The crew is at action stations."

Reed smiled. It was time to pay back the Tenari for Baldry, Tilly, the rest of the Manta's lost crew from both battles, and the colonists they had taken. "Very well. Mr. Grisham, take us to Tenari space."

"Aye, Captain."

The *Black Manta* leapt forward.

Search for the Heart of the Ocean

BY A.J. FITZWATER

THE NORTH WIND STOOD TO attention as the IRATE vessel *Impolite Fortune* sailed past the headlands towards adventure.

Captain Cinrak the Dapper, capybara pirate extraordinaire, breathed it all in, her mind's eye turning the scene into words she could slip to a bard for the perfect opening of an epic that should — would — be written if — when — Cinrak returned with her jewelled prize.

The grinning waves. The beaming sun. The figurehead meant to represent and yet not represent Rat Queen Orvillia straining to be off, reaching to embrace the open ocean. There, atop Shag Rock, chiffon streaming, Locqualchi, First Marmot Diva of the Theatre Ratoyal, shrilling out the 'Ode to the Ocean'. Before, on the docks, Locqualchi telling Cinrak she better come home alive or so help her, she'd kill Cinrak herself. And the

Impolite Fortune herself, gleaming hard as the jewel she was setting out to find.

Cinrak blew her marmot lover a final farewell kiss then saluted claw to brow for the North Wind's spectacular contribution to the day.

"Everything ship shape and ready to be fancy free, ser," said First Mate Riddle, a patchwork rat, snapping a salute paw to chest.

"Open her up, Riddle m'lass."

"Yes, ser!" Riddle slipped her eyepatch to the other side and glared with an empty eye socket down the deck. "You heard the cap! Let 'er fly!"

The excited crew sang open the snapping sails which whispered taunts to the North Wind. As the breeze stiffened, Cinrak clutched her portfolio tighter. The North Wind could get frisky when excited. It would do her no good to lose years of hard-won secrets to the greedy water.

One pouting snout stood out. Riddle twitched her head towards a young grey chinchilla skulking near the down ladder. Cinrak sighed, straightened her purple paisley bow tie, and pulled at the hem of her green silk waistcoat.

Time to deal with the new cabin girl.

"With me," Cinrak growled in passing.

The girl put her head down and followed. Cinrak could almost take it as an insult, but she remembered well her own first day on an IRATE vessel.

Cabin door clicked shut. Desk drawer lock clicked, hiding the portfolio. The pirates of IRATE loved each other, but at the end of the day they were still pirates.

Cinrak drummed forepaw claws on the immaculate desk top.

"Competition be fierce for the apprenticeship you be doin'," she said. "Ev'ry cabin girl from the *Impolite Fortune* have become respected commanders in the IRATE fleet. Ye balance looks good, m'girl, but your mind be elsewhere."

The little chinchilla folded her arms. She was of age to serve with IRATE, but her thin arms, delicate paws, and drooping whiskers needed plenty of discipline to deal with the heavy work and merciless weather.

"Yes, ser," the grey chinchilla sighed.

"Minerva, is it?" The girl looked away, clenched her jaw. Cinrak thought of how the youngling had winced when her mother had smothered her in farewell kisses. "I promised yer m'arm you'd be in fine and safe hands. An' that comes with the IRATE lifetime guarantee. But you gotta work with me here, Minerva. If it be a boy or a girl or a school or a desert caravan that be callin' yer name, ye betta be tellin' me now. Us IRATE pirates not be takin' disrespect."

The restless and heavy silence grew, getting itchy around the edges.

Deepest Depths, thought Cinrak. *Maybe it would be best if I dropped this little one off at the next port.*

The chinchilla burst out, "It's not that I don't want to be here, ser!" then she looked everywhere for her escaping words.

Cinrak sat back. "Go awn." She gestured towards a stool. The girl slumped down with a sigh.

"I do respect the Independent Rodent Aquatic Trade Entente, oh, I do, ser!" The chinchilla found her animation, black eyes gleaming. "I've wanted nothing more to be a pirate and serve on the *Impolite Fortune* and meet the people of the deep since I was a wee one, but I..."

Something familiar in the set of her whiskers, something deep in her dark eyes, made Cinrak decide. "I be listenin'. That's what a good captain does."

The chinchilla lifted her chin, flicked her whiskers once. "I am not who my m'arm told you I am. My name is Benj, and I am a boy. A cabin *boy*. If that means I must be displaced from serving on the *Impolite Fortune*, so be it. But please, ser. I do so want to meet the mers. And there's something about the ocean, something out there, I can...smell it. If you must, set me ashore again, just don't send me back home."

Cinrak blinked once. Oh. A lost boy. This was *much* easier to deal with than a homesick apprentice.

"Deepest Depths, Benj. On Orvillia's Crown, I swear yer most welcome here. The *Impolite Fortune* welcomes crew of many genders an' fluidities. Ye be need guidance of that nature, talk to Cookie. Or Second Mate Zupe, they like to be a boy sometimes."

A sigh like a great weight left Benj, and on the return breath, his chest swelled up. His smile finally crept in, if a little late to the party. "And you?" he said in a tiny voice.

Cinrak straightened her bow tie. "I be happy to teach you a thing or two 'bout dapperness. It in me name."

"Ser, thank you, ser."

"Now. Go find First Mate Riddle. She be showing ye how to make bunk. Then see what supplies Cookie needs run fer dinner."

"Yes, *ser!*" Benj's salute smacked whip smart against the breast of his leather jerkin.

"And Benj?"

"Yes, ser?"

"We be makin' a pirate of ye before this mission is over, and ye'll earn your name addendum."

"Yes, ser!"

The cabin door slammed, and the room winced.

Cinrak chuckled and retrieved the secret portfolio. Maybe she'd become more ship m'arm than captain to the boy, but thems the wave breaks.

THE SHADOW TRAILING THE *IMPOLITE Fortune* made Cinrak nervous, and it took a lot to make her nervous.

And this shadow was a lot: too succinct to be cloud reflection, too precise to be a fish roil. Too early for whales this far south, and too far off share for a bank of inktons.

Cinrak didn't believe in monsters, except when she did.

Three days past Merholm, the shadow dissipated when Cinrak gathered the crew on deck for an evening feast. Everyone came dressed in their best frills and frocks, silks and stockings. Deck feasts were a prelude to some important announcement, and the *Impolite Fortune's* turn of direction had had the crew muttering for days. They heartily tucked into the platters of chilli or lemon doused fish, paella, cornbread, and orange grain pancakes. Cinrak decided to wait until they were well into their cups of cinnamon rum and honey whiskey before making her case.

As she practised her speech in her head, her gaze fell on Benj; he was a good, fluffy boy, faithful to mer-hair anemone tea. Cinrak often found him on deck late at night staring moonily down at the swift-still water, a cup of the sweet red beverage in his hand. It even sounded like he was whispering to the Paper Moon when it peeped shyly from behind clouds.

He wouldn't be the first apprentice to have a sweet love affair with the delicate celestial.

Cinrak banged her cup for attention.

"As ye can see by how well the North Wind blows, our journey didna end with the entente renegotiations at Merholm. I hope ye all enjoyed yer time partakin' of the archipelago's wonders and getting acquainted with our mer friends."

While the crew hollered and whistled, Benj blushed. The charming mers had fascinated him, and he'd spent hours in their library stuffing sea lore into his small big brain.

"But that be only the first phase of our mission," Cinrak continued. "I be sorry to inform ye, we be not on a mappin' and patrol of the southern coasts."

"Coast five days back-thataway," someone yelled, and others laughed.

Cinrak took a deep breath. "I be blunt. The mission we undertake is a folly of my ego. The journey be difficult, treacherous, and one into the unknown. One which, in the end, will restore Queen Orvillia's crown to it's rightful place of beauty an' style 'mongst all the great jewels in the land. She be deservin' only the best since I broke it asunder. Therefore, I go in search of...the Heart of the Ocean."

Excitement rippled through the crew. Not a strand of fur moved on Benj's body.

"I be not expectin' any o' this crew to fall in line with my wild schemes. As always, once ye assessed the rules of engagement, ye be more than welcome to dissent. There still be opportunity to make a swing towards the Gargan Peninsular, and I'll let any crew member off at Gigantia and collect them on the way back."

"That's if we come back," Riddle joked.

Cinrak let the feels have the run of the place for a moment: laughter, drinks swilling, quills and teeth and claws clicking, voices chittering.

"But ser," broke in one of the deckhands. "The greatest jewel in the world is said to be guarded by the fearsome kraken, as tall as the queen's castle with tentacles longer than ten vessels nose to tail!"

"Which is why, m'dear, we not be partakin' of the flesh of the inkton," Cinrak explained. "Kraken's cousins have proven intelligent and good friends of Rodentkind. Friends not be eatin' friends. The mer archives tell us, yes, once beasts of Kraken's size did exist. It be not our place to tempt The Depth's wrath."

The entire crew undulated two digits in a V shape of warding. Except Benj whose black eyes widened, and he sat straight up. Cinrak hoped superstition would come to him soon. All good pirates needed it.

Cinrak continued. "After years of research an' consultation with mer scholars, a bit of falling on the good side of Our Chaotic Lady, an' a touch of ego, I come to the conclusion we must go to The Edge of the World."

This knocked the air out of the crew and the North Wind. The South Wind kept its own council, and a good right it had to do so. The oceans did not give up their secrets lightly.

"The edge of the world, ser?" someone yelled. "Everyone knows the world is round. Just look at them horizon!"

Someone else shushed them with 'read a book of human-tales'.

Cinrak stilled the ruddle by holding up a forepaw. Benj's whiskers quivered, emphasizing his stillness.

"The Edge of the World not be a myth or a human-tale. It be a riddle which points towards a great force of the natural world."

Now Benj's eyes were bulging out of his skull. Disappointment chipped out a little of Cinrak's pride. She had hoped the cabin boy would be tougher than this.

Someone tapped Cinrak on the shoulder.

No. All crew were at the table.

Some*thing* tapped Cinrak on the shoulder.

A shiny wet tentacle slid into Cinrak's vision. And kept going. And going. Undulating up onto the *Impolite Fortune's* deck.

As the quivering Paper Moon pulled a cloud across its face and the rising Moth Moon peeked over the horizon, the crew dissolved into screaming, flailing chaos.

THE KRAKEN HAD A LONG, globular, and moist name.

"But she says you can call her Agnes until you get the hang of the rest of it," Benj said, stroking a tentacle tip. The tentacle wriggled gently. A single castle-window sized eye peeped over the rail. The kraken's orange spade-shaped head went up and up and up, slicing against the blue sky.

Cinrak closed her eyes for a moment, pretending she was below decks with the rest of the crew . If one couldn't see the beast maybe it would stop existing. It hit Cinrak: Benj hadn't been mooning at the water all those nights, he'd been talking to the kraken! Cinrak strained her ears in Agnes' direction, but all she could detect was a hum like the wind strumming its favourite tune in the riggings.

"What be—" she attempted and failed the full name. "—er, Agnes wanting?"

"She's excited that someone came looking for her," he said. "She wants to help you find the Heart of the Ocean. She's lost it too. She's lonely, and she says it's nice to have friends round these parts."

This was all a bit too much. The tiny cabin boy translating for a monster who would barely make a morsel of him. The *Impolite Fortune* tracked all this time. A lonely monster of the Depths becalming the ship with a hug. Her reputation wouldn't live it down if word spread that Cinrak The Dapper had almost wet her second-best pair of pants.

"Agnes wants to know why you're looking for the Heart?" Benj said, quiet, like he was apologizing. Agnes blinked affirmation, her eyelid nicking a few splinters off the railing.

Cinrak straightened her vest and bow tie. Despite the big fright, she was proud of Benj. She didn't know well how ocean or star magic worked, but perhaps there was a bit of the chinchilla in the kraken, or the other way around. Honesty, a pirate's mainstay, was the best solution.

"As I be responsible for breakin' apart Queen Orvillia's crown to set free the Star of a Thousand Years, I bear responsibility for replacin' the crown jewel with something equally, if not more, magnificent. The fabled Heart of the Ocean be the perfect solution. A prize worthy of Cinrak the Dapper and the Queen's legend. But if Agnes is the Heart's guardian, I be more'n willing to negotiate custody of the jewel."

A few more of the crew had crept above deck, rodent faces vacillating between dread and wonder.

Large tentacles wiggled, setting the startled ocean a-slosh. Benj chewed his whiskers, absent-mindedly stroking the tentacle. "Agnes says there may be the possibility of a deal."

Cinrak beamed.

"There's a slight problem. The riddle of the Edge of the World. It's not much of a riddle at all."

The crew held their breath.

"It is, in fact, a gigantic whirlpool."

The crew groaned.

Fear swirled in Cinrak's broad chest, but she reminded herself a good captain only showed enough fear to display how they'd overcome it.

"As I suspected." Cinrak took a deep breath. "Ay, if Agnes be so kind as to cease cuddlin' the ship, we may get underway to assess the problem."

The tentacles shivered in apology and released the ship. The riggings sighed, the Paper Moon peeked out from behind a cloud, and the North Wind whistled softly in relief.

"Agnes says you will have never seen a drain such as this one. Those of her ilk who weren't killed by it have simply...left. She is the last." Both kraken and chinchilla gestured towards the excitable stars popping into existence. "There is an additional problem. The drain is encapsulated by The Bruise."

The crew and ship groaned louder.

"Ahh, the riddle wrapped in an enigma! So that be what that great storm hides. Ay, Captain Cinrak the Dapper never been one to swim away from a challenge. Nor is she one to leave a friend in distress. Whether they be friend on the ocean or in the ocean, we can always come to an amicable agreement."

Life fell into a strange routine as the great kraken joined the retinue. Thrill-fear lifted Cinrak's fur every time she caught a glimpse of the fabled beast leading them on. Agnes knew nothing of borders — the ocean was Everything and Everywhere for her. She turned them due south towards where even the heartiest of maties feared to sail.

Though the North Wind quivered at the peril it pushed them towards, the beneficial weather took them beyond Here Be Dragons. Cinrak would not allow her crew to be lulled into a false sense of complacency. They did storm drills every day.

Eventually, Agnes won over the timid crew members. By day, she would intimidate balls of fish towards the ship, so they never went hungry. At night, she provided shadow puppetry with the assistance of the exuberant Moth Moon. Benj watched on, proud as a parent, rapping out a beat on a drum. He didn't seem in thrall to the kraken. In fact, beneath the salt-steel that was becoming his pirate way, there remained a gentleness Cinrak couldn't help but admire.

Try as she might with all the languages of the ocean and sky, Cinrak couldn't taste the magic of this ocean creature. When Benj was otherwise occupied, Agnes demonstrated to Cinrak her easy power, chasing sea things with big teeth. Once, Cinrak watched fascinated and horrified as Agnes casually cronched a shark, tearing them apart with terrifying efficiency and feeding the struggling beast into the concentric carnassial circles.

THE BRUISE.

Cinrak smelled the broken, heavy air through darkness even before the oily storm wall slid its silky fingers over the horizon. The rest of the crew woke to the odious clouds to go with their hardtack and tea.

Even Agnes hesitated, swimming agitated circles around the ship. The crew tried to ignore it; she had become something of a mascot and even the timidest crew member had respect for her oceanly talents.

Cinrak ordered the anchor dropped and started her calculations all over again. The storm was bigger than rumour had suggested. The roar of the wind and drain was audible even at a safe distance and above the determined heave-ho songs of the crew.

"What says Agnes?"

Cinrak found Benj in his usual spot by the figurehead. He'd knotted a green scarf to represent his growing rope skills and respect for his captain's Dapperly Arts. Along with his new muscles and groomed fur, she couldn't help but be proud of her protégé.

Benj's smile gave no assurance. "Brave is scribed in her blood, ser, but I can tell she is a little...concerned. She says the whirlpool has grown since she was here last."

Cinrak repressed a sigh. She had hoped out of all involved, Agnes would have some idea of how to penetrate the boiling purple and blue clouds stabbed with eager lightning. It was not like Cinrak the Dapper to back out of a challenge, but she had the whole crew to think about. Best take a hit to her reputation than a hit to the *Impolite Fortune*.

A cough.

"Sorry to barge in, ser, but you'll be wanting to see this," Riddle said, unpatched eye hot with hope.

The crew parted to let the captain and cabin boy through. The sun beamed a spotlight on Colombia, a mer, sitting precariously on the starboard railing combing out his waist length auburn beard and hair.

"Captain Cinrak!" The mer air-kissed Cinrak's cheeks. "So lovely to see you!"

"Cut the starfish poop," Cinrak grinned. "Yer a long way from home."

"Our scouts informed us you'd made it this far *and* that you had a friend in tow." Colombia winked at Agnes who blinked back, her eyelid sending a curious dolphin scurrying.

"You knew a kraken still swims." Cinrak folded her arms.

Colombia took no offence. "Of course. We're all friends in the waters. Honestly, we didn't think dear—" Colombia pronounced Agnes' full name with ease, "was associated with any of this." He gestured towards the boiling storm. Agnes waved back.

"So why she be attachin' herself to the *Impolite Fortune's* fortune?" Cinrak asked. "What be so different about our attempt to sail over the Edge of the World and retrieve the Heart of the Ocean compared to all other ships that failed?"

Colombia leaned forward and looked up through his long lowered lashes. "Magic."

Cinrak threw up her forepaws. "Deepest Depths!"

"It's true." Colombia combed out a hair knot. "She can taste it on the ship."

In her head, Cinrak catalogued the small charms she kept in her cabin and the abilities of her crew. Some of them, like her, had small skills in weather work, but nothing that could soothe such a storm and certainly nothing on a wizard's level. That meant...

"Benj?"

"Me?" The cabin boy trembled.

"So it's you who can talk to her." Colombia's sharp grin turned on Benj. "Congratulations. One in a century."

"M... Me?"

Colombia placed a meaty, hairy hand on Benj's shoulder. "You're made of stars, m'boy. Tell me what you can taste on the air."

The crew stepped back as Benj closed his eyes and took a deep breath.

"Emptiness," Benj intoned, his voice taking on a deeper timbre. With the health benefits of Night Rose tea, Cinrak knew he'd come through puberty fine. "A black hole that goes deep into the...no, not the ocean or the earth. Into a void, a nothing. There's water there, but it's not water." His furry forehead screwed up at the contradiction. "I can feel...far away, a heart beating."

Cinrak's fists and jaw ached. The jewel, pulsing under some beautiful light! So close! But so far!

"Good, good," Colombia soothed, iridescent fin tips twitching with delight. "What else? Spread your senses wider. Soar up, like the star you are."

"The water we can see, is...not as smooth as we're lead to believe. It...runs rapidly across ragged rocks. Huh." Benj opened his eyes. "So that's what those old maps in the library meant."

"Explain," Riddle asked.

Thinking of her secret maps, Cinrak nodded as Benj spoke.

"Millenia ago, there used to be a series of merholm scattered far out into ocean," Colombia explained, serious as a swordfish. "But the ocean never sleeps. Volcanos, glaciers, heat, cold. Those islands are now underwater. What we know as coastline today has been changing and will keep changing, so slow you can't see it. But sometimes, like the Edge and Bruise here, very fast."

"For ev'ry magical action, there be a natural reaction," Cinrak said.

"Correct," Colombia said. "Just like you can't take a star from the sky and put it into the queen's crown without the stars being upset."

Cinrak grimaced.

"Oh, my dear heart!" Benj gasped, leaning far out over the railing. "Why didn't you tell me?"

Agnes dipped low in the water, the tip of her remorseful eye peeking out.

"Tell ye what?" Cinrak asked, heart already aching.

"Magic made this mess! Agnes worked with her beloved, Xolotli, to protect the Heart," Benj said. "But even the best and longest of loves can go through rocky times, and they had a, uh, disagreement about how best to protect the great Heart from pirates. In a fit of anger, Xolotli banished Agnes from their ocean home. Xolotli's agitation was so great the Edge formed above them, preventing Agnes from returning once her temper had cooled."

The crew either snuffled or attempted to look staunch. It was a love story for the ages.

Colombia chimed in. "None of the other kraken-kind could help Agnes because the Edge was too strong. They all eventually departed the ocean for the stars, perhaps attempting to find a solution."

"She's been swimming the oceans for hundreds of years, alone?" Riddle wailed into her kerchief. "That's terrible! Cap'n, we have to do something!"

Cinrak chewed her whiskers. "Even with me best calculations one ship couldna possibly hope to defeat the storm, let alone survive the drop into the drain."

"The rocks!" Benj gasped, his eyes widening. He turned to Colombia. "You said the old merholm were submerged, but some of them would have had hills and mountains that would be near the surface now, yes?"

"We've swum around a few and collected artifacts and samples," Colombia confirmed. "But the closer to the drain, the more treacherous it becomes. Even a group of strong mer linked together can't battle such a current."

Benj whirled to his captain. "You still have your famous merhair rope that helped you win the race of the stars, Cap'n?"

"Of course." She brought it out as her best boast on rare occasions. "But it be only a ten span at best."

"But it is a link to the stars."

Colombia nodded. "We come from the same material as kraken and stars."

"Air, ocean, made of the same stuff, just different states." Benj's eyes shone like the stars. "With Agnes' strength, the merhair rope, the crew's skill, and a series of underwater tethers, we might be able to make our way into the drain. Together."

"I'm going to sing up a few extra nearby scouts," Colombia said as he plopped down into the water. Agnes patted him as gently as she could on the head. "A little extra muscle wouldn't go amiss. If that is all right by you, Cap'n."

All eyes turned to Cinrak. She shrugged and grinned. "Do'na look at me. Seems Benj and Agnes have this well in hand."

Benj bounced in place and clapped his forepaws. "Let's get Agnes back together with her beloved!"

The crew cheered. Agnes waved a half-dozen tentacles.

Cinrak rubbed her forepaws in anticipation. The most precious jewel in the world was so close, she could almost taste its glittering candy facets and the eternal gratitude of her queen.

CINRAK DIDN'T KNOW WHERE THE wind's scream ended and the crew's cries and ship's tortured creaks began.

The first tetherings and tentative excursion into the outer rim of the storm had gone well. Both anchors were linked to merhair, which was linked to Agnes, who held fast to underwater rocky pillars and swung them further inwards. But now the crew and mer scouts were tiring. There wasn't any rain, but the crashing waves kept everyone soaked.

Strapped to the figurehead, Benj yelled instructions as Agnes inched along the submerged rocks. Having an enormous eye upon the precariously close ocean floor made things a little easier, though every channel was a close call.

A jerk, a groan of anchors, and a sudden flash-clamber of iridescent scales as the merfolk tumbled on board.

"What gives!" yelled Cinrak through her boomer from her place in the crow's nest.

"Current is too much!" Colombia yelled back. "It's all Agnes from here on in!"

"She be all right?" Cinrak called to Benj.

Benj lifted his own boomer. "She's hating it! And loving it! This is the furthest she's ever made it into the drain!"

"Tell her she can stop at any point. Her safety comes first!"

Benj saluted understanding.

The *Impolite Fortune* shuddered forward through another narrow channel.

A hundred nights fell all at once over the ship, and thunder pressed its invisible hands against Cinrak's ears. But this thunder kept going and going and *going*. The dark sound laughing them into the storm's maw was no beast; here was the gigantic drain, an intertwining of magic and nature writ large.

The world seemed to simply end. The clockwise-rushing water fell into a darkness so complete the night sky would die from envy. It swallowed everything: sucking the soul out of what remained of light, flinging the shrieks of the crew down and stomping on them, tearing breath from chest leaving only iron-salt fear on the back of the throat.

This was it. The Edge of the World, leading to the void. A nothing. A thoroughfare to death.

But there. A flicker. A tiny sliver of silver promise. A throb. Another. A flutter of light to hold hope close.

Way down below. The Heart of the Ocean. Beating.

The crew lashed the mers to themselves and tied all to the inner cargo rings. Cinrak had never known rodents and mer to work in such harmony before. It was a beautiful sight amongst chaos.

"That's it," Benj boomed. "That's as far as Agnes can go! It's all down from here!"

"Deepest Depths, deliver us safely to your soft shores," Cinrak invoked through gritted teeth.

The timbers of the *Impolite Fortune* creaked such a protest, tears sprang to Cinrak's eyes. Was this it for her dearest ship? Was the best beavercraft in the business falling apart?

And what of poor Agnes? Was she tearing apart down there too?

Aaaaaghhhrooooohhhhhhhh.

A great groan rose, diamond hard pressure against Cinrak's senses.

The Depths...were answering her plea?

Aaaaarrrrrroooooooohnnnnggggh.

No, there was Agnes, her great eye gleaming as bright as a constellation of starfish on summer solstice.

"Strap yourself down!" Benj shouted. "She's gonna let go the tether!"

Aaoooooogggggahhhh.

"What?!"

"We're going in!"

Cinrak's paws burned as she slid down the guide rope. She whisked the cabin boy the last few meters and tied them both to the scurry of crew.

Ooooooooooaaaaarrrhh.

"What is that?!" Cinrak yelled.

"The call of the ocean!" Colombia cried, ecstatic.

"Deepest Depths, that's something *living*!"

"The ocean lives!"

"It's Agnes' beloved!" Benj yelled.

"They'd be too far down..."

"Here we go!"

The world tilted. The boat and crew screamed in unison.

Falling forever, into a silence so profound it could write its own epic.

Tiny glimmers of light rose from the depths of the void, like sunrise on the edge of whiskers.

A coruscation of green-purple-blue from cephalopod skin, tentacles curving over every possible edge of the ship. Agnes cuddled the *Impolite Fortune* as, impossibly, the kraken and ship floated in mid-air.

Cinrak blinked at the dancing sparkles. They reminded her of racing stars running backwards. The air tasted of petrichor and an indefinable sweet tang, like oranges, sword blades, and kisses all mushed into one.

"Whu...?" she blundered.

Some of the crew blubbered. A few silently wept. Most gazed in awe.

Oooooohhhhaaarrrhhhoooo crooned the moan. It came from all around now.

The sparkles moved upwards faster and it took Cinrak a moment to realize the stars weren't moving, the *ship* was. Going down down *down*. What sort of cushion would Agnes make for the biggest frigate of the IRATE fleet? Probably a very squishy one. They'd never get the smell of squid out of the drapes.

She was dead, Cinrak decided. Definitely dead. And Locqualchi would have her guts for garters.

A gentle bump put paid to Cinrak's cleaning nightmare. The *Impolite Fortune* protested audibly as Agnes withdrew her embrace, but the kraken took not one splinter with her. The ship settled into its new medium with a sigh of contentment.

When Cinrak dared a look, the light from the uncountable stars showed a medium rippling like water, giving way like cool molten glass under her touch, but not wet. The ocean-that-was-not-ocean Benj had burbled about.

"Deepest Depths," Cinrak breathed.

"Indeed," Colombia sighed, hands clasped in front of his hairy breast, smile as big as a sunfish. "That is where we are."

Ooooooohhhhhaahhhhh affirmed the occupant of the endless sky-under-ocean.

A beast even more enormous than Agnes swum above, around, below in the not-water. Rainbows shimmered across see-through skin, which revealed pulsating, squirming organs in gorgeous jewel tones. Spine and skull curved like the finest of marble carvings, and it was strange to see the beauty in their movement as whalebone was usually only viewed in the repose of death. .

"It's a glass whale," Benj sighed.

"We thought they were all extinct." Tears shimmered in Colombia's beard. "Gone to the skies with their kraken-cousins."

Agnes whirled around the undulating glass whale, tentacles describing things too large and delicate for rodents and mers to understand.

Cinrak too took a moment to enjoy being alive. Her ship had survived, though some of the sails and her green silk vest were tatters. At the beautiful sight of lovers reunited, the crew danced and wept, the mers slapped their tails and sang. Benj watched on with a beatific smile bending his whiskers, paws clenching and unclenching in time to the tentacular spectacular.

Cinrak waited. She had spent a long time searching for the Heart of the Ocean, but Agnes had spent much longer away from her beloved. A few more moments before the jewel was in her hands wouldn't matter.

With a relenting, soft *arrroooogghhh,* the glass whale allowed Agnes to wrap her arms around them. The embrace was so delicate and loving for such huge beasts, stray tears on her furry cheeks caught Cinrak by surprise.

Benj grinned. "Agnes says their name is still Xolotli."

Cinrak paused in winding a rope. "Still?"

Colombia sucked his whiskers. Something like comprehension snuck thief-like across his face. "I think...it would change if something was taken away from here."

"The Heart," Cinrak nodded. "That makes sense. They be the guardian of the jewel."

An upward lilting *arroogh*. An affirmation. Did the whale understand rodent tongue?

"Get to it, ye lot," Cinrak coughed. "We needin' to be ship shape so we be figurin' how to get back up top."

The crew were sluggish to turn away from the sight of the wondrous reunion between the beasts, but to their credit, they held fast to their IRATE values: ship first.

"Alright. I guess there bein' a cave or a chest or a pedestal round here," Cinrak murmured to Benj and Riddle.

"It's in a chest..." The cabin boy started to say, and that was all Cinrak needed. She sent Riddle scampering to launch the captain's sculler.

"But, ser," Benj tried again, tugging on her arm.

Cinrak frowned him into silence. "We've upheld our end of the bargain, now it be Agnes' turn."

"No! You can't!" Benj blurted, front teeth showing. He was perilously close to insubordination.

"We problee do'na be havin' much time, Benj. Now the anger an' magic of them hundreds-a years be dissipatin', that drain'll collapse in on itself. We do'na wanna be here when that happens."

But Benj planted his feet and folded his arms, whiskers aquiver. "No!"

Cinrak's nostrils flared. "Benj," she growled, straightening to her full capybara height.

Benj planted his small self between the captain and the unfurled rope ladder. "You can't have the Heart!"

Colombia and the mer scouts gathered at the rail, looking between the unfolding scenes in the not-water and on board. The rest of the crew put their heads down and made busy. They all knew that look on their captain's face.

"This ain't a negotiation," Cinrak growled. "Agnes promised."

"To lead you to the Heart, not let you cut it out of the ocean!" Benj was on the verge of tears, but to his credit he stood his ground. Cinrak would keep that in mind when she decided his punishment.

Chest puffed, Cinrak stepped face to face with the cabin boy. "I ain't arguing with ye. Under IRATE law, a deal is a deal. You gotta be learnin' to toughen up that heart a' yours, boy."

A gasp, like a spring breeze across a prickleberry bush. The mers. *Propriety be damned*, she thought. Cinrak the Dapper's reputation came as salty as the ocean.

Forceful in her anger, Cinrak swung about to face the judgment of her mer friends and smacked snout to wet leathery appendage.

Agnes reared up over the ship, eye apologetic but tentacles an impenetrable wall. Whichever way Cinrak tried to dodge, the tentacle in her face followed.

Benj placed himself between the tentacle and his captain. "Agnes says you can't have the Heart of the Ocean."

"But she promised!"

Benj pointed at the now relaxed glass whale blowing curious spouts. Such a sight, water in, water out. "*There* is your *chest* with your prize. It is an *actual* chest. An *actual* heart!"

"Oh." The entirety of the revelation replaced Cinrak's breath with silence.

And what a beautiful heart it was. An enormous, scintillating ruby shot through with veins of sapphire and pink diamond. It pumped prodigiously, pushing plasma through the plump pellucid physique.

"Well." Cinrak coughed around a plethora of emotions. "We ca'na be puttin' that in the queen's crown now, can we?"

XOLOTLI HAD OCEAN MAGIC TO spare. From what Cinrak could ascertain from Benj's loving burbles, the whirlpool had gotten away from her, the power of the void self-sustaining. Now that she had her love and control back, she deftly broke the bonds on the Edge of the World and let the drain disperse. The *Impolite Fortune* rode the ocean wall up and up, supported again by the soft weight of Agnes' tentacles.

The strange star-like lights sunk back into the depths, embraced by the void like an impenetrable night flipped on its head. Cinrak's heart wanted to flow with them. It made her feel so small and yet so large at the same time. The stars still had lessons to teach her.

Upon reaching the surface, the mers began whistling in excitement. The dissipation of the water walls had revealed the submerged archipelago. The mer quickly rescued gaping fish and set to exploring the seaweed-draped ruins.

While the crew and mers fussed over the persistence of their respective homes, Benj sat atop the highest point on the main island, silent and strong as a masthead. Agnes and Xolotli swum excited circles around each other and the islands. With The Bruise gone and the ocean calm, the tableau glittered iridescent beneath the excited Moth and Paper Moons and stars.

Cinrak approached her cabin boy carefully, forepaws crossed across her broad chest. "I, yuh, have come teh apologize."

The wee chinchilla's eyes widened at the unexpected opening. "Why? You're the captain. You make calls as you see fit."

"But I didna listen to ye. I bin so focused on my reward, agin. I wouldna ever be hurtin' a creature to take what I be needin' or wantin'. 'Specially one so beautiful as Xolotli."

A wistful sigh escaped between Benj's whiskers. "They are that." Belatedly, he stood and snapped a salute, fur making a damp little squish beneath his fist. "But in the end, you failed to get what you promised."

"Neh." Cinrak shrugged. "Ye learn to make the best o' a situation. I found the Edge of the Earth, tamed the great whirlpool, and reunited lovers. That in itself will be makin' a great epic I can sell to the bards for years ta come. An' look. The mers have found a part of their lost home. They be happy too."

"But what about the queen's crown? Won't she be mad?"

"She'll get over it. 'Sides, sometimes I be thinkin' a jewel ain't what make a leader great. Orvillia is a good woman, but she be needin' to find her own heart, an' not be takin' it from the ocean. Or the land."

Benj stared at his captain, open-mouthed. Cinrak chuckled and slapped him on the back. "Eh, let me be tellin' you 'bout ogre socialism sometime, young kit."

Agnes forestalled any further brusque sentimentality by rising high in the water, tentacles flailing as the mers whistled and laughed.

"What be botherin' her now?" Cinrak asked.

"Well, er, she has a gift for you, ser."

"Does she now."

Agnes swam as close as she dared and Cinrak clambered down the slippery rocks to greet her. "This gift better not be a hug," she grumbled.

Agnes unfurled a leathery fist, the tip ending perfectly before Cinrak's blunt snout. Balanced on the tip of the tentacle was a jewel the size of Cinrak's fist, striated with perfect sweet rosiness, a flash of diamond star, and a blue as dark as the deepest ocean. It smelled like the crackle-taste of stars.

"She says...oh." Benj gasped sweetly. "It's a piece of whale-fall from the deepest trench. It's been down there for so long the pressure of the water and remnants of its sky cousins have rendered it into something new."

"Like pieces of the earth deep in the earth," Colombia said, coming closer to inspect the proffered gift.

"Whale goop and star poop," Benj giggled.

"A piece of dead whale turned jewel," Cinrak breathed, touching a claw tip to the stone. Sure enough, it tingled like the star had tingled beneath her thighs when she rode it. "How marvelous. I never be thinkin' of such a thing. Are ye sure?"

Agnes blinked and shook the tentacle a little, 'here, take it.'

Cinrak took the stone and rolled it gently between her fore-paws. It gave off a warmth unexplained by the eons spent below in the freezing dark. "What part of the whale it bein'?"

"Heart," Benj said.

An enormous whale heart compacted down to this? Cinrak saluted and bowed to Agnes who waved her tentacles back. "Yer kindness will never be forgotten-" She clicked and slurped her way through the full name.

She slipped the stone into the Alice pocket of her vest for safekeeping. So, she got her heart after all. Did she deserve it? What had she just said about jewels and crowns and queens? She needed to think on this one.

The North Wind, having searched frantically all around The Bruise since the ship disappeared, finally found them and blew a warm sigh of relief. Xolotli blew rainbows, the ocean kissed the stones, and the *Impolite Fortune* groaned through its litany of aches.

"All aboard!" Cinrak called.

When she reached the railing, she looked down to find Benj gathered with the mers who were staying to investigate the uncovered islands.

"Hey!" she called. "It be time to go!"

From the rise in his now tatty vest and scarf, Cinrak could see Benj was gathering his courage.

"I think—" His voice cracked downwards. "I'm staying here. Agnes needs me."

Perhaps, Cinrak thought, it was the other way round.

Benj continued, "The mers need me too." Colombia slapped him on the shoulder with his long fin and nodded. "What I learned back in Merholm, what I've learned from Agnes and Xolotli and my m...magic. My place, for now, is here."

There was no use in giving a speech about IRATE duty, but Cinrak gave it anyway, out of duty. Riddle collected Benj's kit from below deck and threw it down.

"Not sure how you gonna keep it all dry though!" she laughed.

"I'll learn quick," Benj grinned, saluting the first mate.

Something pinched hard in Cinrak's chest. Her own jewel-like heart, dusting off memories of discovering bow ties and girls and ocean delights? Or a little throb of the whale heart hidden in her vest?

"Take care, ye salty wee scrapper," Cinrak called as they cast off. "We be back soon, ye can count on that. Not fair ye get to have all the fun! Oh, an' Benj? I got ye pirate name! A-Benj the Ocean Star!"

He laughed at the pun. "It's perfect! Thank you!"

"Yer welcome."

"Give my best to Orvillia and Locqualchi!" Benj roar-squeaked, tears in his eyes.

"That's *Queen* Orvillia to you, young mer-fur," Colombia chuckled.

The shimmer of mer and whale song followed the *Impolite Fortune* for as long as the stars stitched the sky together. As dawn peaked over the horizon and the sun sparkled a yawn, sending the Moth and Paper Moon off to their beds, the glass whale blew one final rainbow salute, and Agnes made intricate signs with her tentacles Cinrak thought she could almost read.

One more salute to kraken and whale and Cinrak wiped her salty-sweet cheeks dry and turned her snout towards where her two other loves made home.

About the Contributors

Ginn Hale, "Treasured Island"

Award-winning author Ginn Hale lives in the Pacific Northwest with her lovely wife and their wicked cat. She spends the rainy days observing local fungi. The stormy nights, she spends writing science fiction and fantasy stories featuring LGBT protagonists.

Ashley Deng, "The Seafarer"

Ashley Deng is a Canadian-born Chinese-Jamaican writer with a love of fantasy and all things Gothic. Currently working through a degree in biochemistry, she spends her spare time overthinking genre fiction and writing. She cycles back to pirates more often than she'd like to admit.

Joyce Chng, "Saints and Bodhisattvas"

Joyce Chng is Singaporean. They write science fiction, YA and things in between. Joyce is also the co-editor of *The Sea is Ours: Tales of Steampunk Southeast Asia*. They can be found at @jolantru and *A Wolf's Tale* (**http://awolfstale.wordpress.com**).

Ed Grabianowski, "The Doomed Amulet of Erum Vahl"

Ed Grabianowski has worked as a contributing writer for *io9* and *HowStuffWorks*. He's also the singer and lyricist for a rock band called Spacelord. This is the first Jagga story, but not the last.

Mharie West, "Serpent's Tail"

Mharie West learnt to read with one hand to enable reading while eating, showering, and most other life tasks. She likes writing fantasy, sci-fi and historical fiction. She studied Vikings and Anglo-Saxons at university and blogs about them at **https:// wordeswif.wordpress.com**. "Serpent's Tail" is her second publication.

Megan Arkenberg, "Between the Devil and the Deep Blue Sea"

Megan Arkenberg's work has appeared in over fifty magazines and anthologies, including *Lightspeed*, *Asimov's*, *Beneath Ceaseless Skies*, *Shimmer*, and Ellen Datlow's *Best Horror of the Year*. She has edited the fantasy e-zine *Mirror Dance* since 2008. She currently lives in Northern California, where she's pursuing a Ph.D. in English literature. Visit her online at **http:// www.meganarkenberg.com**.

Elliott Dunstan, "Andromache's War"

A long-time resident of Ottawa, Elliott Dunstan is in the last year of a Classics degree at Carleton University, which ended up being the basis for "Andromache's War." Elliott has been previously published by Battleaxe Press and In/Words Magazine & Press, and has self-published a poetry chapbook.

Geonn Cannon, "Rib of Man"

Geonn Cannon lives in Oklahoma. He is the author of several novels, including the Riley Parra series, which is currently being produced as a webseries for Tello Films. He also writes official tie-in novels for Fandemonium's Stargate SG-1 series. An archive of free stories can be found online at **geonncannon.com**.

Su Haddrell, "A Smuggler's Pact"

Su Haddrell is a British writer from Worcester, UK. She has had stories published by Fox Spirit and Phrenic Press. In addition to writing, she also plays the drums and organises the UK's only Judge Dredd convention. She loves rum, her cat, her boyfriend and movies where things explode within the first 14 seconds.

Soumya Sundar Mukherjee, "The Dead Pirate's Cave"

Soumya Sundar Mukherjee, an admirer of engaging speculative fiction, is a bi-lingual author from West Bengal, India, writing about stuff strange dreams are made of. His works have appeared/will appear in *Occult Detective Quarterly* and the anthologies *Mother of Invention* and *Hidden Menagerie*, among a few others.

Matisse Mozer, "Rosa, the Dimension Pirate"

Matisse Mozer is a writer and librarian living in lovely Los Angeles, California. If he's not writing obviously-anime-influenced stories, he's probably buying imported action figures, despite his bank account's protest. He's also likely to be retweeting memes on Twitter as @thecopperhikari.

Caroline Sciriha, "A Crooked Road Home"

Caroline Sciriha lives in Malta, where she works as a Head of Department of English in a Secondary School. She writes fiction—especially fantasy—whenever her day job allows. Her short stories have appeared in anthologies and magazines, including *Beyond Steampunk, Mind Candy* and *New Myths*.

Peter Golubock, "After the Deluge"

Peter Golubock is a teacher, writer, and pie enthusiast. He lives with his family in New Taipei City, Taiwan.

Michael Merriam, "Tenari"

Michael Merriam has published three novels, two collections, and over 90 short stories and poems. His novel *Last Car to Annwn Station* was named a Top Book in 2011 by Readings in Lesbian & Bisexual Women's Fiction. He lives in Hopkins, MN with his wife and two ridiculous cats. **www.michaelmerriam.com**

AJ Fitzwater, "Search for the Heart of the Ocean"

AJ Fitzwater is a dragon wearing a dapper meat-suit living between the cracks of Christchurch, New Zealand. Their words of import can be found in *Clarkesworld, Beneath Ceaseless Skies, Glittership, Shimmer Magazine,* and many other venues of repute. They survived the trial-by-wordfire of Clarion 2014, and is a two time winner Sir Julius Vogel Award winner.

About the Editor

CATHERINE LUNDOFF IS A TRANSPLANTED Brooklynite who lives in scenic Minnesota with her wife, a fabulously talented bookbinder and artist, and the two cats who own them. In former lives, she was an archaeologist and a bookstore owner, though not at the same time. These days, she does arcane things with computer software at large companies and hangs out at science fiction conventions.

Her recent works include short stories in *The Cainite Conspiracies: A Vampire the Masquerade V20 Anthology*, *The Mammoth Book of the Adventures of Professor Moriarty*, *The Mammoth Book of Jack the Ripper Stories*, *Respectable Horror* and *Tales of the Unanticipated*, and essays in *Nightmare Magazine: Queers Destroy Horror* and *SF Signal*. Her books include *Silver Moon* and *Out of This World: Queer Speculative Fiction Stories* and the Goldie Award-winning collections *Crave* and *Night's Kiss*. She has also co-edited or edited two other anthologies: *Hellebore and Rue: Tales of Queer Women and Magic* (with JoSelle Vanderhooft) and the Spectrum Award-winning anthology *Haunted Hearths and Sapphic Shades: Lesbian Ghost Stories*. **www.catherinelundoff.net**

ABOUT
QUEEN OF SWORDS
PRESS

QUEEN OF SWORDS IS AN independent small press, specializing in swashbuckling tales of derring-do, bold new adventures in time and space, mysterious stories of the occult and arcane and fantastical tales of people and lands far and near.

Visit us online at **www.queenofswordspress.com** and sign up for our mailing list to get notified about upcoming releases and offers. Or follow us on Facebook at the Queen of Swords Press page so you don't miss any press news.

If you have a moment, the author would appreciate you taking the time to leave a review for this book at Goodreads, your blog or on the site you purchased it from.

Thank you for your assistance and your support of our authors.